G000254312

19

SURREY

Overdue items may incur charges as published in the current Schedule of Charges.

L21

First edition published in 2018 by Heddon Publishing.

ISBN 978-1-9995963-4-7

Cover design by Catherine Clarke

Book design and layout by Heddon Publishing.

www.heddonpublishing.com
www.facebook.com/heddonpublishing
@PublishHeddon

To Sophie and Harper
Omnia Vincit Amor

CONSEQUENCE OF CARDS

Trust your friends, but always cut the cards.

Prologue

In poker, the line between fact and fiction, truth and bluff, reality and deception, is blurred. Knowing which side you and your opponents are on marks the difference between success and failure.

Life is much the same.

Card 1

The Stake: the amount a player buys in for and can bet in a game.

Las Vegas, 11 July 2009
JACK'S HAND

'Maybe he got lucky?' Tom said, scratching his wiry beard.

'I doubt it,' said Jack. 'If he picked someone up last night, he would've called by now; to brag, if nothing else.'

'OK, so let's think. Can you retrace your steps? I left you in the restaurant at nine and came back here. What happened after that?' Charlie looked down at his black G-Shock.

Jack thought for a moment. 'Well, we settled up in Maestro's and bar-crawled along the Strip. We must have been in the Sahara Casino for about an hour. Piers was with us then, right?' Struggling to remember, Jack looked to Tom for reassurance.

'Yeah, yeah, he'd scored that bag of coke, remember? And he was charging round the casino like he owned the place, pulling all the levers on the slot machines.

Basically, being a total dick and annoying the hell out of everyone. Me included.'

'Yes,' Jack quietly agreed, though in truth his sore head was struggling with the details. He found himself thinking back to their first night of excess in Sin City. He was exhausted, jet-lagged, and his memory was hazy, but he did have a vague image of Piers annoying the geriatrics on the One Arm Bandits.

Tom's voice broke his chain of thought. 'We got chucked out of the casino and moved on to a club, I think.' He checked the wristband he was still wearing: 'The M-A-D-H-O-U-S-E,' he read slowly.

Jack noticed a similar green plastic band on his own wrist. He'd obviously been at the Mad House as well but his mind was drawing a blank. A series of flashbacks jolted his brain into action, like a jump-started car.

Kitty. Sindy. Honey. High Rollers. Dom Pérignon. $100 bills.

The images flickered through his brain like strobe lighting, making him nauseous. Piers wasn't in any of them. Just half-naked women and gratuitous excess.

'He was definitely with us when we got there. I remember him ordering a bottle of champagne and then spraying most of it all over the place.' Tom winced at the thought.

'What was the time, exactly? Who else was there?' Charlie's size fourteens tapped on the marble floor.

'God knows. They don't have windows or clocks in these places. They want you in there 24/7. Time was the last thing on my mind, if you know what I mean.' Tom raised an eyebrow at Jack. 'Then again, perhaps you don't, Charlie?'

'Try and remember,' Charlie said. 'Visualize Piers – what was he doing? What sort of state was he in? Did he talk to you at all?'

'Err – we had quite a few dances...' Tom said vacantly.

'We weren't really bothering each other. Sorry, Charlie, I honestly can't remember much. Maybe my drink was spiked. I have no idea how I even got back to the hotel.'

Jack sensed Charlie's frustration. 'I'm sure he's fine, mate. Let's give it another hour or so and then we'll ring the front desk and see what they suggest. This type of thing's probably quite normal here.'

Charlie continued abruptly: 'Were any Chinese men hanging around in the club?'

'What?' Tom said, throwing Jack a knowing look. 'No. I don't think so. It wasn't the men I was looking at though, mate.'

A phone rang, startling Jack and Tom.

'Where's it coming from?' Jack stumbled around their palatial suite, trying to locate the landline. His brain was stirring, like a teenager getting out of bed, goaded by the irritating ringtone. 'Where the hell is the bloody thing?'

The gaudy furnishings of the six-bedroom, 22,000-square-foot Caesars Palace Presidential Suite were a sight to behold. It was typical of Las Vegas; over-the-top, excessive, obsessed with superlatives. Desperate to be anything but average, anything but ordinary. But, like so much of the superfluous glitz and glamour of America's favorite playground, this was nothing but a superficial veneer. Beneath the surface lay something entirely different.

After three more discordant rings, Jack finally found a phone hanging on the wall behind the private, fully-stocked bar.

'Answer it, JD, it could be Piers,' ordered Charlie just as Jack picked up the receiver.

'Hello? Jack Davidson speaking.'

'Listen up. You wanna see ya greasy little friend again? We've got him right here, an' he's gonna catch a bullet if you don't do exactly what I say.'

What the hell? This could not be happening. In Jack's

mind, Piers was still on a winning streak, or lying by a pool somewhere – surrounded by bikini-clad women fascinated by his posh English accent.

Jack looked across at Charlie and Tom; he could feel the blood draining from his face. Pressing the speaker button, he waved them over.

'Do not contact the authorities,' the guy spoke fluent gangster – his voice sounded like a cliché and Jack would have probably laughed, had the tone not been so chilling. 'Do not contact his family. Do not try to be heroes. The rules of my game are simple. Hand over half a million dollars … and ya'll get to see him again.'

'We don't have that sort of money,' Jack pleaded, trying to manage expectations like he was talking to one of his corporate clients. Making sure he wasn't promising something he couldn't deliver.

'Listen. Don't harm him,' Charlie called out before Jack had a chance to speak again. 'We'll find the money. But put him on the line first, so we know this isn't some kind of sick hoax.'

There was a long pause, followed by muffled noises, then two or three voices. Jack strained to hear but couldn't make out a word. After some shuffling there was a distant, low-pitched whisper then finally heavy footsteps before a familiar voice came on the line.

'It's me … Piers. Please just do as they say and get me out of here. They aren't messing around. They're bloody mental. They've got weapons. They'll kill me if you don't do exactly what—'

The line went dead.

Card 2

The Call: To match a bet.

Las Vegas, 11 July 2009
CHARLIE'S HAND

Charlie marched into the state-of-the-art kitchen. He took a sharp steak knife from the drawer, slotted it carefully into the inside pocket of his navy-blue corduroy jacket, and returned to the main atrium.

'Listen. You two stay here in case we get another call.' He strode across the shiny marble floor and stepped into the suite's private elevator.

'Hang on. Where are you going?' Jack cried out. 'Shouldn't we talk about—'

'Don't do anything until I get back,' Charlie ordered.

The elevator doors closed before Tom or Jack had a chance to reply. Six seconds later, Charlie arrived on the ground floor and the doors opened to the dazzling gold-and-white lights of the hotel's gigantic lobby. It was a mesmerizing view; an attraction in its own right.

Crowds flock to Caesars Palace just to gawp at the classical furnishings and marvel at the statues, sculpted ceilings and water fountains in its lobby. Today was no exception; the place was overrun with tourists, staff and paying guests.

The style didn't appeal to Charlie in the slightest. Measured and stoical, phrases like "excited" and "impressed" could rarely be applied to him. To his mind, Caesars Palace was just a reproduction, a fake. It was faux-classical and faux-Roman. In Charlie's opinion, Italy was the place to go for real classical architecture; authentic statues and domed ceilings with ancient paintings of demigods, chariots and horses. Italy, the true provenance of Julius Caesar. Not the middle of the desert in Nevada.

The bright lights and gratuitous luxury hadn't impressed him when they'd first arrived at the hotel and they weren't going to distract him now as he stepped out of the elevator and scanned the busy lobby.

There you are.

He zoned in on a Chinese man in a black suit, incongruous amid a crowd of tourists. Charlie was certain he'd seen this man before. His training had taught him to follow his gut and right now it was telling him that this man was trouble. He had a feeling it was time to face Trouble head-on.

He approached from the side, out of the man's field of view, then, at less than five meters away, reached into the pocket of his jacket.

'Piers – Piers, is that you? Yes, yes – OK,' Charlie spoke hurriedly, loud enough for anyone around him to hear. 'OK. Calm down – I'll be at Serendipity in ten minutes. You can tell me everything when I get there. I'll meet you out the back.'

He slipped his iPhone 3 back into his jacket pocket then marched across the lobby and out of the hotel. As he eased through the gaudy, gold-framed doors, he caught a reflection in the glass.

Trouble was following him.

Card 3

Offsuit: Cards that are not of the same suit.

Cardiff, 12 December 1991
JACK'S HAND

The rain was relentless: fierce, cold, Welsh rain. It had taken Jack fifteen minutes to navigate the multitude of steps from the Student Union and now he was standing on the road in a torrential downpour. He was drunk and he'd forgotten his coat. Had he been sober, he would have run back up the stairs and retrieved it from the club. *Bugger that,* he thought. *It's freezing. I'm going home. I'll pick it up in the morning.*

He'd spent the whole evening drinking. Snakebite & black followed by tequila, whisky & Coke, and then bottles of cheap lager. Starting at 5.00 pm in the Talybont Social and ending the night in Solus, in the Student Union. He'd been drinking with a friend from his course, out on the beers with the Law Society rugby team. Jack was naturally competitive but he couldn't keep up. He wasn't a natural drinker but he was too stubborn to accept that his limit was well below the average student's.

'Jack?' a vaguely familiar voice called from behind. 'What are you doing out here? It's freezing.'

Jack swiveled round. A tall, dark figure was moving toward him, holding out a jacket. He squinted to try and make out who it was but it was too dark and his retinas were stinging – pickled by the alcohol, frozen by the winter rain. He felt dizzy and nauseous, the dance music from the club still ringing in his head. He lunged awkwardly towards the large silhouette, stumbled, and threw up a purple-colored liquid all over the sidewalk.

'Jack, are you OK? It's me – Charlie. Charlie Preston … your roommate.'

Jack felt a little better as he wiped his sticky mouth. 'How come you always seem to pop up, out of the bloo?' he slurred, 'As if you're phlollowing me or shomething. It's kind of weird.'

'Here, put this on. You'll catch a death of cold.'

'Thanks, Mummy,' Jack mocked as he took the jacket and put it on. It was like wearing a tent, it swamped his slight frame, but it shielded his body and much of his legs from the cold and the rain so he was grateful.

'Let's get you back to the flat. I was on my way home anyway.'

As they turned, the wet, blustery air hit Jack like a fist to the face and he felt his brain revolve inside his head. He swayed across the sidewalk erratically, stumbling like a clumsy toddler. Charlie grabbed him under one long, muscular arm, using the other to hail a taxi.

The two of them ambled along the road in silence for a while but the cabs weren't stopping. One pulled over eventually but as soon as the driver realized the state Jack was in, he sped off in search of another fare.

'I'm abtholutely fine, I'm not that drunk, let go of me, you masshive queer,' Jack slurred, wrestling free from Charlie's arm.

'I'm fine, offisher, look, I can walk in a shtraight line.' He stopped and tried to raise his hand to attention but lost his balance and staggered out into the road.

An oncoming Fiat Punto careered toward them, swerving at the last moment and missing Jack by inches. The brakes slammed on and the car skidded to a stop thirty meters away.

'Holy shit, that was close,' Jack said as he lay, soaked to the skin, on the side of the road. Suddenly, he felt totally sober. Charlie held out his huge spade-like hand and lifted him back to his feet.

They looked toward the car and watched as its doors swung open. Four young men climbed out. It was clear they weren't coming to see if anyone was hurt. The driver let off a volley of abuse: 'Stupid student scum. I could've crashed, you fucking twats.'

He made a beeline for Charlie, bristling with rage. His three friends were right behind him. 'I can handle them,' Charlie said calmly.

As the unrelenting rain lashed down, Jack's heart rate quickened. He registered what looked like a rolling pin in the hand of one of the aggressors. *Why a rolling pin?* Before he could answer his own question, the "Baker" lunged forward and cracked him over the head.

In the seven or eight fuzzy seconds before Jack lost consciousness, he witnessed a sequence of events unravel like scenes shot with an 8mm camera.

Charlie crouched and spun in one single motion, deploying a roundhouse kick to the driver's face and stopping him in his tracks. The driver collapsed and with two smart steps Charlie was in front of the Baker, who was swinging his rolling pin wildly. In a flash, Charlie dodged the baton and, his fist springing out like a malicious jack-in-the-box, jabbed the Baker in the Adam's Apple. Deprived of air and clutching his throat, the Baker dropped his weapon. It fell to the ground right next to Jack's rain-soaked face. There was a name printed in black on its side. Wilson. *Of course – a baseball bat.*

The bat clattered noisily in the background as the movie reel rolled on. Jack saw Charlie snap the third man's wrist and break the nose of the fourth. His movements were balletic, like a performance artist's – deliberate but deadly. As the rain continued its assault on Jack's throbbing head, his eyelids grew heavy. The movie switched from color to monochrome to silent. Then it faded to black and the curtains closed.

***

JACK'S HAND

The next day, Jack woke up in his bed in Talybont with a bandaged forehead and two black eyes. His brain pushed against his fragile skull like it was trying to escape, only the strapping around his forehead holding it in. His eyes were half stuck together and his vision was blurry but he could see that someone had left a glass of water, painkillers and a handwritten note on the bedside table. He picked up the note and read it.

At the third cup, wine drinks the man.
CP.

Jack smiled. He'd barely spoken to Charlie before last night but he knew now that his quiet, enigmatic roommate would become a friend for life.

Card 4

The Motivation: A limit on the amount a player can win or lose in the play of a single hand.

For Jack, the night of 25 June 2009 was just like any other Thursday night. Until it wasn't.

He had met up with two of his less irksome clients for after-work drinks. They'd gone to a cocktail bar in Soho; the kind of place that had become so popular it had lost its cool. But Jack didn't know this and nor did anyone else in the bar, except the manager and his long-suffering staff.

The very fact that the place was crammed with bankers, accountants and lawyers marked the beginning of the end. The infestation of City Boys was bad news – a barometer of a business in decline. Much like the bankers, who were still living in a pre-credit-crunch world, unaware of their imminent redundancies or the real fallout from the global financial crisis, the cocktail bar had become a victim of its own success. Unlike the banking industry, the government wasn't going to step in and bail it out. Soon, another fashionable venue would take the limelight and this one would wane in the wings like an ageing actor.

Jack stood at the bar with his clients. He was waving a fifty-pound note, trying to catch the attention of the stony-faced bartender while half-listening to the conversations around him.

'It's just a liquidity problem; it has nothing to do with insolvency...'

'The last thing I need is to have my pension decimated – three bloody years before I retire.'

'... it's on the market just to keep Flossie at Habs for her AS-levels. It's just a bridge until I get my bonus next year.'

'You'll be lucky to keep your job – I hear Smythe Wilkinson laid off another 500 from middle office...'

'Three Old Fashioned,' Jack shouted at the bartender, who replied with a contemptuous nod.

'Christ, he's got a face like a slapped ass,' said one of Jack's clients. 'Cheer up, squire. It could be worse. You could be long Lloyds Bank shares, like poor Andy here,' he shouted obnoxiously as he slapped his colleague on the back.

'Piss off, Timothy.'

All the white-collars in the bar wore suits. The usual mix of blues, grays and pinstripes. Jack was no exception. He sported the same ensemble every Thursday: a navy-blue handmade suit, white monogrammed shirt, and a baby-blue Hermès necktie. Bright red socks provided a flash of color between the hem of his pants and his Crockett & Jones crocodile loafers. He felt exceptional but he looked little short of ordinary. Despite his efforts to stand out, he blended in, undetected, with the rest of the white-collars.

'Hey. I've just seen that twat from KKR come in. The one who stiffed us on the Irish deal last year,' Timothy yelled, just as Jack had finished paying for their drinks.

'Let's get out of here, this place is a sausage fest anyway,' shouted Andy.

They bolted their cocktails, jostled their way out through the sweaty male crowd and hailed a black cab to Mayfair.

The evening followed a familiar pattern. Cocktail bar after work, nightclub in Mayfair, and a huge bill at the end of the night. Business development was part of Jack's job. Anything his clients wanted, he paid for. Spear, Collier & Horn ultimately covered his expenses so he effectively had carte blanche when it came to entertaining. Most of his clients knew this all too well.

It was 11.10 pm when he eventually decided to leave the nightclub and abandon his two clients. They were too distracted to notice him leave, covered as they were in a rash of young Essex girls. Jack closed the tab, stuffed the VAT receipt into his leather wallet and walked out into the humid summer night.

He jumped into the first cab he saw, gave the driver his home address and sat back; pleased he wouldn't be spending the night in a strip club with two middle-aged dads. He stared through the window as the cab crawled along the city's streets, observing the drunken crowds pouring out of pubs and wine bars; grown men and women behaving like feckless teenagers. A young girl tripped over in her high heels, ending up on the sidewalk swearing at the gawking spectators, her leather skirt up round her middle, revealing a pair of black lacy knickers.

'There you go, fella – eyes left – look at them pins, I wouldn't mind a go on that crumpet, I tell ya,' said the portly cabbie as they slowly rolled past.

Jack noticed a white price tag on the flesh-colored soles of the young girl's high heels. He hated that. *Attention to detail,* he thought as the cab rolled on.

The taxi passed seedy late-night restaurants with

flashing signs reminding drunk passers-by that they were hungry.

'Driver,' Jack shouted. 'Do you mind dropping me at Kebab Kid? I fancy a Chicken Shawarma. You know where I mean?'

'Yeah, no worries, fella. The boys down the club rave about that place. Prefer Caspian myself. You ever been there? You know, next to Blockbusters off the Edgware Road? Elleva find that one, gets busy though, specially this time of year, long nights an' that. You'll have a queue right out the door. Worth the wait though, fella – I'll tell you that for nothing. They put turmeric and coconut in the pita bread – that's their secret – bake them in house, you know? Run by a Lebanese family. Three sons. All got these bushy beards. I mean, say what you want about immigration, fella – but I reckon...'

Jack had already zoned out. He had lived in London long enough to know that you never really have a conversation with a cabbie. They'll talk at you for the entire journey if you give them half a chance, occasionally asking questions but never letting you respond. You're just expected to listen – literally a captive audience, trapped inside the back of their cab – to their opinions on everything from immigration to casual dining.

***

JACK'S HAND

'MICHAEL JACKSON IS DEAD. MICHAEL JACKSON IS DEAD,' yelled a man running down the road, hands flailing in the air like a wind-dancer.

Jack heard this as he stood at the front of the line in Kebab Kid and his heart seemed to stop for a moment. They were just four words but they came as a shock.

His new iPhone 3 vibrated inside his pocket.

Where are we going, JD? CP

Jack smiled. It was over fifteen years since anyone had
called him JD. At once, it made him feel young and
carefree, as if he was a student again. A second vibration,
another text, this one from an unknown number.

How much, JD?

The subdued line in the kebab house had suddenly come
to life; drunken revelers now involved in animated
debates with cab drivers, or tapping away at their
phones, texting their friends, searching for news. There
was a total change of mood. The untimely death of a
megastar had breathed life into all of them. The irony
was not lost on Jack. His mood changed, too. The initial
sadness subsided, replaced by a mixture of relief, unease
and excitement. His heartbeat seemed stronger now
than before, as if the news of Michael's death had caused
it to reboot.

'Chicken or lamb Shawarma, mate?'

Jack didn't hear the question. His mind was
elsewhere.

'Mate? Jewunchickinorlam?'

He'd lost his appetite. The significance of the news was
just beginning to sink in. He left the morbid buzz of the
garish kebab house and wandered off down the street.

Michael Jackson was dead and after more than fifteen
years, Jack Davidson had finally won.

He ambled down the road, his mind whirring busily,
then stopped in the middle of the sidewalk, took out his
iPhone and answered the first text.

I'll let you know soon.

He turned right, onto his street, enjoying the feel of the warm midsummer breeze against his grinning face. He stopped again by the freshly painted gate of his newly refurbished Victorian townhouse then answered the second text.

Who is this?

Within seconds the phone vibrated again.

It's Piers. How much is in the account, old fruit?

The flood of memories seemed to trigger a dopamine release, making the hairs on the back of Jack's neck stand up and his skin tighten. He smiled as he typed his response.

One million pounds.

Card 5

The Table Stakes: A limit on the amount a player can win or lose in the play of a single hand.

London, 25 June 2009
JACK'S HAND

'What time do you call this?'

Jack jumped and dropped his front-door keys. They clattered on the mosaic floor. It had only been laid a few weeks ago and as he bent down he noticed a tiny crack on one of the white ceramic tiles. It unsettled him. Grabbing the keys, he looked up and saw Amelia standing in front of him. She was wearing her Louis Vuitton heels. *Damn it,* he thought as he remembered that it was date night.

'I made a reservation at Luna Nuova. Alessandro held our special table. I had to lie to him and say your mother had been taken to hospital,' she seethed. Jack's girlfriend was Italian, her temperament fit the traditional cliché.

'Alessandro?'

'The Maître d'. Why can't you remember these things? His eldest is at school with Bella's daughter, Olivia.'

Jack had no idea who she was talking about.

'Unbelievable. You have such a crap memory, Mr. High-and-Mighty-I'm-a-Partner-at-an-International-Law-Firm.'

'Is she OK, though?'

'What?'

'Is my mum OK?'

'How would I know? I haven't spoken to her since Christmas.' His question had thrown her off-track and for a moment he thought he'd derailed the scheduled steam train of abuse. The moment was short-lived.

'Why didn't you ring me or send a text or something, and why didn't you pick up your bloody phone when I called?'

'Look, I'm sorry, darling. I was working on the telecom acquisition. You know I don't always have time—'

'You haven't been working late. I can smell the whisky from here, you liar. Who the hell were you with?'

'Relax, Amelia. I was with Tim Johnson and Andy De Souza from King Investments. We went for a few drinks in Soho after our meeting. I'm sorry you had to lie to Alice and Drew.'

'Alessandro,' she yelled, turning up the volume. 'I bet Andy De Souza is a woman, isn't she? You'd rather spend time with her than your own girlfriend.'

Jack breathed in then exhaled slowly. He counted to three. He was well practiced by now.

'No, Amelia. *Andrew* De Souza is a forty-year-old man from Walthamstow. He's got two young children and bad breath. He's the general counsel at King Investments and a very important client. I've billed over half a million pounds to his firm in the last quarter. Anyway, I said I was sorry.' He paused and half-smiled. He knew exactly how to get out of this. 'Listen, have you heard the news about Michael Jackson?'

'What news?' Amelia rose to the bait. 'Don't tell me

he's changed his tour dates.'

'No, darling. He's dead. Apparently he died of an overdose earlier today.' His voice was warm. Soothing. 'There won't be a tour,' he finished gently.

The strategy worked. Amelia looked stunned and confused, then her mood changed visibly, as if someone had flipped a switch inside her brain. She eased forwards, arms outstretched.

'Darling, why didn't you tell me sooner? That's awful. I can't believe it. I just feel so … numb.' Her voice was breaking as she spoke, as if she was about to cry. She put her arms around him and they held each other for a moment, each lost in their own thoughts.

Amelia was a huge MJ fan. She'd told Jack about her teenage obsession – posters in her bedroom, memorizing the words to so many of his songs. It didn't matter about the high-profile court cases or accusations of sexual abuse; as far as she was concerned, Michael Jackson was the victim.

Jack, on the other hand, appreciated the guy's music but he was trained as a lawyer and the case against Jackson was far too strong. Nevertheless, that hadn't stopped him buying tickets for Jackson's next London concert. Amelia had been ecstatic when he'd presented them to her; jumping up and down and behaving like a teenager. Maybe the ten-year age gap was too much, Jack had thought to himself at the time.

'Hey, come on now, darling, there's no need to get upset.' There were tears welling in Amelia's eyes. 'It's not like he was a member of the family, is it?'

'You wouldn't understand. I loved him,' Amelia said as the tears began to roll. 'I love him. I still love him.'

As she nestled into his arms, Jack looked across and noticed that, once again, she had failed to place her front-door keys in the little wooden bowl that stood in the center of the half-moon console. Rebelliously, she'd left them instead on top of the antique walnut table.

Jack was a creature of habit. Everything in his world had to have a place, otherwise it was superfluous. Coats belonged on the coat rack – not on the floor, the couch, or the stairs. Footwear belonged in the shoe tidy inside the wardrobe in his custom-built dressing room – not next to the door, or in the bedroom, and never in the living room. Even the books on the bookshelf were ordered by size and color. If a book didn't suit Jack's display, he'd discard it. It was less a matter of tidiness or cleanliness, more a matter of order. He couldn't understand why Amelia failed to follow the same basic domestic protocol despite his tireless efforts to correct her behavior over the nine months they'd been living together.

In Jack's head, the keys belonged in the bowl, like it was their home. Failure to comply with this simple system was an affront to the natural order of things; in fact, almost a personal attack on him. Amelia's persistent failure to understand the bowl's importance upset him but she was strong too and he knew he stood little chance of changing her. He held back the urge to criticize, remembering the reason they were still in the hallway.

'Amelia, did I ever tell you about a game I played at university, with Charlie, Tom, Vincent and Piers?' he whispered, soothingly.

'No,' she said, quietly wiping her nose with her hand.

'Well, it started back in '91. Basically, we each picked a celebrity, paid some money into a joint bank account, and agreed that whoever's celebrity died first would be the winner. The prize was to plan a trip for all the players, using the money in the joint account.'

Amelia didn't respond.

'I picked Michael Jackson and now that he's dead I've got to organize that trip.'

Several seconds passed before Amelia could find the words to reply. 'What the hell are you talking about?' she said finally, breaking their embrace and stepping away from him. 'Are you still drunk? Is this some kind of internet joke? Are you filming this? Is Michael even dead?'

'It's not a joke, darling. There are no hidden cameras. And yes, unfortunately, he really is dead.'

'Liar. Who are you really going away with? It's that bitch from work, isn't it? The one who always says you're not available.' She gave him a look of disgust.

Amelia was hotheaded, always suspecting the worst. Every late night at work, every phone call taken in private, every last-minute dinner cancellation, she jumped to conclusions and accused him of lying whenever he tried to explain. Luckily for Jack, her moods were capricious; she jumped in and out of them with such frequency that these days he didn't worry too much about trying to placate her. Instead, he picked up her front-door keys and placed them in the wooden bowl. They joined his Porsche 911 keys in one metal mass. He felt a little better.

'There's no girl at work, Amelia. I've told you that a hundred times. Ruth is my PA. It's her job to answer my calls. Look. I'm sorry, but this isn't about you; or us, for that matter, darling. It's about me and my old mates from Cardiff. We've been playing this game for over fifteen years. I'm not going away with another woman. Honestly, you must know that by now, but this game is important. There are strict rules and a binding contract,' he explained.

'A binding contract?' Amelia looked ready to explode. 'Jack Davidson, you lying, selfish bastard. Who the hell are these people? You've never mentioned them before. Come on – what kind of a name is Piers, anyway? You've just made it up.'

It was a fair point, Jack thought; he hadn't mentioned them before. The truth was, he hadn't really been in contact with any of his old mates since they graduated in '93. They had all gone their separate ways after that and apart from the financial update Jack emailed every year, he'd had very little contact with them at all.

'Amelia, it's out of my control. It's a trip for the players of the game. Not the wives and girlfriends. Please try to understand.'

'Don't be so ridiculous. Is this sick game another figment of your imagination? If you think I'm letting you go on vacation without me – with people I've never heard of – you've got another thing coming. God knows what you'll get up to. Old university friends? For Christ's sake, you're not eighteen anymore. You're a middle-aged, boring lawyer. All our friends are married with children and you think you can jet off and gallivant around on some make-believe bachelor's party without a bachelor or even a goddamn wedding to go to. There's no bloody way you're going. No way. End of.'

Jack sighed. 'Look, as I've just told you, I'm in charge of organizing the trip of a lifetime, Amelia. Of course I'm going. It'll be amazing. I've got a million pounds to spend...' He said it in an effort to justify the importance of the trip but immediately regretted opening his mouth.

'A million pounds! Are you mental? What are you going to spend that sort of money on? Whores? Drugs? Gambling? You could buy me an engagement ring with it and pay for the whole of our wedding, for Christ's sake, instead of pissing it up the wall with some friends you haven't spoken to in nearly two decades.'

Amelia was shaking by now and this time the drama seemed almost genuine. Her mother was a model from Milan, her father an interior designer from London. She was blessed with good genes but as Jack watched, her porcelain skin turned blotchy. Strands of long black hair stuck to her oval face, obscuring the faint mole just below her right eye.

As she stood crying in the hallway, Jack marveled at the way her beautiful face could change so radically with her mood. Some people are more attractive when they smile; others look better when they don't. Whether Amelia was smiling or not, she generally looked amazing, but when her anger took over it always showed in her face. Even her cute mole turned malevolent.

Jack didn't know what to say. Instead, he stood back and silently admired his girlfriend's performance of her own angry drama, hoping it would be over soon and he could finally get to bed.

Amelia had turned twenty-seven only two months earlier but she was desperate to get married and have a baby like all of her friends seemed to be doing. On her birthday he'd given her a pair of pearl earrings from Tiffany's in a little square jewelry box. She'd burst into tears. At the time, Jack had found the whole charade over-the-top and embarrassing. Days later, it had dawned on him that she'd been crying with disappointment.

At work, his attention to detail was commendable. He prided himself on his ability to pick up on the smallest mistakes; to spot opportunities and take advantage of them for his clients, and he had an unrivaled ability to spot a double space or a grammatical error in the documents he spent all day reviewing. Outside the office, the smallest details took on disproportionate significance. He noticed straightaway if a book was missing from the bookshelf in his study or a wine glass put away in the wrong cupboard. When it came to his relationships, however, subtlety wasn't his forte. He was hopeless when it came to interpreting body language.

He suspected that people thought he was punching above his weight with the beautiful, youthful Amelia, and it wasn't that he hadn't considered proposing, but her unpredictable mood swings and petulant jealousy scared the hell out of him. She had started with subtle hints at marriage, moving on to far more obvious suggestions, now resorting to crude ultimatums.

'You're not getting any younger, Jack.' Amelia's performance was continuing on the imaginary stage. Like many Italians, she spoke with her hands. They were now thrashing around like an overzealous orchestra conductor's. 'You're not at university anymore; you're over the hill, past your sell-by date. No way am I letting you swan off to splash a load of money around. Who the hell do you think you are? Some high-fucking-roller? I'll tell you who you are. You're just an overweight, middle-aged, boring lawyer, that's all,' she screamed. There was a moment's silence before she added, quietly, 'And anyway, what are my friends going to say?'

With that, the curtain came down. Amelia twirled round on her Louis Vuitton heels and stomped up the stairs.

What are my friends going to say? Jack rolled the words around inside his head; trying them out for size, putting the stress on different words, changing the delivery each time.

What *are* my friends going to say?

What are my friends going to say?

What are my friends going to *say*?

His mind wandered as he imagined the mental angst that real stage actors must suffer; reading and rehearsing the same lines and then performing them night after night in front of a changing audience. The repetitive nature of their art; the difficulty of making something so stale, so familiar, so boring, appear natural, unrehearsed and original.

What are my friends going to say?

That's a very good question. He considered his reflection as he looked into the gold-framed mirror which hung above the walnut console. He was thirty-seven years old, his hairline was receding, and what hair was left was showing far too much gray.

He let out a deep sigh then inhaled slowly, his mind flashing back to his undergraduate self – a pumped-up rugby ball of vitality, ready to take whatever life had to throw at him. Now more of a deflating ball: misshapen, losing its grip. The side-effects of a sedentary job and too many business lunches taking their toll on his body. He knew that his tailored suits and slim-fitting shirts couldn't disguise this fact forever. The stubbly beard was supposed to make him look more stylish but in reality concealed his growing double chin. *Maybe Amelia is right,* he thought as he took a step toward the mirror. *Maybe I am a five o'clock shadow of my former, clean-shaven self.* He examined his tired-looking eyes and dehydrated skin and made a mental note to drink more water and get more rest. He needed to be on top of his game in the coming weeks.

Jack looked down at the wooden key bowl for a moment and then back into the mirror. *Today is the shadow of tomorrow,* he thought. He reflected for a moment then repeated his favorite mantra out loud.

'Today is the shadow of tomorrow.'

Card 6

The Rules of the Game: A set of explicit or understood principles governing conduct within a particular game.

Cardiff, 13 January 1991
JACK'S HAND

It was Sunday and it was raining. But that didn't matter to Jack and his friends because, like most of the first-year students in Cardiff on God's holy day, they were inside, enjoying the warmth of the pub. Their very own church.

'Here you go, lads,' Tom said as he placed a tray of drinks carefully on the table.

'Did you put it on my tab, old bean?' Piers asked as he picked up the only wine glass from the tray, tilting it toward the window and observing the dark red hues in the afternoon light.

'Of course I did. Oh, and Tasker sends his apologies, he's out of the Malbec, that's a Merlot.'

A harmony of 'Cheers, Piers!' rang out as Jack, Charlie and Vinnie each picked up a pint of Carling and clinked glasses.

'God bless you, Father,' Tom said in a mock-Irish brogue.

'It's pronounced Mer-*low* not Mer-*lotte*,' said Piers before nosing the wine ostentatiously.

Tom's cheeks reddened as he picked up the remaining drink. 'I don't care. All I know is I could Mer-*der* this pint right now.'

Jack smiled at Tom as he emptied half of the glass and took a seat next to Piers at their usual table.

Piers was in his Sunday best – a white Ralph Lauren shirt and a navy-blue sports jacket with gold buttons. He was always the best-dressed student on campus.

Charlie sat in his usual spot, facing the entrance to the pub. As was his way, he seemed indifferent to their schoolboy banter. In fact, he seemed distracted. His eyes searched the room, as if looking for someone better to talk to, though Jack knew that he and the others around the table were Charlie's only real friends.

'Talking of murder,' Jack said, putting down his pint and reaching for his leather satchel. 'Guys, this is it.' He pulled out three sheets of white paper and placed them on the table. 'I printed it off in the Law Library this morning.'

'First of many contracts you'll be drafting, I'm sure,' Vinnie said.

'I guarantee none of them will be as jolly fun as this one, old fruit,' said Piers, swilling his glass around then sipping his wine judiciously.

'Now listen, guys. I know over the last term we've discussed this game ad infinitum,' began Jack.

'Ad nauseum,' interrupted Piers.

'Seriously,' said Tom, 'can you two pack it in with your Latin phrases? You sound like a pair of prize pillocks.'

'Nice alliteration, Tom,' said Vinnie.

'That's when you use words with the same—'

'Piss off, Piers.'

'Anyway, children, if I may continue,' said Jack, 'what I've done is formalize all of our conversations, debates and discussions about the rules of the game over the last few months. I've tried to cover as many eventualities as possible, as you'll see when you read these three sheets of paper. The premise of the game is straightforward but there are all manner of things that need to be included in a legal document: a schedule of payments; the type of account they'll be paid into; the consequences of non-payment, or death of a player; how new players can join the game, and all the other boiler-plate clauses that make a contract legally binding. The process was actually quite involved. It took a few drafts to get it right.'

'You're going to make a great lawyer, JD, I'm sure of it. Well done, we appreciate all your efforts,' Vinnie said as he glanced over the contract.

'Who's ever going to want to talk to you at a cocktail party?' said Tom. 'This is like the most boring part. It's supposed to be fun, remember? Each of us picks a celebrity – we've already done that. We all pay money into a designated account – we can open one tomorrow – then we wait for one of the celebrities to die and whoever picked the poor sod wins the game and has to organize a trip for everyone else. Boom. It's that bloody simple. You've made it a whole lot more complicated by taking weeks to draw up an unnecessary contract. I mean, talk about over-egging the pudding.' Tom finished the rest of his Carling. 'Come to think of it, JD, you *are* going to make a great lawyer.'

'Listen. The contract's important. We need a legal document that sets out clearly what needs to happen under different specific circumstances. It'll remind us exactly what we've agreed. Suppose, three years down the line, Piers, say, decides he can't afford to make the monthly payments. We'd need unequivocal evidence of what we agreed would happen. If I'm to be the custodian of all this money, I want the rules of the game to be absolutely clear for everyone.'

'Agreed. It's important we set all this out properly,' said Charlie.

'As if Piers wouldn't ever be able to afford anything,' said Tom.

Piers smiled. 'Well, quite, but that's not the point, is it?'

'So what did we decide would happen if someone misses a payment?' Vinnie asked.

'You stop paying, you stop playing,' Jack and Tom said in unison.

'Jinx,' they said at the same time then high-fived.

'The contract provides that any player who misses more than one payment forfeits their rights to the money and the game. It's the two-strikes-and-you're-out rule we talked about, remember? I know it's harsh but it's the only way to keep everyone playing,' said Jack.

'OK, so let's say Fidel Castro drops down dead in two years' time; which I'm positive he will, by the way. How much money will we have?' Tom asked.

'If we all keep on paying, there should be around eleven thousand pounds in the account and you'd have to organize the trip for us all,' Jack replied.

'Havana, perhaps?' Tom said with a grin.

'It's a big responsibility, JD. You sure you're OK looking after all the money?' asked Charlie, his arctic-blue eyes fixed on Jack.

'I'm not going to run away with it, if that's what you're implying, Charlie, and, to be honest, I'm disappointed if you don't feel you can trust me.'

'Hold on. No one's questioning your integrity, JD,' said Tom. 'Charlie was just checking you appreciate what you're taking on. I wouldn't want the stress of it myself. Or the temptation. I can barely manage my own finances.'

'Well, exactly. No one else put their hand up, did they?' Jack mellowed a little. 'Listen, I'm happy for someone else to do it but I thought the decision was made.'

'We did agree, JD, you're right. It makes more sense if it's you,' Vinnie said. 'We wouldn't be playing this game if we didn't trust each other, right?'

Charlie picked up the contract and turned to the schedule at the back.

'Payments go up quite quickly, don't they?' he said. 'D'you think we'll be able to afford this?'

'We've taken inflation into account. Piers reckons the purchasing power of sterling will reduce over time so we've factored that in,' Jack replied defensively, looking across to Piers for support.

'That's right, old bean. The real value of the fund will decrease unless the payments go up in line with inflation. But fear not, chaps, our salaries will be a lot higher, because there's wage inflation as well,' Piers explained with his usual bumptiousness.

'I guess if anyone knows about finance, it's the soon-to-be-Bachelor of Economics heir to a mining dynasty,' said Tom. 'I wouldn't worry about it, Charlie. After graduation we'll all get well-paid jobs: joining the army will give you plenty of disposable income. Jack will be a high-flying liar ... I mean *lawyer*. Vinnie will be teaching at some posh school and Piers, well, Piers won't need to work, but he'll have more money than the lot of us put together.'

'What about you, Patto?' Vinnie asked. 'What are you going to do with your marine biology degree? It's not exactly a vocational course, is it?'

'You look after your own game, Vincent. I intend to do all right for myself and if I don't I can always count on Father Upwell here to look after me.' Tom smirked as he nudged Piers in the side. 'Anyway, there's no way Castro is going to live past graduation. So let's not get too worried about any of this, shall we?'

'I reckon Arnie will keel over first – all those steroids can't be good for the heart – and Charlie'll make us all trek to the North Pole or something equally tedious,' laughed Jack.

'God, no,' said Tom, putting down his empty pint glass. 'Let's sign this thing quick before I change my mind. Then we can really get down to business. It's Sunday, after all, we're at church, there's drinking to be done, and Father Upwell is buying. Thanks be to Piers.'

'*In Vino Veritas,*' Piers declared with a beam. His perfectly straight white teeth were slightly tainted by the red wine but they still looked three shades brighter than everyone else's.

'Amen to that,' Jack said, pulling a pen out of his satchel and signing his name with a flourish.

Card 7

Deuces: A Pair of Twos.

Las Vegas, 11 July 2009
CHARLIE'S HAND

A snake of taxis lay patiently outside Caesars Palace, moving with the menace of an immortal serpent; every time the head was cut off, its yellow body would slither forward and a new head would regenerate. Charlie marched past the dawdling, shopping-laden hotel guests and stepped up to the snake's head.

'Where you going, sir?' said the taxi driver in a fake-sounding classic American accent. Michael Jackson's *Black or White* was blasting from the radio.

'Serendipity,' Charlie called as he climbed into the back of the cab.

The driver switched the radio off, turned to Charlie and gave him a bemused grin. 'You sure, Mister?'

Charlie nodded, his eyes fixed on the taxi's wing mirror as they peeled away.

'Sure thing, sir. A fare's a fare.'

Charlie looked at the driver in his Hawaiian shirt then at the permit displayed on his dashboard and concluded that Malik S. Ahmed hadn't been born in the USA. He was probably from India or Pakistan originally. A first-generation immigrant. In the United States long enough to have adopted the accent and picked up the brashness of a typical US taxi driver. Like Caesars Palace – pretending to be something he wasn't.

The ride to Serendipity took less than two minutes. It was walking distance from the hotel; Charlie could have got there just as fast on foot. He was a little embarrassed when the taxi pulled up outside but he handed over a ten-dollar bill knowing he wouldn't get any change. 'Have fun then, sir. Don't eat too much sundae,' Malik S. Ahmed said before driving off with the same bemused grin on his face.

Serendipity was a curious venue, bright pink and playful – a girly girl's paradise. Charlie marched into the restaurant and was at once struck by the colorful décor – it could have been designed by the love child of Willy Wonka and Alice in Wonderland. The walls were dripping with bright rainbow pinstripes and a large pink clock with blue eyes and bright red lips painted on its face hung on the wall. It was 6.45 pm.

Time for some answers.

A kid's party was in full swing in the restaurant. Three tables were covered in a bounty of chocolate, sweet treats and ice cream. Ten screeching kids were bounding around the restaurant with careless abandon, E-numbers surging through bloodstreams like amphetamines. *Irresponsible parenting,* Charlie thought to himself as he filed past. The waiters were too distracted to notice Charlie march through the dining area toward the back of the restaurant.

The washrooms in Serendipity were underground, and some distance away from the dining area, as if they'd been added on as an afterthought. They were dirty and smelly; a total contrast to the rainbow room upstairs. *Typical,* Charlie thought. *All show and no efficacy.* He stood behind the dank, yellow-stained door, fully expecting Trouble.

Charlie was fast. He overpowered the man with brute strength and close-quarter combat skills as soon as the guy entered the room. The speed of Charlie's hand, and the element of surprise, were enough to lock Trouble's arm in a tight hold and slam his body against the damp, greasy wall. As the man's head bounced back, Charlie used it to crash through the cubicle door. Within a second, he pulled the steak knife from his jacket pocket and forced it up under the chin of his would-be attacker. Trouble sat, stunned and defenseless, slumped on the toilet seat, Charlie pressing the blade hard against his throat.

'Where's Piers? Where are you keeping him?' Charlie shouted in Trouble's face, spraying him with saliva.

'Calm down, Captain Preston,' Trouble said with surprising composure. 'We're looking for him too, you know.'

Charlie stared into Trouble's dark brown eyes and studied him closely. He didn't seem flustered, nor did he seem to be bluffing. Charlie could usually tell when someone was lying. He was unsettled by the fact that Trouble knew his name and military rank, though. What else did this guy have on him?

'Why are you following us?' Charlie asked in a more measured tone, slowly pushing the tip of the knife into Trouble's neck, piercing the skin and drawing blood.

'OK. Stop.' The guy was starting to lose his composure now. 'We work for Mr. Lee. Don't do anything you'll regret. We are trying to keep Piers out of trouble. He's a valuable asset.'

The words tumbled out of Trouble's mouth then his body relaxed and he raised his hands in resignation. Charlie noticed his black leather gloves.

'If you're keeping him out of trouble, why has he been

kidnapped?' Charlie asked.

It was the same question he'd been repeating to himself but as he waited for Trouble's response, Charlie felt the sensation of cold metal pressing up against the back of his head.

'That's a very good question, Captain Preston,' said a voice from behind.

Charlie slowly lowered then dropped the knife, raising his hands in surrender; bracing himself for the inevitable.

Trouble stood up and punched him hard in the face with his gloved fist. Blood pumped to Charlie's right eye. It was an unusual feeling. The texture of the soft leather glove reminded him of his days in the ring, when he'd boxed for the Adjutant General Corps.

'That was for making me bleed,' Trouble said.

'Turn around,' the voice from behind commanded. 'We've no interest in hurting you. We just want to know where Piers is.'

Charlie turned slowly, his hands aloft. First he noticed the Beretta 92S pointing at his head. Then the guy who was holding it. The man's dark brown eyes, his face, even his black suit, seemed to be a mirror-image of Trouble's. Maybe Charlie's swelling eye was playing tricks on him? He shook his head and blinked hard. It made no difference.

'Let's all just relax, go upstairs, and have a sensible conversation,' suggested Trouble's double.

Charlie gave a quiet sigh of relief at the knowledge he wouldn't be spending his last moments in a neglected toilet in the basement of Serendipity. He glanced around the room, looking for any more surprises, then nodded in agreement.

The three men returned upstairs, to the manic cacophony of the psychedelic restaurant. They sidled uneasily into a hot-pink booth in the corner, as far from the riotous kid's party as they could get. By now the place was almost full but the three of them stood out like bruises on a child. Charlie sat opposite Double and Trouble. He had a clear view of the restaurant's main exit over their shoulders. There were enough witnesses around for him to relax. In any case, if they'd wanted to hurt him they would have done it by now.

He looked at Trouble, then at Double, then Trouble again. Now that they were sitting side by side, their similarities were even more pronounced. They were the same height – around six foot – they had the same athletic build, and each wore a black suit with white shirt unbuttoned at the collar. Both had a grade-two haircut. They looked almost identical – twins, maybe? Charlie stopped himself. Was it innate racism, making him think all Chinese people look alike? If so, it annoyed him; he expected better of himself. His mind flashed back to the times he'd noticed them before, always skulking in the shadows. He'd never entertained the idea that there'd been more than one man. As he sat in the booth looking directly at them, he struggled to find a single physical feature that distinguished Trouble from his Double.

'Let's introduce ourselves properly, shall we? My name is Mr. Yin and this is my associate, Mr. Yang. We work for Mr. Lee. Mr. Harald Lee.' There was a pause as the words "Harald Lee" hung in the air. 'Your friend, Piers, is in debt to Mr. Lee.'

'We're guessing you're his protection or something?' Mr. Yang cut in.

Charlie fixed them with his granite-hard stare. 'Is that what he told you?'

'We've not spoken to Piers. He doesn't even know we're following him, but we know how bodyguards behave and you fit the bill. I guess the army pension is not what it used to be,' Mr. Yin said.

'You couldn't be further from the truth,' Charlie said.

'He's an old friend of mine.' His cold, hard stare gave nothing away.

'So far, Piers has been paying the interest on his debt. Our job is to ensure that continues until Mr. Lee is repaid in full,' added Mr. Yang.

'How much does he owe?'

'Two hundred and fifty thousand pounds, plus interest. Currently five-and-a-half thousand a month.'

A spotty waitress in a pink mini-skirt bounced over to their booth and interrupted their conversation, eyes on her notepad. Her words melded lazily as she spoke, 'How y'all doinfolks? What can I getchy'all today? We got the deep fried Snickers sundae on special all this week.' Her eyes wandered slowly from the notepad to the booth. She took in the two Chinese men with their matching black leather gloves, then the white guy with the black eye, who looked too big for his seat. Her acne-sprinkled face fell.

Charlie broke the uncomfortable silence and ordered a Scotch.

'Coffee. Black,' said Mr. Yin.

'White coffee, and I'll take one of those sundaes,' said Mr. Yang without looking at her.

The waitress turned to Charlie, tilted her head and widened her eyes. He half-smiled and nodded, letting her know he was OK and she disappeared in the direction of the bar.

'But if Piers has been kidnapped like you say he has,' Mr. Yang said, 'how come you were talking to him on your cell in the hotel lobby?'

'He wasn't,' snapped Mr. Yin. 'He just wanted us to follow him.'

'We haven't seen Piers since last night,' Charlie admitted. He looked down at his black G-Shock. 'We had a call about twenty minutes ago, saying he'd been kidnapped and demanding half a million dollars. The accent was American. We don't know how many people we're dealing with or how he was kidnapped.' He paused for a moment and narrowed his eyes. 'I thought you two were involved. I know you've been following us. I clocked you in London at Hardbodies, then at Heathrow, and again when we checked in to the hotel.'

'But aren't you supposed to be protecting Piers, Captain Preston?' Mr. Yang said, with a smirk on his face. 'And you've let someone kidnap him?'

'Look. I don't know what you've been told, but I'm just an officer on vacation in Vegas with my old university friends. If what you're telling me is true, you're the ones who should've been keeping an eye on him.'

The spotty waitress returned, placed the drinks and dessert hastily on the table, together with the bill, and scurried away. Charlie picked up the Scotch and held the glass in front of him. He could usually tell whether whisky was genuine without even tasting it. A rich, dirt-flavored aroma and subtle caramel coloring distinguished it. *Everything has a tell,* he thought to himself. He bolted the whisky in one gulp. As he'd suspected, it wasn't authentic; more like cheap bourbon. Another imitation.

He stared at Mr. Yin and Mr. Yang and wondered how Piers had become indebted to their boss. Charlie had heard about their infamous leader, the Dragon Master of the 14K; the largest and most feared Triad gang in the UK. Mr. Lee was famously associated with drug-trafficking, illegal gambling and extortion. A very dangerous creditor and Piers owed him money.

'Thank you both. This has been useful. Enjoy your dessert, I'll leave you to pick up the check,' he said as he slid out from the booth.

'We'll be keeping an eye on you, Captain Preston,' Mr. Yang answered, before tipping a spoonful of multi-colored ice cream into his mouth.

'I'm sure you will, but try not to lose sight of what you're supposed to be doing. I've heard Mr. Lee doesn't tolerate mistakes.'

Charlie strode past two squabbling kids and out of the restaurant. He stopped in the parking lot outside Serendipity, turning to Caesars Palace and staring for a moment towards its uniform gray columns.

Card 8

The Fold: To discard a hand and forfeit interest in the current pot.

London, 26 June 2009
JACK'S HAND

Jack woke up at 6.15 am, walked into his bathroom and took a shower. He preferred showers to baths. He'd rather be on his feet, being pelted by hot water, than lying still in a bathtub; it better prepared him for the challenges that would undoubtedly rain down on him during the day ahead.

He would often spend up to an hour in the bathroom, although Amelia berated him for it. Today, he stood under the head of the power shower, giving his face a pummeling as he thought long and hard about whether or not he should go away. He massaged an invigorating scrub into his face and neck and felt the tingling sensation of the menthol unclogging his tired pores, removing his dead skin and stimulating the blood flow to his face.

As he washed his hair he thought about the money in the account. The stakes were higher now than they had ever been. There was enough cash for a complete new start. He could jump off London's corporate carousel, leave the country; sail to a remote island somewhere in the South Seas. He daydreamed about white sand beaches and turquoise seawater as he rinsed the shampoo from his scalp.

Feeling refreshed and energized, he stood drip-drying in front of the bathroom mirror, a white towel wrapped high above his waist, continuing his morning routine by applying a nutrient-rich regenerating serum under his eyes to help reduce the dark circles he had noticed the night before.

He automatically picked up Amelia's toothbrush from the basin and returned it to the glass tumbler attached to the wall. It fell against his. The white bristles pressed up against one another as if locked in a passionate embrace.

His mind drifted. He thought about proposing to Amelia. He didn't have a ring, but that didn't matter. He imagined her delighted face when he asked her, and pictured that same expression as she floated down the aisle towards him in Farnham's quaint stain-glass-windowed village church. He could picture the scene vividly in his mind's eye; the strapless ivory lace dress, the bouquet of white avalanche roses in her petite hands, the Manolo Blahnik bridal shoes that only she would see – her father walking by her side, a look of relief, pride and reluctance drawn confusingly across his face. Jack could imagine every little detail with unnerving clarity, exactly as she'd described it to him time and time again.

He stroked the stubble on his chin, tilted his head, and examined himself in the mirror. Then he opened the cabinet and took out the Taylor of Old Bond Street shaving set that one of his partners at work had given him for landing his first big client. He filled the basin with hot water and used a flannel to soften the skin and encourage the pores in his face to open up. He applied shaving gel to his face and circled the shaving brush over it, to work up a lather. The soft badger hair of the brush seemed to command his stubble to stand to attention and prepare for a reckoning. He'd have loved to have used a cutthroat razor but he didn't trust himself. He'd rather submit to a Turkish stranger, he thought, as he reached for his Gillette safety razor.

Ten minutes later, he looked and felt totally rejuvenated. His skin was smooth, rehydrated and firm, his mind clear. He cleaned the washbasin methodically, removing the traces of hair and foam. He tidied up the bathroom, stowed everything away neatly in the cupboards, and mopped the wet floor around the washbasin and shower, before strolling into his dressing room and inspecting himself in the mirrors. As he dried himself, he could hear the morning birdsong outside his window. The aroma of Brazilian Arabica coffee wafted through from the kitchen.

He put on the salmon-pink shirt that he always wore on a Friday, with his navy-blue Hugo Boss pinstripe suit and his black wing-tip brogues. He struggled for a few seconds with the silver cufflinks Amelia had given him for Christmas, before striding through to the kitchen to join her for breakfast. It was 7.20 am.

Time for a fresh start.

'It's over, Amelia,' he announced as he sat down and reached across the table for the handle of the cafetière. 'I want you to leave. I don't want you living here anymore. I'm sorry.'

It was a bright morning and a ray of sunlight streamed into the kitchen, illuminating them both and exposing their relationship. There was a brief moment of tranquility as Jack poured the steaming, almost-black coffee into the white bone-china cup.

'You better be kidding me, Jack.' Amelia's face slowly

turned pink as she registered that he was deadly serious. 'Is this because of – you seriously need to – you think you...'

She couldn't finish her sentences. It was as if her brain was short-circuiting. Her face was the shade of a Pink Lady now. His least favorite apple, Jack thought. Her pupils were small and dark, like peppercorns.

He tried to stay calm as he spoke. 'I'm sorry but it's for the best, Amelia. Last night I finally realized what's wrong with our relationship. It's not fair on either of us to carry on with this pretense any longer.' He hoped she might just agree, pack her things and leave without fuss.

'Pretense. *P-r-e-t-e-n-s-e?* PRETENSE!' Amelia shouted. Jack knew an Italian storm was brewing. He braced himself. 'What a joke. You are the one pretending, Jack Edward Fucking Davidson. You *pretend* to like your job, *pretend* you're still cool, *pretend* to be rich, *pretend* to like your friends.' She stiffened and gasped for air, incandescent with rage. 'Let me tell you something. I've been *pretending* you are funny, *pretending* to like your family. My friends even *pretend* they like you, and guess what, Jack? I was *pretending* when I said I loved you. You ungrateful, miserable shit. I hate you. I fucking hate you.'

Jack picked up his coffee and moved it out of the line of fire. A volley of spittle was shooting from Amelia's mouth with each angry word. It wasn't just her appearance which altered as a result of her temper; her language changed as well. Her mouth became a weapon of mass destruction. Jack wondered whether this might be the last time she'd aim her belligerence at him, and began to feel vindicated by her revealing testimony.

I rest my case M'lud, he thought as he turned to stare out of the window, in an effort to blank out the continued abuse. The morning sky seemed implausibly perfect. Not a single cloud. He observed two birds perched close to one another on a nearby branch. Robins or sparrows; possibly chaffinches, he guessed. He didn't really know. Their heads moved robotically, right and left, while their petite bodies stayed perfectly still. One of them cocked its tiny burnt-orange head to one side and stared back at him. He locked eyes with the curious bird for three or four seconds until it flew off.

Minutes later, Amelia stormed from the kitchen. Still hurling abuse, she crashed out of the house, knocking the wooden key bowl onto the tiled floor, where it broke into two distinct pieces.

Jack remained seated at the kitchen table, eyes closed. He took a deep breath, exhaled slowly, and thought about the prospect of flying away.

Card 9

The Bluff: A bet made with a hand that is
mathematically unlikely to either make money or
disguise patterns of play.

London, 26 June 2009
TOM'S HAND

'We really need to assess our outgoings. We can't keep
burying our heads in the sand. A lot of these luxuries we
can do without, can't we?'

Tom Patterson didn't reply. He was sitting in his
kitchen in deflated silence. His right hand wrapped
around a mug of steaming black coffee. He'd felt numb
ever since the redundancy. Life wasn't supposed to be
like this. He had worked at UBG for the last fifteen years,
coming up through their graduate scheme in '94. A loyal
employee, practically married to the job, he hadn't done
anything wrong. He'd seen UBG change through the
years – for better or for worse, through sickness and in
health – but he'd stayed the same, faithfully by its side.
Nevertheless, the decision had been made to let him go.
Of course, he hadn't been the only one to lose his job, but
he had taken it personally.

His boss had broken the news on Tom's first day back from his honeymoon in Mauritius; he was to be part of the third round of redundancies that year. *Necessary to rationalize headcount and right-size the business I'm afraid, Tom. More losses than we realized.* Tom could not believe that he was now just another sad statistic – one of the 12,000 employees axed by UBG since the economic meltdown a year before.

'Seriously, Tom. It's been a whole month now,' Victoria said. 'You have to pull yourself together. I'm sorry you lost your job but we need to deal with this situation head-on and not keep putting it off until tomorrow. You need to start applying for a new one. Why don't you ask Jonny to help you out? He seems to know everyone in the city.'

Tom kept quiet.

'Or why don't you try a career change?' she continued. 'What about marine conservation? I thought that was what you really wanted to do.'

'I didn't *lose* my job,' Tom replied after a pause. He hated her way of saying it – like she was calling him a loser. 'It was taken from me.'

'Fine, but however you want to say it, we are where we are. We need to stop spending so much, at least until you get something else. The redundancy payment won't last much beyond Christmas at this rate. Not unless we make some drastic changes.'

'Agreed. So why don't you stop getting your hair and nails done every two weeks and stop shopping in the farmers' market every other bloody day?'

'Don't take this out on me, darling. It's not my fault.'

'Or you could sell your wedding dress,' Tom continued. 'I mean, it cost your parents an absolute fortune and you only wore it once. It's only two months old – practically brand-new. Why don't I call the boutique and see if they'll buy it back?'

'There's no need to be like that.'

'I'm sorry, Victoria. I didn't mean to snap. It's just ... well, I guess, I feel like I'm letting you down.'

She smiled at him. 'Let's approach this sensibly, shall we? Just take a look at our outgoings. Surely we can cut back on some of these payments?' Victoria handed him a bank statement with several figures highlighted in bright yellow.

'Seriously? I don't believe this,' Tom snatched the statement from her, feeling at once embarrassed and annoyed. He knew she was right, but he hated the thought she'd been snooping around, examining his spending habits ... and she was calling him frivolous. The cheek of it! He shot a glance at the highlighted expenses: golf club, Sky Sports and Movies package, gym membership, wine club, magazine subscriptions and monthly fees for his various private members' clubs.

'We don't need any of this stuff, do we? Not really, I mean,' Victoria said in a calming tone.

'Hang on. Hang on. These are all essential and isn't it funny how they only relate to me? What about the cost of that second car you insisted on in January? We don't need both the Mercedes and the Audi, do we? How about we sell the Merc; you barely drive the thing anyway.'

His wife seemed to ignore his barbed comments and pointed to the statement in his hand. 'What's this eleven-hundred pounds a month we're spending here?' She was pointing to a standing order with the reference: "Famously Dead".

Tom felt blood rush to his cheeks. 'Oh, that. That's for ... insurance,' he replied hesitantly. 'Life assurance. I can't stop paying now or the whole policy will be worthless.' He avoided her gaze. 'Basically, if I die, you get millions of pounds. Enough to pay the mortgage off in full and allow you to live in luxury for the rest of your life. You'll be rich and famous and I'll be famously dead.'

It was the first lie he had told her since they got married. He hated her interrogation but he knew that if he was honest about his university game she was bound to demand that the payments be stopped.

Life as newlyweds had been tough; since Tom had lost his job, they seemed to be arguing almost daily. The healthy tan and positive attitude he'd brought back from their honeymoon had been rapidly eroded by his sudden lack of income. He had been made redundant at work and now his wife was making him feel redundant at home.

'You know what, Victoria? I really could do without all of this right now. I'm going to get some fresh air. I need to clear my head.'

He stuffed the bank statement in the back pocket of his jeans. Leaving his wife standing in the kitchen, he walked outside and down the street, towards the cluster of shops which surrounded the village park. It was nine o'clock on a sunny Friday morning and the fresh air was a welcome reprieve from the stale atmosphere at home.

As Tom strolled past the Yummy Mummies pushing their babies in designer prams, he considered himself lucky that at least he and Victoria didn't have any kids to worry about, like so many of their friends did. He then thought about the dreadful task of having to apply for a job. Victoria was right but the market was competitive and very few banks were recruiting at his level. Besides, they could take their pick of redundant bankers washing around London, all chasing the same few jobs. It was going to be tough. He thought about starting the process of pulling together his résumé and the ignominy of trying to sell himself to parochial recruiters who would then try to sell him to prospective employers; the internal tests and demeaning interview after demeaning interview. He'd be competing alongside younger, hungrier applicants; people who would take the job for far less than he felt he was worth. The whole process would be tortuous and belittling, every knock-back met with obvious disappointment and concealed derision from his friends, his family and his wife. At his age and with his experience, he shouldn't have to prove himself all over again. The very thought of all the effort was exhausting.

After a five-minute walk, he arrived at the local newsagent's. He pushed the door open, pausing on the doorstep to scan the tabloids on display outside. His heart skipped a beat as he registered the headline in large black letters shouting at him from the front page: 'JACKO DEAD!'

'Michael Jackson is dead?' Tom asked the newsagent excitedly after picking up the *Daily Mail* and hurrying into the shop.

'Yes, Mr. Patterson. Terrible news. Only fifty years old. Can you believe it? Three years younger than me. Tragic story. My daughter had tickets to see him. She's absolutely devastated.'

Tom couldn't believe it. He stood staring at the newsagent, a peculiar smile across his face. 'Thank you,' he said at last. 'That's the best news I've heard in months.'

He paid the confused-looking newsagent, left the shop with a spring in his step, and walked down the street until he reached the village green. *I guess I'll cancel that life insurance policy after all,* he thought as he sat down on the park bench with a smile on his face and read about the unexpected death of the King of Pop.

Card 10

The Family Pot: A deal in which every player calls the first opening bet.

London, 26 June 2009
TOM'S HAND

Tom finished reading the article, took his cellphone from his jeans and scrolled down his list of contacts. He was surprised to find he still had a number for Piers Upwell. Without giving it much thought he pressed the call button and took a deep breath.

'Hi, is that Piers? It's Tom Patterson ... from Cardiff—'

'Thomas Andrew Patterson, how the devil are you? Goodness, I was just thinking about you, funnily enough. It's happened hasn't it, old bean? It's bloody well finally happened.'

'Yes, mate. It has,' Tom said. He felt goose bumps, hearing Pier's posh voice. 'Typical of JD to win, though, lucky git. I bet he can't wait to tell us what's in store.'

'And I for one can't jolly well wait, either. I'm about due another vacation, Tom, I can tell you that much. I need to get out of this place. D'you know how much is in the pot, by the way?'

'No.'

Piers paused for effect, before announcing gleefully, 'One million pounds!'

'A million? Seriously? Holy shit. Poor old Vinnie. Must be four years since he stopped paying. Just after his second child was born. Said he couldn't justify it any more – I reckon his wife got to him.'

'Vinnie – married and a daddy? I always thought he would be the last to settle down. Good on him.'

'Are you still in touch with Jack and Charlie, then?'

'Haven't heard a peep from any of the old gang. I spent a few years traveling around after we graduated and fell out of touch with everyone. Awfully silly, really. Made sure I kept up my payments though, unlike Vincent. Gosh, he will be livid when he hears the news about Wacko Jacko. Poor sod. Still, more fun for us, I suppose.'

'Yeah, I've been rubbish at keeping in touch, too. This reunion is well overdue. I suppose JD's still a hot-shot lawyer?'

'I guess so. I'm surprised you two didn't stay in contact. You were such good mates at Cardiff. I haven't actually seen anyone since graduation. JD did text me last night, though. That's when he told me about the million pounds. Not sure what he's planning, mind you. He's keeping it all rather cryptic at the moment but we'll find out soon enough, I'm sure.'

'We've got so much to catch up on. Fifteen years – so much has happened.' Fond memories of university slowly began to stir. 'Where are you living nowadays?' Tom asked.

'I'm back in the UK. Burnt a few bridges back in Oz so I'm living with a friend in London for a while.'

'Excellent. Why don't we meet up? I'm free today if you fancy a drink.'

'Not working today then, old bean?' Piers asked.

'No … I had some leave to take. I've got a few errands to run this morning but otherwise I'm available.'

'Perfect. Kensington Roof Gardens, then, around 2pm?'

'Looking forward to it.'

Tom hung up and smiled. Then his phone beeped with a text from an unknown number:

TP. The K of P is FD. Long live the K of P. JD.

Tom's smile transformed into a knowing grin.

***

TOM'S HAND

Tom was standing at the bar in Kensington Roof Gardens when his friend walked in, twenty minutes late. Piers looked much thinner than he had at university and he seemed to have lost his famous sartorial flare.

A plain navy-blue T-shirt and jeans hung loose on his slender frame. He wore white trainers but Tom didn't recognize the brand. Piers' face looked old and slightly drawn and his once-bright teeth and perfect smile seemed insipid.

'Patto, how are you doing? You haven't changed at all,' Piers approached with his arms wide open.

Tom noticed a small hole in the armpit of his T-shirt. 'Piers Lawrence Fraser Upwell,' he stated. The name sounded pompous but Tom used it fondly

'It's been too long. Look at you! By Jove, the years have been kind,' Piers said as he brought Tom in for a friendly hug.

The comment made Tom feel uncomfortable. Was Piers being sarcastic? And should he repay the compliment, even though Piers didn't look good? In fact, Tom felt a little embarrassed by his friend's scruffy appearance. They were, after all, in a trendy private

54

members' club. Piers' lank hair was swept back and it was clear he was trying to hide the bald patch over his crown.

'Thanks, Piers. You're looking good, too. Can you believe we haven't seen each other since graduation?' Tom smiled. 'I remember it vividly – singing in the Student Union at the end of the night, arms linked, pissed out of our minds – so relieved to have actually graduated. Gabrielle was at number one with *Dreams* – that's what we were singing.'

The two looked at each other and began to sing at the same time, Piers' loud, plummy accent making Tom want to laugh. Then they lapsed into an awkward silence. After several seconds of observing one another through the bittersweet lens of nostalgia, Piers spoke again. 'Let's get some drinks in, shall we? We've a lot to catch up on. Why don't we start with some Extra Cheeky Vimtos, for old time's sake?'

They eased across the room and took up a couple of stools next to the bar. Apart from a few staff and a Chinese man sitting surrounded by small plates of food at the far end, the club was practically empty.

'Two Extra Cheeky Vimtos please, young man,' Piers said with excitement.

The twenty-year-old barman stared back vacuously.

'It's what we drank at university in the '90s, old bean. Blimey ... kids of today,' Piers said, winking at Tom. 'They have no idea, do they? Right,' he looked back at the barman. 'Get a pint glass, young man. Add some crushed ice, one shot of vodka, one shot of tequila, two shots of port and a bottle of WKD Blue. That's it – the drink of champions.'

The barman shot them a look and began to prepare their drinks in silence.

'So tell me, old boy, what the devil have you been up to since '93?' Piers slapped Tom on the shoulder.

'Oh well, nothing exciting, really. I got a job straight away on the UBG graduate scheme and moved to London. I've been with the bank for fifteen years. I'm a Senior Credit Analyst. I live in Richmond in a detached house with a garden and a double garage. I married my long-term girlfriend, Victoria, in Wiltshire this year and we had a three-week honeymoon in Mauritius.' He didn't want to admit yet that he no longer worked at the bank. Why spoil the start of their reunion with such depressing news?

'Well, in that case,' Piers grinned, 'commiserations on becoming a banker and felicitations on becoming a husband. That's truly fantastic. I'm so pleased for you both. I look forward to meeting your better half.'

'Two Extra Chinky Vin Teas,' said the barman as he placed the fizzy purple concoctions down in front of them. 'Would you like me to open a tab?'

'Please,' Piers said quickly, picking up his drink. 'Cheers, Patto,' he said. 'Let's drink to our reunion, to an amazing trip, and to your new wife.'

'Cheers,' Tom said. They clinked glasses and he took a sip. 'God, that brings back a well of purple memories. I used to love this stuff. It only cost a pound in the student union, didn't it? Probably more like fifteen in here.'

'Don't worry about that, old boy. I'll pick up the tab today, just like in the good old days at church, hey?'

'Thanks be to Piers,' Tom replied in an Irish accent. 'Hey, speaking of picking up the tab, remember the time those third years tried to make you pay for their drinks in the Union and Charlie came to the rescue?'

'Goodness, it was so long ago, I don't think—'

'You must remember, though?' Tom continued eagerly. 'Those nobs were with the First XV. Three of them, wearing match ties and blazers. I think they'd beaten Swansea that day and they'd been on the sauce since the final whistle.'

'The rugby team thought they ran that place,' said Piers.

'Charlie asked them to leave you alone and they got all rowdy. It was three against one but Charlie could handle himself, couldn't he? Jesus, he was hard.' Tom paused for a moment. 'I think that was the first time I ever saw him in a fight. He basically embarrassed them in front of the whole bar. Everyone was watching in stunned silence. Don't you remember? They smashed that glass over his head and he didn't even flinch. He just stood there and stared at them with those piercing eyes. Then he knocked them out with three swift punches and dragged them from the club by their rugby ties. It was so cool. I can't believe you don't remember.' Tom took another sip of his drink. 'I wonder what he's up to now?'

'I think he joined the army not long after graduation,' Piers replied. 'He's probably getting paid to beat people up in the name of queen and country now.'

'Fair play. I'm pleased for him. I always thought he was better suited to the military than life as an accountant or something equally as boring. I could never work out why he was on the same course as you. Anyway, what the hell have you been doing, Piers? I bet you've got some interesting stories to tell?'

Piers took a sip of his drink and folded his arms. 'I wanted to see the world after university, you know, before starting a proper job, so I flew to South America and traveled around.'

'Not in your own private plane, I hope?'

'Commercial flight. Even flew cattle-class. I wanted to feel like a proper traveler, you know?'

Tom smiled.

'I lived in Sao Paulo for a month with an old school friend, who was working as a hack for one of the national papers in Brazil. Then I spent a bit of time as a cowboy living and working on a ranch in Argentina.'

'Did you get to ride around on a horse with a lasso?'

'I did, as a matter of fact. That was the best part,' Piers took a sip of his drink. 'I walked the Inca trail. And after I'd seen enough of South America, I flew to Asia and bummed around Thailand, Indonesia, Vietnam, Cambodia and Malaysia. Do you know you can live like a king in Cambodia for as little as fifty dollars a day?'

'I would've thought you could live like a king anywhere you wanted, Piers. The amount of money your mother has, you could practically buy Cambodia and declare yourself their supreme leader.'

Piers ignored the comment and downed half his drink.

'I remember the day we met like it was yesterday,' Tom said with a smile. 'You were wearing a white Ralph Lauren rugby shirt with a light blue collar, jeans and those mustard-colored loafers.'

'My favorite pair.'

'God, they were hideous,' Tom continued. 'You had your sleeves pulled up – I even remember your watch: expensive-looking, with a red-and-blue face. You were the first person I ever met who owned a Rolex.' Tom smiled but Piers didn't seem to react. 'You were barking orders at two men as they carried your stuff into our flat at Talybont. You even had a computer. You musta been the only student in our building who had one back then. Oh, and then you spoke! I can remember your exact words, I'd never heard anything like it.' Tom mimicked Piers' posh accent, '*Well hello there, old boy. I'm Upwell, Piers Upwell. How do you do? Shall we go to the local watering hole and check out the totty?*'

Tom grinned broadly and eyed Piers, who was looking down at his empty pint. 'Hey, what's the matter? I didn't mean to offend you, mate. I mean, come on, that wasn't such a bad impression, was it?'

'No, no, it's not that,' said Piers. 'I miss that Rolex. It was the only present my mother ever gave me. I got it on my sixteenth birthday when I was at Eton. She'd even had "Happy Birthday Son" inscribed on the back. I treasured that watch, not because it was a limited edition but because it had an intrinsic value that was, quite frankly, priceless. And when that Welsh bastard pinched it,' he said the word "bastard" with a long "aaaah" sound, 'I was devastated. I felt I had lost something so much more than a watch.' Piers looked Tom in the eyes and continued. 'It was like a security blanket, if you know what I mean?'

'I do know what you mean, mate. I had a blanket for years when I was a kid. It had pictures of Paddington Bear all over it. I used to call it "Pad". My mum told me I was inconsolable for weeks when I lost the thing. I cried myself to sleep and wouldn't speak to anyone for days. But over time I grew to cope without it. Sometimes it's good to lose your security blanket – it teaches you how to deal with things on your own.'

Tom ordered another round of drinks from the barman. He'd never seen Piers so emotional. 'Talk about "born with a silver spoon in your mouth",' Tom joked. 'Can't believe I just compared my grubby old "Pad" with your limited edition Rolex.'

'It's silly really,' Piers said, his tone still downbeat. 'I was a little boy, when she sent me to Eton. I was thousands of miles from home, far away from her and my brother. She gave me as much money as I needed; I could buy anything I wanted, but the thing I really longed for didn't have a price – I couldn't buy time with her.'

'I'm sorry I mentioned the Rolex, mate,' said Tom, slightly taken aback by Piers' revelation. 'I didn't realize you were still brooding about it. Anyway, listen, I refuse to sit here and feel sorry for you. And you shouldn't feel hard-done-by, either. Most people would give their right arm to be in a privileged position like yours, so chin up and get over it.'

Another round of Extra Cheeky Vimtos arrived and Tom tipped his back in seconds. 'So tell me – I'm intrigued – what jobs have you had since graduation?'

'Well, I was a ski instructor in Austria for two seasons and I managed a school friend's bar in the South of France for a summer. Then I was a super-yacht purser in the Caribbean and I did a stint as a lifeguard in California, too. I had to quit the modeling agency in Paris after a few months – all the models were crazy as hell, they have to be some of the worst people to work with. They're so demanding and petulant when they don't get their way. Honestly, Tom, the atmosphere was toxic; I had to get out of there. Let's see … what else? Oh yeah, I taught English to some students in Nepal and I've done a bit of financial consulting off and on for the family business.'

'Wow, you have been busy. I suppose if you've got a family fortune to fall back on it's easier to leave the boring desk jobs to suckers like me who have to work for a living.' Tom paused. That familiar sense of inadequacy and jealousy was beginning to surface already. 'Sorry. I didn't mean to sound so bitter.'

Piers shrugged, finished his second Extra Cheeky Vimto, and ordered two pints of Guinness.

'I can't drink the black stuff anymore without thinking about that time you made me drop a dissected penis into that pint glass in the Taf,' said Tom, trying to steer the conversation back to safer ground.

'By far the funniest and strangest thing I've ever witnessed,' said Piers. His face lit up as he thought of it. 'How the hell did you pull it off? I still can't believe you didn't get caught.'

'For one horrible second, I thought he might have seen me messing with his drink. Lifting the penis from the dissection room was the easy part, getting it into that poor sod's pint of Guinness without anyone noticing...'

'Was a masterstroke,' laughed Piers. 'How you had the nerve to do it in the first place, I'll never know. What a legend.'

'I didn't have a choice. Don't you remember? I lost that poker game. It was either do everyone's chores for a week or take the dare.'

'I would have taken the chores, to be honest.'

'Yeah, but you'd have paid someone to do them for you.'

'Maybe,' Piers replied with a wry grin. 'But let's face it, I wouldn't have lost the game in the first place.'

'Yeah, you were so obsessed at uni, you got us all hooked.' Tom laughed. 'Remember teaching JD and me Texas Hold'em for the first time? We came back from lectures and you were in the kitchen with Sally something and Lizzy Ashton from the flat upstairs. The cards were out, you'd plied them with Archers & lemonade and Lizzy was wearing nothing but her knickers when we walked in. It was eleven in the morning. Absolute genius. I wonder what Lizzy's up to now?'

'I don't gamble anymore,' Piers cut in. Tom noted his friend's expression and paused. Had the incident in the Dragon's Den put him off poker altogether?

Piers finished his Guinness and placed the empty glass on the bar. 'Let's talk about something other than poker, shall we?'

The barman cleared the glass and Piers ordered a Jack Daniels & Coke. Tom had barely touched his Guinness. This was going to be a heavy session.

'So Charlie joined the army, hey?' He was repeating himself, but it was the best way Tom could think to change the subject. 'I suppose he was never really that interested in studying. I swear he used to spend more time in the gym than in lectures.'

'Funny chap, wasn't he? All the girls loved him but I don't remember him ever having a girlfriend. The rest of us had our fair share, mind you. Who was the girl who came knocking on your door at night when she was drunk?'

'Bethan Matthews,' Tom said in his best Welsh accent. 'Sober, she never said a word to me – I'm not sure she'd even have recognized me.' He paused, took a sip of his Guinness. 'I always thought Charlie might be gay. Tall, handsome, square-jawed – and those piercing blue eyes. He looked after himself but never seemed much interested in women. JD and I thought he had a crush on you, he spent most of his time at university following you around like a shadow.'

'No way,' Piers protested with a laugh. 'Anyway, it wasn't just me he followed. He came to JD's rescue more than a few times, too. There was that night Jack nearly got run over on his way back to the flat and those four Valley boys jumped him.'

'God, yes. I wasn't there but I remember Jack telling us about how Charlie saved his life that night.'

'D'you know what, Tom? I can't wait to have the old gang back together. Why the devil has it taken us this long?'

Tom had been wondering the same thing. They'd all graduated with such promise for the future. Maybe they didn't want to compare lives; maybe they weren't all happy with their lot. A pair of aces can be the best two cards you'll ever be dealt, but they don't guarantee a winning hand. He considered his own situation: a redundant ex-banker with a huge mortgage, new wife, and no means to continue their comfortable lifestyle. The prospect of his future made him bitter. This wasn't exactly the ideal time for a reunion. *Let's just enjoy the here and now,* he thought; *reminiscing about the past.* He tipped back the last of his Guinness.

'I guess life just gets in the way sometimes, Piers,' Tom said. 'And by the sounds of it, you were having far too much fun to give a second thought to your old mates anyway. But look, it doesn't matter now. I truly believe that the friends you make at university will be friends for life; the passing of time won't change that. Great friendships can lie dormant for years but then you'll pick up exactly where you left off, right?'

'I couldn't have put it better myself, old boy; I only hope the others feel the same way.'

'They will, I'm sure, and this trip is going to be awesome, we'll be talking about it for years afterwards.'

Tom called the barman over. 'What's he eating?' He nodded his head towards the Chinese man at the end of the bar. 'It smells delicious.'

'Honey-glazed pork ribs,' said the barman. 'That's his fourth plate.'

'Two of those, please, and some cashew nuts.'

'Anything more to drink, sir?'

Tom looked at Piers. 'Fancy a bottle of red?'

'Only if it's full-bodied and comes from Australia,' Piers replied with a smile.

'2000 Penfolds Grange Shiraz?' the barman suggested.

Piers nodded in approval. 'A good vintage, just like you,' he smiled at Tom. 'Quite complex, wiry undertones, full-bodied, with a big nose.'

Tom laughed at the jibe. At £299 a bottle he was glad he wasn't paying.

'Shame about Michael Jackson,' said Tom after a moment's silence. 'I was convinced Fidel Castro would be first to pop his clogs.'

'So, Tom, what would you have done if you had won?'

'Well, as you can imagine I've given that question some serious thought...'

Card 11

From The Bottom of the Deck: A sleight-of-hand technique in which the bottom card from a deck of playing cards is dealt instead of the top card.

Las Vegas, 11 July 2009
CHARLIE'S HAND

Charlie headed back towards Caesars Palace. He was unsettled. He was no closer to finding Piers but he had uncovered a secret that gave him cause for concern. The Triads were shrewd and suspicious and he knew he would have to tread carefully from now on.

As he turned onto the asphalted walkway he observed three lads ahead, bragging loudly about the strippers they had been with last night. Their accents were unmistakably Welsh. *What are the chances?* Charlie thought. He didn't believe in God. His time in the army had made it difficult for him to reconcile religion with the horrors of war. Charlie believed in things he could see and understand; facts, evidence and scientific theories with probable outcomes. But occasionally things happened that science couldn't explain. Things that caused Charlie to wonder whether there was someone or something watching over him; guiding his path. He marched double-time towards the three Welsh lads. He was not going to let this opportunity pass.

Time for revenge.

'Excuse me,' he called out. 'Do you guys have the time?'

Two of them turned around warily, their faces pinched with hostility. The other continued walking.

'What was that, butt?' the tallest of the three chimed as he stepped forward, a Lucky Strike balancing between his chapped lips.

'What are the chances?' Charlie said without surprise. 'I met your friend in London,' he pointed to a lad in a white Adidas tracksuit.

'Hey, Geraint,' the tall one called out. 'This old man reckons he knows you.'

They stood staring at Charlie as their friend joined them.

Charlie held their gaze.

'It's good to see you again, *Geraint*. I just wanted to know if you had the time.'

'You're that queer from the airport lounge. Why you acting like you know me, butt?'

'What do you really want, boyo?' the tall one spoke again, taking a final drag on his cigarette and flicking it to the ground in front of Charlie. 'Cos you sure as hell don't need the time. You're wearing a watch, you posh English prick.' He pointed to Charlie's wrist.

Charlie observed the three lads closely, his military brain crunching a series of calculations.

'Very astute,' he said, glancing briefly at his black G-Shock. 'I don't need the time. What I need, in actual fact, is for you to step aside so that Geraint can give me *his* Rolex.'

The three Welshmen looked at each other and then cackled in unison.

'Go fuck yourself, old man,' said the tall one, grinning

confidently as he took a step closer. 'Do you have any idea who his dad is?'

Yes I do, Charlie thought as he fixed him with his granite-hard stare. The tall lad's smile suddenly vanished and his eyes narrowed, flashing with menace. The next moment, he lunged forward and swung a right hook at Charlie's head. Charlie was expecting the attack and bobbed to the left, propelling his knee into the body of his aggressor. With his left fist, Charlie struck the lad on the side of the head then watched as he collapsed to the ground, his arms hardly lifting to protect his face from the asphalt.

The other two turned and darted off, gaining a twenty-meter head start. Charlie sprinted after them, long strides allowing him to cover the distance quickly. The two lads splintered, one running along the sidewalk, the other fleeing left into a nearby park. Charlie followed Geraint into the leafy space, drew up behind him and jumped forwards, tackling him to the ground. A muted cry escaped his lungs as all 260 pounds of Charlie landed on top of him on the manicured grass.

'Get the hell off me, butt,' he wailed as he tried to wriggle free. 'You've broken my arm, you fucking psycho.'

Wasting no time, Charlie suspended his huge fist above the moving target then slammed it down. The target stopped wriggling. Grateful that the park was close to empty, Charlie calmly removed the Rolex from Geraint's limp wrist, tucked it safely into the pocket of his corduroy jacket and then leant in close and whispered into his ear, 'Tell your dad you gave the watch to Mr. Hilfiger.'

Card 12

The Raise: To increase the size of an existing bet in the same round of betting.

Las Vegas, 11 July 2009
JACK'S HAND

'So how much do we have left, then?' Tom asked. He scratched his facial hair and a shower of white skin cells landed on his black jeans. His eyes were bloodshot from lack of sleep and his skin dehydrated from a combination of alcohol and air-conditioning.

Jack was pacing up and down. They had only been in Vegas for two nights but already they'd hemorrhaged a lot of money. He knew roughly how much was left; he'd been keeping a mental record. Last night had been expensive: the meal at Maestro's; their pub crawl along the Strip, and their bill at the Mad House had come to nearly $50,000. The first-class return flights and Presidential Suite had already been paid but the bar tab, service charge and extras were yet to be settled. These would no doubt run into tens of thousands of dollars.

'We've only got about £150,000 left. That's roughly $250,000.'

Jack thought about asking Tom how much of his own

money he could access at short notice. He was curious to know what sort of nest egg Tom had amassed since university. But he thought better of it in case he was asked the same question. He certainly didn't want to reveal his own finances.

'Can't we just call the police? Or his mum? She's supposed to be a billionaire, remember?' Tom said sarcastically as he walked towards the bar. 'And where the hell's Charlie? Captain Preston should know what to do.'

Tom reached for the Rémy Martin and a crystal brandy glass. 'Fancy a stiff one?'

Jack shook his head.

'Why don't we gamble what's left – turn the 250 into half a million? We could double our money in less than a minute. Bosh. Easy as that. Head downstairs to the Forum casino and put it all on black,' Tom said as he poured himself a cognac. 'Or red.'

Jack laughed but he wasn't convinced his friend was joking.

'Seriously, JD, it's not such a bad idea. Maybe not roulette but poker? You and Charlie were proper good at Cardiff and we are in a gambler's paradise after all,' Tom said, lifting the glass to his lips and taking a swig.

'Have you forgotten what happened the last time we played poker together?'

The night at Cardiff's Dragon's Den casino was burned into Jack's memory. Piers had come close to losing his eye. The look of terror on his friend's face had given Jack nightmares for months.

'Yeah, but you guys actually won that night. We're in Vegas now, JD. No one's going to steal your winnings.'

Tom did have a point. Charlie had been a brilliant poker player back at university, with an uncanny ability to get inside people's heads, read their body language and get the better of them from across the table.

The noise of the elevator interrupted their conversation and they both turned towards it, watching anxiously as the light flashed and the doors parted. Charlie reappeared and without saying a word marched into the master bathroom then locked the door behind him.

'Where the hell have you been?' Tom shouted through the bathroom door.

There was a slight delay before Charlie responded, 'I went to that club you were at last night to see if I could find out anything. Got into a spot of bother. Nothing serious. One of the doormen didn't like my questions.'

'You alright, mate?' Tom asked. 'You're kind of freaking me out a little. You've been gone for an hour and we need you focused, Charlie. Listen, we've got to come up with a plan. Bottom line is, we don't have enough money for the ransom. There's only $250,000 left and we're running out of time.'

Jack could hear the sound of running water. 'Are you taking a bath?' he shouted in disbelief, throwing Tom a worried look.

'I think better when I'm in the bath.'

***

CHARLIE'S HAND

Charlie stood in front of the gold rococo mirror in the palatial master bathroom. His eye had already swollen up nicely.

He looked down at his bloodied fist. He hadn't felt anything but the skin on his knuckles had opened up after the second punch. He remembered Mr. Yang's leather gloves and, for a brief moment, thought about buying a pair. Reaching into his corduroy jacket pocket, he took out the watch and placed it on the marble-topped surface next to the washbasin. As he washed his hands and stared into the mirror, he tried to assemble his thoughts. Crimson-colored water lapped around the gold washbasin then disappeared through the plughole.

He got undressed, draped his corduroy jacket on the back of the decorative French chair and climbed into the steaming water. The bath was gold-plated and stood impressively on lion-clawed feet in the middle of the vast room. Charlie sat back and turned his head to the side, facing the mirror. The watch lay in front of him. A Rolex GMT Master II. The distinctive red-and-blue face was staring back at him. It was 8.35 pm.

Time to come up with a plan.

***

TOM'S HAND

Tom tipped back his second cognac within half an hour and felt a sudden urge to call Victoria. He'd sent her two texts in the seventy-two hours they'd been away, and both messages had contained lies.

'Need to check in with the good lady wife, let her know I'm alive,' he mumbled as he pulled out his cell and slipped from their suite into the opulent corridor for a bit of privacy.

'Hello? Victoria Milton speaking,' she sounded slightly out of breath as she answered their house phone.

'Hi darling. You're a Patterson now, don't forget,' Tom said proudly.

'Yes. Sorry. Force of habit, I suppose – it still feels strange. Anyway, how's New York? How are the interviews with Jonny's colleagues going? It was so good of him to do that, wasn't it?'

Tom took a deep breath. 'Well, actually I've been

meaning to tell you something – I've not been completely honest with you, darling.' He paused, hardly daring to imagine the reaction on the other end of the line. He looked down at his cell. 'For Christ's sake... Useless piece of shit.'

'That was quick. How's the ball and chain?' said Jack as Tom returned to the suite.

'Bloody battery died again. I hate these new cell phones. That Steve Jobs is a latter-day Charles Ponzi. I swear he's just conning us out of our hard-earned cash. They're all aesthetics and no utility.'

'Your wife must be a real saint.'

'How so?' Tom said as he looked for his charger.

'Most of my friends wouldn't have had a chance of getting a pass from their other halves for a trip to Vegas.'

'Yeah, she's great,' Tom said quietly.

'Not like my ex,' Jack continued. 'She went ballistic when I told her about our Famously Dead game. Didn't take it very well at all. Probably didn't help that she was an ardent Michael Jackson fan. I'd say your wife's a rare breed, mate. Definitely a keeper.'

Tom didn't respond. He stopped looking for his charger, walked towards the bar and poured himself another cognac.

***

CHARLIE'S HAND

Charlie sat in the steaming bath with his eyes closed. The peace and tranquility of the water seemed to cleanse his mind; away from life's dirty distractions he could think with more clarity.

Should he tell the others about the watch? His mind flashed back to the Dragon's Den. He remembered the look of abject terror on Piers' youthful face. The broken wine bottle millimeters from his eye; the malicious grin on his attacker's face.

Take his watch as well, Gethin. That'll be worth a few quid for sure, butt.

As he lay in the bath, the familiar feelings of failure resurfaced. The sense of panic, vulnerability and fear as he'd watched Piers under threat of his life and had felt, with the gut-wrenching shame, there was nothing he could do to help. He didn't want to go back to that place. Yet he sensed it was happening all over again. Piers in danger while Charlie stood by, watching helplessly from the sidelines, unable to protect his friend.

Opening his eyes, he looked at the watch again. 8.55 pm. He turned his conversation with the Triads in Serendipity over in his head. He believed what they said. He was usually a good judge of character; he could sense when someone was lying. It was a natural gift, refined in the military police. Mr. Lee had ordered Mr. Yin and Mr. Yang to keep an eye on Piers. They had no reason to kidnap him and if they wanted to hold him to ransom, they would surely be asking for a lot more money. Their job was to protect Mr. Lee's investment. Though why Piers owed the Triads so much money in the first place, and why he hadn't just paid his debt to Mr. Lee, was still a mystery.

Charlie sensed Mr. Yin and Mr. Yang would be following him more closely from now on and he wondered how he might use this to his advantage. But if the Triads weren't responsible for Piers' kidnapping, who was? Whoever they were, had they any idea of their hostage's true value?

***

JACK'S HAND

Jack was standing at the bar, pouring himself a glass of

Talisker ten-year-old single malt when Charlie finally reappeared, wearing a white Caesars Palace bathrobe, at least two sizes too small for him, his muscular frame barely covered by the white Turkish cotton.

'I'll take one of those. No ice,' Charlie said calmly.

'So now that you've had a nice, long soak in the bath, mate, have you any idea what we're going to do?' Jack asked as he handed him a glass of whisky.

'Should we call the police or contact his family?' asked Tom as he joined them at the bar. 'I know they said not to...'

Jack poured another glass of single malt and handed it to Tom.

'Too risky. We can't jeopardize his safety,' said Charlie. 'In these sorts of situations, when there's so little intel to go on, you play it safe. Pay the ransom. Keep the hostage alive.'

'So we're going to just hand over half a million dollars?' said Tom.

'How can we if we don't have it?' Jack said, disappointed that this seemed to be the only plan they had. He had been hoping for a rescue strategy that didn't involve parting with any money.

'I guess Piers would do the same for us, right?' Tom said, looking at Charlie. 'Jesus, man. Those doormen roughed you up a bit, didn't they? You're going to have a real shiner in the morning.'

Charlie didn't comment on his appearance. 'I'd like to think that we'd all make the right decision if it came down to it ... Piers included.'

Jack took a large swig of whisky and looked away.

'So what's the plan?' Tom asked, scratching at the stubble on his neck.

'Get your suits on, gents,' Charlie commanded. 'It's time to make some money.' He finished his single malt and walked towards his bedroom suite.

'I hope your suit fits better than that bathrobe, mate,' Tom called out after him. 'You're showing more skin than some of the girls we met last night.'

Card 13

Four of a Kind: A hand that contains four cards of the same rank.

Cardiff, 12 May 1992
JACK'S HAND

'Some people say it's just a game of chance,' Tom said, 'but that's utter bollocks. There's an element of luck in any game you play but to be a good poker player you need the right skills – an understanding of the game, and the players, in front of you.'

The five friends advanced down Hemingway Road towards the Dragon's Den casino. 'Take Charlie here,' Tom continued, 'he's one of those players who can read body language and facial expressions. JD, on the other hand, is more of a math genius, who likes to calculate the odds.'

'Genius has nothing to do with it,' Jack interrupted, with a smile, 'I spent a whole week studying the outcomes and memorizing the probabilities. It's a very useful skill to have.'

'What about you, Tom? What are you good at?' Vinnie asked.

'I'm going to do what I do best, Vincent. Stay vocal and

play aggressively,' Tom said confidently. 'Goad the other players into betting when they shouldn't. It worked well last time we were here. What you have to appreciate is that most people in the casino at this time of the morning are lads looking for somewhere to continue drinking after hours – too drunk to know they're being manipulated.'

'Come on, Patto. We all know you got lucky last time,' Jack said. 'If you hadn't hit that club on the Fifth Street you would have walked away with sweet F.A. It was dumb luck; nothing to do with your powers of manipulation. Don't forget, we've played enough poker with you to know your game inside-out.'

'Whatever,' Tom shot back, 'we'll see who wins tonight, JD. Twenty pounds says I fare better than you.'

'Done,' said Jack. They smiled at each other as they shook hands in front of the entrance to the Dragon's Den. It was 2.25 am.

'ID,' grunted a bored-looking doorman standing outside the red-and-black painted building.

The five friends pulled out their wallets and flashed their student cards. The doorman's expression was one of hostile resentment but he waved them through. Jack was used to the animosity; there was a peculiar juxtaposition between the student and the non-student species in and around the city. Like a symbiotic relationship, each believed the other to be the parasite.

"Student-bashing" was a sport enjoyed at weekends by local Cardiff thugs. As a result, most students didn't dare venture out at weekends, staying close to the student union and student-friendly pubs around campus instead. But Jack and his roommates weren't like most other students. As long as they were with Charlie, they felt safe, even in the shadiest quarters of the Welsh capital. They shuffled past the doorman and climbed the red-carpeted stairs towards the card rooms. The casino seemed quiet as they stopped at the top, in front of the card room doors.

'OK. From now on, let's keep our interaction to a minimum and try not to draw attention to ourselves. We are not here to make trouble or friends. We're here to make money,' Charlie said with his usual authoritative tone.

'Quite right, Charlie. Mum's the word,' Piers said excitedly. 'Now, let's go and make some dosh for the summer, my dear boys.'

Jack gave him a look. 'You're hardly going to blend in wearing that,' he said, pointing at the red, blue and white jumper Piers was wearing.

'You're a walking advertisement for Tommy Hilfiger,' joked Tom.

Piers ignored them both and handed Jack, Charlie and Tom a crisp £50 note each. 'Righty-ho, Vincent you stick with me and observe,' Piers said cheerfully. 'One day, when you've got more experience under your belt, like these three, it'll be your turn to earn your keep, and I'll let you play with the big boys.'

'That sounds weird on so many levels,' Tom said.

'You sound like a pimp,' said Jack as he slipped his note into his empty wallet.

Charlie nodded. 'Now remember, let's avoid going head-to-head with one another but if we have to the player with the least chips folds as early as possible. That way we increase our collective chance of winning.'

'Absolutely, Charlie,' observed Piers, 'it's a team effort tonight, chaps, so leave your egos at the door. Let's go forth and conquer.'

As they pushed through the doors into the card room, a fog of silence settled upon them along with the smoke-filled air. All eyes trained on the five fresh-faced students as they crossed the threshold into the dimly-lit room. The place had a feel of exclusivity about it, like they had intruded on a private game. Piers and Vinnie headed to the bar and ordered a bottle of red wine. Tom eased towards the far table while Jack and Charlie took up seats at the table closest to the bar.

'Evening,' Jack said politely as he sat down.

The dealer stared at the newcomers, his face locked in a permanent sneer of derision. 'Texas Hold'em. £50 buy-in. Minimum £25 re-buys with no limit. The small blind is £1.50 and it goes up every twenty minutes. We play until there's one winner, got it?'

Four old men with frozen stares sat at Jack and Charlie's table, each of them smoking cigars and drinking what looked like whisky. Four younger men were playing on the other table. They looked shifty and seemed far less drunk than Jack would have liked. Aside from the two dealers and the barman, no one else was in the low-lit, smoky room.

Two hours passed and several hands were dealt, chips reluctantly exchanged and whisky drunk. Charlie and Jack were on vodka & soda, being careful not to down too many. Tom was knocking back pints of Extra Cheeky Vimto, which rapidly accelerated his boisterousness. Already, he was cursing a lot and winning very little. Forty minutes later, after his last reckless hand, he bellowed a drunken slur at the poker deities, stood up theatrically and joined Piers and Vinnie at the bar.

It was now 5am and the game at Jack's table was beginning to get interesting. Charlie was chip leading and Jack had the third largest stack. The other four men had barely spoken but it was evident they knew each other; there was a clear divide across the table. The dealer was obviously betting against Jack and Charlie, despite being closer to them in age.

After pleading noisily for Piers to give him more money, Tom finally kicked his bar stool to the floor and skulked off, leaving empty-handed. No one paid any attention to the petulant exit; they were too engrossed in the cards in front of them.

Jack had been studying the old man across the table closely and sensed he had a read on him. The man was using his vices to mask his shortcomings; when he picked up his cigar and smoked it confidently, Jack reckoned he was holding a good hand. Then, when he pretended to drink – brought his whisky to his mouth but didn't swallow – he seemed to be bluffing. This was his tell and Jack was confident of it.

Jack had a pair of queens in his hand when the Flop was drawn. A king, a jack and a two lay face-up on the green felt in front of them. He was left of the dealer button and so the action was on him. He tapped the table to see what the old man would do. Betting hard, he pushed £100 of chips across the line; over half of his stack. Jack quickly did the math. He had just over a 12% chance of winning the hand. He stared at the man, trying to read his mind, but his face gave nothing away. The other players, Charlie included, folded their hands.

Despite Jack's mathematical head for poker, he occasionally followed his gut. He knew that the odds were against him but he sensed this was the right time to make his move. He decided to match the old man's bet, confident that his pair of queens was strong enough. It was a risky play but it wasn't Jack's money; he could afford to lose, for once.

When the Turn, the fourth card, was flipped over by the dealer, Jack observed his opponent closely. It was a jack of diamonds. He now had Two Pair; queens and jacks. It was his turn to bet. '£100,' he said aloofly, knowing full well that his opponent didn't have enough chips to call.

Jack placed his chips in the middle of the table and stared straight at his opponent. The old man held his gaze and whispered in a course Valley accent, 'Alright then, boyo, let's see what you got, shall we?'

The old man pushed his remaining chips into the pot with an air of confidence and called, 'All in.' He reached for his cigar from the ashtray, inhaled, and blew a smoke ring in Jack's direction.

Damn it, Jack thought, as the dense ring of smoke grew larger then dispersed before his eyes. He must have a king, or a jack ... or a pair of jacks.

He tried to work out the odds but he didn't have enough time before the dealer announced, 'On their backs then, gentlemen.'

The old man was eager to turn over his cards. He had a pair of twos. Jack flipped over his Queen Pair. The dealer said out loud what everyone was already thinking, 'Full House – twos over jacks plays Two Pair – queens and jacks.'

There was close to £500 in the pot. The odds were heavily against Jack – less than a 10% chance of winning, he calculated. He was annoyed at himself but kept a straight face and hoped for a queen. The dealer burnt a card from the deck, flipped over the River card and placed it next to the other four cards on the green felt in front of them.

Jack could feel his heart thumping.

The queen of hearts.

You little beauty. Jack kept silent, trying to keep his smile to himself. He knew he had been lucky. Very lucky.

'Full House,' the dealer said with an apologetic glance at Jack's opponent. 'Queens over jacks, beats twos over jacks.'

The old man rose from his chair slowly, leaving his cigar burning in the ashtray. His face was pinched with scorn. It was only as he stood up that Jack appreciated how fit the guy was for his age. He must have been in his late sixties, perhaps even into his seventies. He might have been a doorman or an ex-rugby player. As he moved under one of the lights in the dank and smoky room, Jack noticed a scar running from the top of the man's right eyebrow and across his forehead, finishing somewhere on his bald pate. He left the table muttering under his breath and perched on a stool at the bar, one foot on the floor – as if he knew the wooden frame wouldn't take his full weight.

Meanwhile, Piers was slumped at the bar, looking bored and uncomfortable, oblivious to Jack's good fortune. Vinnie was drunk and tired and had lost interest about an hour before. There were only five players left now. The other table had long since finished their game and the young men had crept out unnoticed earlier in the morning.

It took about a dozen hands before the game eventually came to a close. Charlie and Jack had systematically scooped up the rest of the chips from around the table before going head-to-head with one another. Their three opponents headed for the bar to join the old man, whose face was still pinched with anger, a vein on the side of his head pulsating like a decapitated earthworm.

After a few hands, both Jack and Charlie went all in. They would both be winners at the end of the night. Charlie won the final hand and the dealer counted out the winnings on the table in front of them. There was £1,355 in the pot in a mixture of scruffy bank notes. Not a bad return for a few hours' work, Jack thought. Charlie thanked the dealer and tipped him £30.

Just as he was putting the money into his wallet, the silence was broken by the sound of smashing glass, followed by a high-pitched squeal.

Jack turned. The old man had Piers by the neck and was holding a shattered wine bottle up to his right eye. One of the man's cronies took a menacing step towards Charlie and said in a thick Valley accent, 'Listen, butt.

Hand over the money and the queer can keep his precious eyes. I'm not joking. Gethin here has done a lot worse for a lot less, like.'

In spite of the darkness and the stale smoke, there was enough light to see the fear on Piers' reddening face. His head was now enveloped by the bulbous arm of his attacker, his eyes twitching frantically while the rest of his body hung limp, in a state of surrender.

A glimmer of hope surfaced when Jack registered the barman, half-hidden behind the bar as he slowly emerged with a thick wooden bat raised high above his head. *Has he the nerve to use it on Gethin's bald head?* Jack wondered. Seconds later, his question was answered.

'Arghhhhshittinhell,' shouted Vinnie as he sprang off his stool and stumbled backwards onto the floor, clutching his head, trying to stem the blood that was pouring out.

'Stop. Take the money,' announced Charlie with enough volume to drown Vinnie's cries.

'Let our friend go and we'll hand over the cash,' Jack called out.

'How's 'bout you boys give us the cash first and then I'll let go of Hilfiger here, so he can run back to his boyfriend, like?'

'OK, fine,' Charlie said quickly. 'Just don't hurt him.' He reached into his wallet and handed the wad of bank notes to the guy standing next to him, who looked like a carbon copy of Gethin but without the scar.

'Take his watch as well, Gethin. That'll be worth a few quid for sure, butt,' the barman said, pleased with himself.

'Have the watch. Please. Just let me go,' spluttered Piers. Trembling with fear, he took it off and held it out. Gethin released Piers, took the watch and stood still for a few moments to admire it.

Charlie rushed over to help Vinnie to his feet as Jack and Piers scrambled for the exit.

'Now piss off, you student scum, and don't be coming back here, mind,' the barman called after them as they staggered out of the room.

Card 14

*The Starting Hand: The initial set of cards dealt
to each player before any voluntary betting takes
place.*

London, 3 July 2009
JACK'S HAND

*You're not young, Jack. You're a middle-aged, boring
lawyer. Past your sell-by date.*

Amelia's words still chimed in Jack's head. Perhaps
she was right.

He had been getting more and more anxious about the
reunion. The four of them had hardly seen each other
since graduation. Jack's life had changed drastically
since Cardiff, when they were last together – young,
naive and full of hope for the future. What did everyone
look like now? It had been such a long time; too long,
really. Would they even recognize each other? He
wondered who had aged the worst, lost the most hair,
gained the most weight ... hoped it wasn't him. What
would they make of his life? Would they be impressed or
apathetic?

Almost a week had passed since Michael Jackson's
death and Jack had been busy planning the trip. At work,

he had been spending most of the day thinking about how to spend the money. His deals were suffering and a few of his clients were starting to complain about his lack of attention to their transactions. Several partners had also remarked that he seemed to have lost his focus recently. He didn't care. In truth, he had lost focus. What did he care about some rich clients' next IPO or merger? He had his own plans to make.

Time to make a change.

***

JACK'S HAND

Jack arrived at Hardbodies of Mayfair at exactly 6pm on Friday night. He had arranged to meet everyone there at 7pm and wanted to be sure he was the first to arrive. He took a seat at the table he'd reserved, facing the entrance. Four black spiral-bound manuals lay in front of him, next to a crystal glass of Yamazaki whisky.

He'd prepared the contents of the manuals meticulously – his blueprint for the trip of a lifetime. It had taken him the best part of his working week to consider, research and plan the whole trip, with a little help from his PA and the reprographics department. The flight details; the hotel; the restaurants where they would eat; the shows they would see; the golf courses they would play, and the casinos they would visit. He'd listed the best nightclubs and strip clubs as well as everything they needed to see and do while they were in Vegas. The manual was a compendium of the adventure he had in store. He had been extremely thorough; included every little detail. Full itineraries, with every aspect covered, from the name of the chauffeur picking them up from McCarran International Airport to the suggested dress code for each event he had planned. Emergency phone numbers, insurance details, time differences – no detail had been omitted.

Each manual was personalized and contained a checklist of the information Jack needed in order to finalize the bookings: passport details, dietary requirements, personal requests, etc.

For Jack, the manuals were imperative, representing the time and effort he had expended in planning the trip. They showed off his attention to detail and also, he hoped, his transparency and honesty, because the last tab contained a full breakdown of how the money would be spent – every last pound of the full one million. Every monthly installment since 1991 and the interest accrued was shown on the ledger. Jack had spent a very long time preparing it.

What are MY friends going to say?

As he sipped on his whisky and waited for his past to walk back into his life, he tried to suppress the jittery sensation in the pit of his stomach. His thoughts were clouded with feelings of insecurity. He looked down at his watch – a Franck Muller King Conquistador. What would his old friends be wearing on their wrists?

For Jack, success was being seen at the best restaurants, living in the smartest part of London, and keeping an appropriate timepiece underneath his shirt cuff. He lived in a world where his job title and the car he drove seemed more important than the direction he was going or what he did for a living. Jack's self-worth was intrinsically linked to his salary, bonus and bank balance. Deep down, he knew his view of life was toxic. Constantly worrying about material things meant he never felt content but he was traveling so fast on the gravy train that he was scared to jump off.

He glanced at his watch – 7pm exactly – and stared at the entrance to the bar. A smart-looking gentleman with horn-rimmed glasses and a full head of gray hair strolled in. *Bollocks,* Jack thought. He couldn't believe it. It was Lord Jeffrey Neilson-Davis, the managing partner of Spear, Collier & Horn. Typical. Jack turned away and hoped his boss wouldn't spot him.

He rehearsed a few scenarios in his head, in case Lord Neilson-Davis came over and asked him what he was doing at Hardbodies: *I'm meeting some prospective clients, old friends of mine – owners of a successful start-up looking to raise finance to acquire one of their competitors.*

But when he looked back again he noticed that his boss was not alone. He was standing at the bar with a young woman. She looked like one of the Russian prostitutes who made a good living working Hardbodies and other classy establishments. Perfect for hunting down wealthy and powerful men. Jack had spent enough time in these places to know that if you attract a certain class of patron, you will always attract a certain class of hooker.

Unbelievable. The dirty swine.

Lord Neilson-Davis was a pillar of the justice system, a Law Lord with a coruscating intellect. He was most famous for his dissenting opinion in the Court of Appeal's decision in Pod's Pies Limited v Pope & Others [1981], when he'd argued that meat pies should be granted separate legal personality; a position that was later upheld by the House of Lords and changed the landscape of corporate law for a few brief years. He was also renowned for his charity work – tackling problems like sex trafficking and human rights. Jack knew that Lord Neilson-Davis's reputation would be destroyed if he was caught fraternizing with a working girl. The press would have a field day.

Jack did his best to ignore what was happening in front of him. Keeping his head down, he leafed through one of the manuals, flicking to the Gantt chart at tab six.

Five minutes passed before he looked back towards the bar. He was relieved to see a Chinese man in a dark suit standing in the exact spot his boss and his little secret had occupied moments earlier. Then, finally, he spotted the familiar muscular frame of an old friend. Charlie Preston had arrived.

There could be no mistaking Charlie. The imposing physique, square jawline and no-nonsense aura. His clothes were plain and unpretentious as ever. He strode over confidently and smiled. 'Great to see you again, Jack. How are you?' He stretched out his huge hand. He was still as big as a vending machine. Possibly bigger than Jack had remembered.

'Great, thanks. You look fantastic.' Jack winced inside as the bones of his right hand were crushed in Charlie's grip, whose calloused skin pressed against Jack's soft palm like extra-coarse sandpaper.

Jack waited for Charlie to return the compliment but he didn't; he just stared back at him, a faint smile across his clean-shaven face.

'Let's get you a drink, shall we?' Jack caught the attention of the waitress and Charlie ordered a bottle of beer. Jack hovered over the table, suddenly uncertain whether or not to sit back down. 'So how's life? You look really well. Nice tan. Have you been abroad?'

Charlie stared at him with those same intense arctic-blue eyes. The pupils seemed darker now. Jack felt uncomfortable, like he was under examination. He could almost feel his friend's gaze piercing his skin, as if searching for something beyond the surface.

'Afghanistan. Helmand Province,' Charlie replied after a short pause.

That figures. Jack felt an idiot for asking. Charlie had never been the type to spend time on a sun lounger next to a pool. Military fatigues on patrol in the desert were much more his style.

The waitress arrived with the beer. Charlie picked up the bottle and smiled. His eyes softened slightly. 'It's great to see you, mate. We haven't stayed in touch nearly as much as I'd have liked. It's difficult with my job.' He raised his glass.

Jack picked up his Japanese whisky. 'Of course. I completely understand. It's a sad indictment of our friendship that we had to wait for the King of Pop to die before we managed a reunion but that's life, I suppose. I mean, I only see my brother once or twice a year and we practically share the same postcode.'

Jack moved to sit down. Standing next to Charlie's 6'4" frame made him feel self-conscious. 'So unless you enjoy vacations to war-torn countries, I guess you joined the army?'

'I passed out at Sandhurst in '96 and joined the Adjutant General Corps. I've served with the RMP ever since.'

Jack hesitated, not sure how to respond. 'RMP?'

'Royal Military Police.'

'That's fantastic – I always knew you'd make a great officer. Your dad must be really proud.'

Charlie smiled briefly and stared at Jack with narrowed eyes. Jack felt nervous again. He'd forgotten how serious his old friend could be. Clearly a decade in the army hadn't helped loosen him up. If anything, Charlie seemed more detached than before. Jack had a head full of questions he knew he couldn't ask. *What's it really like? Are we doing the right thing out there? Have you killed anyone?* At university, Charlie had barely mentioned his family. He was a very private person. But Jack remembered a rare moment when Charlie had let his guard down and admitted that he wanted to join the army, like his father.

'I guess you've traveled quite a lot? I had a friend who joined the infantry and he got to go to all sorts of exciting places.'

'Northern Ireland, Sudan, Bosnia, Libya, and two tours of Iraq and Afghanistan,' Charlie replied. His face betrayed nothing. Jack couldn't detect a solitary hint of emotion. Charlie's speech was measured, just as it had been in their undergraduate days. He looked much the same. If anything, he looked better – more distinguished. His hair was still dark and cut respectably short but a few strands of gray were now showing. His widow's peak was still noticeable but, much to Jack's annoyance, there was no sign his hairline was receding.

'Look who it is,' Jack exclaimed, trying to disguise his relief at seeing Piers and Tom enter the bar.

'My boys. My boys,' said Piers as he rushed over to the table. 'How the devil are you both?'

Jack and Charlie stood up to greet them. Charlie stuck out his hand but Piers pushed it aside and gave him a hug. 'Bet you thought you'd seen the last of me, huh, Charlie boy?'

Tom shook Charlie's hand as Piers stepped to one side and offered outstretched arms to Jack. 'Come here, old fruit.'

Piers didn't look at all as Jack had imagined he would. He was unkempt, loose clothes hanging off his wilting frame. When they hugged, Jack expected a waft of Fahrenheit – Piers' fragrance of choice when they'd been at uni. Instead, his nostrils were filled with the pungent smell of body odor.

'It really is good to see you, old bean. I've been looking forward to this moment for an awfully long time,' said Piers.

'Good to see you too, Piers,' Jack said after breaking free from the musky embrace.

At university, Piers had always called Jack and the others "old boy", "old fruit" and "old chap". He'd used them as terms of endearment, proof of his posh private-school education. Now, somehow, the words felt slightly offensive, certainly less than genuine.

'Hello, JD,' Tom called out. 'Is it hugs all round?'

Jack hooked an arm around Tom's shoulders and was pleased to note the sweet smell of cologne. Tom had never bothered at university, insisting that it was a ruse on the part of the fashion houses to cheat impressionable men out of their hard-earned cash; as if sprinkling themselves with scented water would make them more desirable to the opposite sex! Jack smiled, enjoying the irony. *How times have changed,* he thought.

'Good to see you too, Patto,' he said as the four of them took their seats. He waved the waitress over and Tom and Piers both ordered whiskies.

'They do a world-class Japanese one here,' said Jack. 'You should honestly try it. They really know what they're doing. It's called Yamazaki. Their distillery is right next to one of Japan's purest rivers. Conditions are perfect for producing the stuff.'

'Sounds good to me,' Tom replied.

'I'll take a Balblair 1999. No ice,' said Piers, crossing his arms in front of him. 'I'd rather stick to the real thing, if you don't mind. I don't trust the Japs, the same way I don't trust the Chinese. They're all rip-off merchants.'

Jack exchanged glances with a surprised-looking Tom. *Times really have changed.*

***

JACK'S HAND

Sitting at a table in Hardbodies of Mayfair with three familiar, yet different, faces looking back at him felt weird. Jack's friends weren't the eager young students with spotty faces and full heads of hair that he so fondly remembered. It was like looking through a fairground mirror; the reflections were recognizable but strangely distorted. It unsettled him, provoking a peculiar mixture of emotions: pride, excitement, bitterness, resentment and jealousy.

'How's life treating you then, JD?' asked Tom.

Jack felt anxious again, though it was different from the panic he'd felt when he'd seen his boss walk through the door earlier. It was the kind of feeling he might get before a client meeting or an important presentation to his colleagues. He felt exposed, as if he was facing three stern-faced interviewers. He felt the need to sell himself, to justify his position and list his accomplishments and so he gave a verbal résumé of his career to date, explaining how he trained at Spear, Collier & Horn and went on to qualify into the corporate department in '98.

He told them he had spent a year in Hong Kong, working on one of the firm's biggest acquisitions, then how he had been made up to partner two years ago and was already making more money than some of the senior equity partners in his team. And with the formal structure of any professional profile, he included the briefest of personal details at the end: he was a keen golfer with a handicap of eleven and had an interest in fine wine. But, just like most professional résumés, he'd stretched the truth. Jack was a keen golfer but only during the British summer, and his handicap was closer to twenty-one. As for the fine wines, when he'd been made up to partner, he'd been given a single bottle of 2007 Le Montrachet Bouchard Pere & Fils. In truth, he looked to his local wine merchant for recommendations. Just like in a professional interview, Jack couldn't tell how he was doing. He looked at his friends' expressionless faces.

'Didn't get married, then?' Tom fiddled with his wedding band. 'Probably haven't had time, with all the hours you spend in the office.'

'Something like that,' Jack replied curtly.

'What about you, Charlie?' Tom probed, moving the spotlight away from Jack.

'No,' said Charlie, his face unyielding. 'Difficult in my line of work.'

'I've had plenty of offers,' said Piers. 'I've been with hundreds of women from all over the world but never found "the one". They all seem to be just after my family's money. I think I need to find a girl on the same financial level as me, if you know what I mean?'

Tom burst out laughing.

'What's so funny, Tom?'

'Nothing. Sorry, Piers. It's just the thought of an heir to a mining empire trying to avoid gold-diggers,' Tom grinned.

'We're not all as lucky in love as you, Patto,' Piers said, unamused.

Jack was a little disappointed. His friends were clearly unimpressed by what he did for a living – the pride he felt when he told people he was a partner at Spear, Collier & Horn was one of the reasons he'd stayed in the job for so long (and it was a great chat-up line). But they hadn't seemed particularly interested by the partnership itself. He was used to people's indifference to his work, but these three were his friends and he'd really hoped for more.

'What about you, Tom? What do you do nowadays?' Charlie asked.

'Senior Credit Analyst at UBG,' Tom answered. 'In layman's terms, I evaluate the creditworthiness of businesses. I determine whether the bank's borrowers can repay their loans, honor their promises and so on.'

'OK,' said Piers. 'So in your opinion, how did we end up in such a terrible financial mess? If you're that close to the coal face, how did people allow it to get so bad?'

Tom turned to Piers and began a lengthy explanation

of the global banking crisis. Jack was already well versed on the credit crunch and wasn't interested in Tom's carefully rehearsed account of it. He wanted to hear what Piers and Charlie had been doing since graduation.

In any case, it seemed strange that Tom of all people, with his third-class degree in marine biology, was now working as a City banker. He'd never expressed even a passing interest in finance or economics when they'd lived together. Jack thought Tom had wanted to stop over-fishing and study the behavior of marine vertebrates or something equally as virtuous. *Is the parlous state of the economy in any way linked to the number of marine biology graduates working in finance?* Jack wondered.

Even though they were sitting down, Tom was clearly still the shortest of the four – there was nothing the intervening years could have been done about that. Jack was also pleased to see that Tom had put on some weight. *A sedentary job as a "Fat Cat" banker clearly paying dividends in more ways than one,* he thought, smiling to himself. Tom did have the hint of a tan, which gave his skin an artificially healthy look, but the stress of a job in finance had clearly taken its toll – he had lost his boyish facial features to worry lines and crow's feet.

Jack was also pleased to see that he wasn't the only one whose hairline, like the growth of the economy, was in recession. Piers' had receded markedly and Tom had lost a fair amount of his distinctive blond curls. It seemed curious, though, that Tom was sporting at least a week's worth of facial hair – stubble that looked more indifferent than designer. Was UBG more relaxed than the other banks he was used to dealing with?

'So, Tom,' Jack said, 'I imagine a lot of your customers suffered in light of the hiatus we're in. I guess you didn't foresee the credit and liquidity problems brought about by the economic crisis?'

'Well, I mean, I don't suppose anyone could have predicted what happened,' Tom replied defensively, avoiding Jack's gaze.

'Apart from Nouriel Roubini, of course; you know, the economist whose forecasts proved accurate. Or Steve Eisman, Dr. Michael Burry, Kyle Bass, and all the other investors who saw the disaster looming and were on the right side of the trades when the music stopped. A number of my clients made a killing in the CDS markets, shorting sub-prime mortgage bonds,' Jack said, lifting his shoulders and puffing his chest out as he spoke.

'Bloody traders. They should've been drowned at birth,' Piers muttered under his breath. 'Conniving bastards.'

'Anyway, we've not come here to talk about work or put the world economy to rights,' said Tom. 'Let's change the subject, shall we?'

Jack nodded, sensing he had won this little exchange. But any feeling of superiority quickly vanished as he noticed Tom's watch: an IWC Portuguese Perpetual Calendar. It was more expensive than Jack's. *Maybe it's a replica – like the knock-off ones they sell in Thailand,* he thought, trying to find an acceptable explanation that pushed back his sudden stab of jealousy. He settled on the idea that it was a wedding gift from a rich uncle or someone. He glanced across to see the other's watches and noticed that Piers wasn't wearing one and Charlie wore the same black G-Shock he'd had at university. Jack felt a little better about himself. He stood up and raised his glass. 'I'd like to propose a toast to Tom and his new wife. What's her name, Patto?'

'Victoria,' Tom replied proudly.

'To Tom and Victoria Patterson. May you have a long and happy marriage,' Jack announced.

'To Tom and Victoria,' Charlie and Piers responded,

standing up momentarily.

'I guess our invites got lost in the post,' Piers joked as he sat back down.

Jack sensed Tom felt embarrassed by the jibe. He recalled the pact they had once made at university to be each other's groomsmen. Tom had even promised to make Jack his best man. But Jack didn't feel aggrieved; how could he? He'd not seen Tom since graduation.

'Let's get some champagne,' said Jack, deciding to take back control of the evening. 'We've good reason to celebrate. Not just our dear friend's recent wedding, but our long-awaited adventure as well, and we must, of course, drink in honor of the late great Michael Joseph Jackson, without whom none of this would be possible. And, by the way, friends and fellow Famously Dead players, tonight's expenses will be on me. It's about time I repaid your generosity – especially you, Piers. It really is great to be back together again.'

'Thank you, JD, that's very kind of you,' said Tom, as he now stood up. 'And thank you for organizing everything with such scrupulous detail. I look forward to reading your Magnum Opus with a large cup of Tetley's. Typical lawyer. Making more work for yourself. Seriously, though, I for one can't wait until next week – I know it's going to be a real belter. Just like the good old days – the four of us back together.' He raised his glass and declared, 'Here's to making new memories.'

'To new memories,' they roared in unison.

***

JACK'S HAND

As the evening rolled on, it was difficult for Jack to see through the fog of bravado, banter and bluff. He had no way of telling whether any of his friends' accounts of the last fifteen years were true, and he didn't care too much, either. He was interested in the future, not the past; looking forward to Las Vegas, a blank canvas onto which new stories would be painted. It was like being at university again – he had to take everyone at face value.

Time would tell if they were being honest.

Card 15

Two Pair: A hand that contains two cards of the same rank plus two cards of another rank.

London, 5 July 2009
TOM'S HAND

Tom called on his best friend, Jonny Banks, for some much-needed help. He'd first met Jonny at UBG, where they'd started out on the graduate scheme together. They'd been colleagues for four years before Jonny moved on. It had been Jonny who Tom had been out drinking with when he first met Victoria and he still claimed Jonny was the reason she came over to talk to them. The guy was incredibly likable. The type of person who always comes across well at interviews. He had a gift for letting people know just how good he was and how well the position they were offering would suit him; both things that Tom struggled with when it came to himself.

Ever since Jonny had left UBG, his career had skyrocketed. Tom had played it safe, sticking it out with his first employer; slowly climbed the greasy pole to a relatively senior position – then been made redundant. Jonny, on the other hand, had moved five times since leaving UBG and each time he switched he got a better package and a more senior title. He was currently one of the managing directors at the investment bank Hyde Silbermann, in charge of their fixed-income department. As far as Tom could tell, Jonny was earning close to a million pounds a year selling financial products and trading debt securities across a number of markets. His bonus the previous year had been enough to pay for a house on the French Riviera – in cash.

Jonny had once tried to explain his role to Tom but the conversation had left Tom confused and wondering whether Jonny himself understood what he was supposed to be doing. He had a lot of young, ambitious minions working for him, which must have made his work easier, as well as making the bank and its clients an awful lot of money.

Even though Jonny was Tom's best mate, it didn't stop Tom feeling resentful about the way things had played out. He often wondered what his life would be like if he had been as daring in his career as Jonny. He probably wouldn't be redundant, for a start.

He hadn't thought twice about asking Jonny to be best man at his wedding. He'd seemed the perfect choice: a larger-than-life character who lit up a room when he entered. His best man's speech had everyone in tears – especially Victoria, who kept saying how sweet and thoughtful he was to include so many heart-felt observations on the bride.

Jonny had insisted on buying them a present that wasn't on their wedding list: Egyptian cotton bed sheets imported from Italy. It had left Tom feeling a little short-changed, until Victoria had explained just how expensive that particular brand of linen was. She loved the sheets but Tom had been hoping for something a little more extravagant.

Three months on, Tom felt he needed the support of

his best man more than ever yet they hadn't seen each other since the big day. Truth be told, he'd been avoiding Jonny. He'd been avoiding most things, in fact: his family, his friends, and especially the tough decisions about what to do next, now that he was unemployed.

He climbed the steps to Jonny's £3.8 million Georgian townhouse in Chelsea and stood facing the imposing Hague Blue door. He knew the color all too well. His wife was obsessed with Farrow & Ball. It was her specialist subject. She could spot a Mouse's Back or an Elephant's Breath from 200 yards. Their own front door had changed color three times in the last two years on her insistence. It was now the same as Jonny's, only in Tom's eyes Jonny's door looked a richer, more impressive shade of blue.

Staring into the eyes of the lion doorknocker, Tom caught his breath. But he hardly had a chance to lift the heavy gold ring clamped between the lion's teeth before the door swung open. A young girl with a pretty face stood confidently behind the freshly polished brass step. She invited Tom through to the drawing room.

'Good afternoon, sir. I'm afraid Mr. Banks is running a little late. Please come in and take a seat. He will join you very shortly.' She spoke fluent English but it was clear from her accent the girl was Scandinavian. 'Can I fix you a drink, Mr. Patterson?'

'I'll take a gin & tonic if that's OK? And please, just call me Tom.'

'Mr. Banks prefers me to address all of his guests formally. What type of gin would you like, sir?'

'Plymouth Gin. Navy strength. Slimline tonic, Fentiman's if you have it. And a radish – if that's at all possible?' Tom asked for the most obscure gin he could think of, in the hope that Jonny's well-stocked bar might fall short on this occasion.

'Certainly,' she smiled knowingly. 'A discerning taste,

Mr. Patterson.'

The girl turned and walked off towards the bar, her high heels clicking on the dark parquet flooring as she glided across the room with the confidence of a catwalk model. Tom couldn't help admiring her as she left. Damn, Jonny was a lucky man, he thought, just as his best friend came striding into the room.

'Gorgeous, isn't she?' Jonny said proudly. 'Off-limits for you now though, eh? No more fun and games for you, Tommy boy.'

Jonny looked unusually tanned for the British summer. He was trim, with jet-black hair gelled back. He was the same height as Tom but Tom always felt shorter in his company. Especially today, sitting there, all too conscious of his own diminished status in this immaculately decorated Chelsea home.

He fought off the feelings of inadequacy as he stood up and smiled at his best mate. It was good to see him after all.

'I don't know what you're talking about. I was just admiring your...' Tom hesitated. 'Your new furniture.'

'I know,' Jonny said with a grin, 'not like the flat-packed stuff from IKEA that everyone else has around the house, hey, Tommy boy? Although saying that, Vicky's still got a couple of nice heirlooms.'

'Easy, mate. That's my wife you're talking about now.'

Jonny smiled playfully as he grabbed Tom's shoulder and pulled him close. 'I've enrolled Kissy on a massage course. Trying to enhance her skills. You know me, Tommy. I like to sweat the assets,' he whispered.

Tom felt uneasy. His friend could be a real creep at times. He found it bizarre that, despite the fact that Jonny had neither a wife nor children, he felt the need to employ a very young and attractive live-in nanny.

The girl returned with two gin & tonics on a silver tray, the melodic sound of ice cubes against the crystal glass as pleasing to Tom's ears as the girl was on the eyes.

'Would you like your drinks in here, Mr. Banks, or in the smoking room?'

'Let's go through to the smoking room, Tommy. I've just had a very special package arrive from Cuba.'

They followed the girl into the hall and down the stairs to the lower ground floor, location of the billiards room, gym, wine cellar, and the recently refurbished smoking room.

'That'll be all for now, Kissy,' Jonny said after she gently placed the drinks on the mahogany coffee table.

The smoking room, like every other room in the house, was a sight to behold. It was softly lit, with wood-paneled walls and ceiling. There was a bar in the corner with a variety of whiskies on display and it even had a card table to one side. A large oil painting hung above the imposing hand-carved fireplace. Tom was in awe but didn't want to let on so he casually took a seat on one of the three Chesterfield couches. Jonny sat down with him and pulled out one of the humidor drawers from the coffee table in front of them.

'Kissy's not her real name, is it?' Tom asked.

'No. It's Kjersti or something. But Kissy is much more fitting,' Jonny said, with a broad grin. 'Listen, Tommy, I heard about your job. Damn credit crunch. You'll be fine though, honestly mate. It won't last long. The markets will pick up again and you'll get a new role in no time at all.'

Tom hadn't spoken to anyone about his redundancy and was curious as to how Jonny had found out. 'Who told you that?'

'I guess Vicky mentioned it at some stage,' Jonny replied evasively.

'When, exactly?'

Jonny picked out one of his prize cigars, rolled it in his fingers and smelled it theatrically.

'I can't remember, Tommy. We musta bumped into each other in the Farmers' Market last weekend, I guess. Now listen, I've got something that will cheer you up. This bad boy here is called a Cohiba Behike. It's the new line from Habanos, you know, the Cuban tobacco company. You can't get hold of them anywhere right now. They don't even go on sale until 2010. Rare as rocking-horse shit. Of course, I can't possibly tell you how I got them.'

The only language Jonny spoke was English, but he was fluent in Getting What He Wanted. Tom wondered how many times Jonny would repeat the story to his smoking-room guests. He was quite sure he wasn't the first person to hear it.

'I think I'll pass. Not a fan of horse shit,' Tom said with a smirk. He knew Jonny would be pleased with his answer. No point wasting a prize cigar on anyone who didn't appreciate it.

'Suit yourself, Philistine,' he said as he set about meticulously preparing the cigar for lighting.

'So Tommy, Vicky tells me you're not doing too well. She's worried about you, mate.' He warmed the foot of the cigar by gently rolling it between his fingers.

'It's fine. Honestly. Like you say, the markets will pick up and I'll get a job soon enough. My experience has to count for something. Fifteen bloody years at the same bank. I mean *that* is loyalty,' he said, trying to put a positive spin on his situation.

'Yeah. That's longer than most marriages, if you think about it.'

'She's just finding it difficult because I'm around the house all day and she's not in control of the situation. Plus, she's a little worried about having to change our lifestyle.'

'Not the best start to married life, eh?' Jonny said as he sliced the cap off the cigar with his gold-plated guillotine cutter before tapping the end on the glass ashtray.

No shit, Tom thought, playing with his wedding band.

'Did Vicky tell you she'd asked me about getting you a job? You know I can ask around, I've got plenty of contacts who owe me favors, but I wanted to speak with you first, you know, check you're cool with it,' Jonny said without looking him in the eye.

No one else got away with calling his wife Vicky. Tom was pretty sure she didn't like it, but he couldn't bring himself to tell Jonny. In the same fashion, Jonny was the only person who ever called him Tommy. It was as if he had to take something that belonged to someone else and put his individual stamp on it for some sort of leverage or gain. Just like the financial derivatives he sold to his clients; he was repackaging an underlying asset and calling it something different. Sometimes Tom liked it. It made him feel special, like a nickname from school that only your closest friends know you by. Today, it was irritating him.

'Jesus. I can't believe she did that. I didn't ask her to. God, I wish she would just stay out of it. If she really wants to help, she can stop spending so much money and get a bloody job herself.' Tom took a sip of his gin & tonic and decided now was a good time to bring up his plan. 'Anyway. Forget about all that for a moment. Remember at UBG when I told you about the game I was playing with some friends from university?'

'The celebrity death match or something?' Jonny lit his cigar with a match.

'Yes, that's the one. Famously Dead, we called it. Well, we've been playing it since our first year at Cardiff and it's finally come to a head. One of the celebrities died and the pot of money we've been pooling since 1991 is massive. It's a once-in-a-lifetime trip with my old roommates.' As Tom spoke, he felt excitement building in the pit of his stomach.

Jonny took several short puffs on his Cohiba and exhaled slowly, tilting his head upwards so the thick smoke traveled towards the wood-and-brass ship's wheel chandelier that hung from the ceiling. Then he inhaled deeply and blew a solitary, perfect smoke ring that hovered above the coffee table for the briefest of moments before vanishing into the fumes drifting above their heads. Jonny grinned wildly, as if it was the first time he'd ever done it. He looked at Tom. 'Is that a radish in your glass?' he said absentmindedly before asking the question Tom knew was really on his mind. 'How much money are we talking?'

Tom tried his best not to sound too excited, 'A million pounds.'

'Christ, Tommy. That'll be one hell of a trip, mate. Where are you going?'

'We fly to Vegas next week. First class.'

As soon as he finished the sentence, the trip became a reality in his mind. He knocked back his drink and started munching on the cold, gin-infused radish.

'The thing is, there's no way Victoria will let me go to Vegas without her. Especially now that I'm out of work,' Tom said, then paused as if he was searching for an idea. He swallowed some of the radish. 'But if I told her I had an interview in the States...'

Jonny took another theatrical puff on his illicit cigar, a long column of gray-and-white ash hanging dangerously over the glass ashtray. He grinned at Tom. 'Hyde Silbermann has an office in New York, you know?'

Tom hesitated, as if the thought had only just crossed his mind. 'I guess all you'd need to do is tell Victoria you lined up some interviews for me in Manhattan with some of the head honchos at your shop.'

Jonny let the gravity-defying ash tumble into the glass in front of them and smiled mischievously. 'Not a problem, Tommy. Not a problem at all. Just you remember to take pictures.'

They both laughed and high-fived each other, like when they'd worked on the same desk at UBG.

'Maybe I will have one of those cigars after all,' Tom said, swallowing the last of the radish.

Tom and Jonny spent the rest of the afternoon talking about the trip and the rich bounty to be found in Vegas. Of course, Jonny had been there already and done everything there was to do, so he took great pleasure in telling Tom all about what to expect, and which restaurants, casinos and strip clubs were worth visiting.

By the time Tom left Chelsea he was drunk, but excited about heading home to tell his wife all about the new job opportunity Jonny had set up for him in New York.

Card 16

Ace in the Hole: Where one of the pocket cards or 'hole' cards is an ace.

London, 9 July 2009
JACK'S HAND

Jack, Charlie and Tom were sitting in the British Airways first class lounge at Heathrow airport, waiting for Piers.

'Time can change people, though,' Jack looked at his cup. 'Take this as an example. I never drank the stuff at university, just didn't like the taste. Now I couldn't imagine life without it.'

'It's not really the same though, is it, JD?' said Tom. 'It's normal for your taste buds to change as you get older, but this is different. He just seems a lot less gregarious, don't you think? Like he's got the weight of the world on his shoulders. He looks a lot worse than I thought he would, as well.'

'Well, I did notice his fashion sense has waned somewhat and his white teeth seem to have lost their shine. At Cardiff, he was always immaculately turned out – if it wasn't a designer brand, no way was Piers going to wear it,' said Jack taking a sip of his coffee. 'But look around you, we're in the first class lounge, where passengers have paid tens of thousands of pounds for their tickets. I imagine everyone here is pretty rich but look how some of them are turned out. That group over there,' Jack pointed to three young men in their late twenties, noisily playing drinking games at the table closest to the bar. They were all dressed in Adidas tracksuits and trainers.

'Appearances can be deceptive,' Charlie said as he looked around the room. 'In Afghanistan, we had to reprogram our brains: a young boy kicking a football; a single mother pushing a stroller; a frail old couple carrying shopping bags – things that seemed innocent, everyday activities, were being used against us. Soldiers died because they couldn't see beyond them.'

Jack shot Tom a glance.

After several seconds of silence and a couple of awkward sips of coffee, Tom spoke again, 'I guess what I'm trying to say is that if I was worth as much as Piers supposedly is, I would dress a bit better; more like that guy over there.' He pointed towards a Chinese man wearing a smart black suit and white shirt. 'He looks like he belongs in this lounge.'

Jack and Charlie turned to see. No doubt sensing he was being watched, the man picked up a magazine and hid behind it.

Jack and Tom chuckled as they turned back round. 'Busted,' they both said in unison.

'Jinx,' they chorused.

They smiled at each other and returned to their coffees while Charlie kept an eye on the man reading the magazine.

'Despite Piers' appearance, I guarantee no one in this room is as rich as he is; he's still got to be worth hundreds of millions of dollars, notwithstanding the financial crisis, don't you think?' Jack said, looking at

Tom. 'They mine commodities, right? Actual resources the markets need. Not synthetic financial instruments that investors were tricked into thinking they needed. That's the type of solid, reliable business model that can weather any economic storm.'

Tom shrugged. 'I know he had buckets of cash at Cardiff and he always said his mother was a billionaire, but it doesn't really stack up, does it? I mean, look at him now. He doesn't behave like the heir to a mining dynasty. We all know he was flush back then, and always generous with his money, but was he telling the truth? Do you ever remember his family coming to visit? I've checked them out on Google. The internet doesn't seem to have heard of a wealthy Mrs. Upwell, or an Upwell family.'

'What are you saying, Patto?'

'I guess what I'm saying is that maybe he made the whole thing up just to make friends or something?'

'What do you think, Charlie?' Jack asked.

'Here he comes,' observed Charlie as a flustered-looking Piers, wearing ripped jeans, a cotton pullover and a well-worn pair of boat shoes, hurried towards them.

'What time d'you call this?' said Jack. 'Departure time is in half an hour. I specifically said be here by 8pm. Didn't you read the itinerary?'

'Sorry, JD; sorry, chaps. Awful delay on the Piccadilly line,' Piers said as he wiped the rolling sweat from his brow. 'Where's the bar? Have I got time for a quick one?'

'Now we're finally all here, let's get a bottle of Bolli to celebrate the start of our adventure,' Tom suggested.

'Jolly good idea,' said Piers. 'I just need to pop to the little boys' room first, back in a jiffy.'

He dropped his black rucksack to the floor and took off his pullover, revealing a well-washed T-shirt, and rushed towards the restrooms.

Jack decided not to say anything about the rucksack – it was polyester and cheap. *Looks can be deceptive,* he thought. *Charlie may be right.*

'I'll get the champagne,' Charlie said, standing up. 'I need to stretch my legs anyway.'

***

CHARLIE'S HAND

Charlie strode towards the bar, passing the smart Chinese man and trying to take in every detail he could remember. He caught the eye of the bartender as he approached: 'Bottle of Bollinger and four—'

'Scuse me, boyo,' interrupted a young man in a white Adidas tracksuit. 'I was here first.' There was a belligerent tone to his voice.

Charlie stared at him for three to four seconds. 'Sorry,' he said eventually. 'Please, be my guest.' He smiled and nodded at the bartender, detecting a flash of embarrassment in his eyes.

'Another three Guinness, butt, and a glass of whisky for my old man,' the young Welshman looked down at his watch. 'And make it quick, mind. Our flight to Vegas leaves soon and I wanna get another round in after this one, like.'

'Single or double?' asked the bartender.

'What d'you reckon? Double, of course, butt.'

'I'm on the same flight as you, it would seem,' Charlie said politely.

'In that case I apologize in advance for all the noise we're gonna make. It's my last proper blow-out with the boys 'til I tie the knot, like,' his tone seemed friendlier.

'Nice watch,' Charlie said, looking at the man's wrist. 'A friend of mine used to have one just like that.'

'Piss off, you faggot.'

Card 17

Upping The Ante: Increasing the stakes.

Las Vegas, 11 July 2009
CHARLIE'S HAND

As the three of them headed downstairs to the hotel casino, Charlie spotted a Texas Hold'em poker tournament advertised in the foyer of one of the card rooms. The buy-in was $110,000 and it was an open tournament. They signed in and paid the entry fee just before the cut-off time. The three of them had agreed that Charlie was their best chance of winning the prize money and, in turn, the best chance they had of getting Piers back.

A mounting pressure rested heavily on Charlie's shoulders as he took a seat at the brightly-lit card table. Luckily, pressure had been an ever-present aspect of his life in the Royal Military Police. He had learned to harness it and use it to his advantage. Making a mistake in the heat of battle could lead to casualties. Making a mistake at the poker table could be just as dangerous. He knew that losing this game was not an option. It was important for him to remain calm and not let the gravity of a negative outcome affect his performance. This was a card game. Nothing more. The chips were just a way of keeping the score.

Charlie noticed that Mr. Yin had followed them into the card room. But there was someone else at the bar who caught his attention. He recognized him instantly. He'd never been able to forget that face, although he hadn't seen it for over fifteen years.

***

CHARLIE'S HAND

The first couple of hours had gone well and Charlie was pleased with his approach and the cards he'd been dealt. He was chip leading and felt he had a good handle on the other four players still left in the game. He'd been getting good pocket cards and was slowly amassing a sizable stack, while building up a mental record of the other players' tells.

In truth, apart from the odd game on tour, he hadn't played much since leaving university and certainly nothing like the game he was facing now. He was surprised at how quickly he got back into the swing of it, face-to-face against strangers.

Two of the remaining players were clearly foreign; a thick Slavic accent suggested one of them was most likely Eastern European. The other was a very thin, almost malnourished, Arab, with sleepy eyes. They spoke very little throughout the game and when they did talk it was difficult to understand what they were saying – not that poker demands much talking, whatever language it's played in. An understanding of the cards, the chip values and the betting is all that a player needs to communicate successfully.

Charlie preferred a quiet game, happy to let the cards

do the talking. He was more comfortable in the presence of the taciturn foreigners than the other two players, who sat across the table with a pile of black, red and green chips in front of them. They were brash, rude, vocal and American.

The older of the two was an archetypal Texan cowboy. In his mid-fifties, with a graying handlebar mustache, he dressed, walked and talked like a stereotype, even wearing his ten-gallon cowboy hat at the table. The guy couldn't stop talking trash. He loved the sound of his own voice. Charlie found him deplorable and it was clear from the faces of the two other foreigners that he wasn't alone.

The other American, though less of a caricature, was equally loathsome. He was smartly dressed, in a dark suit and burgundy shirt, chest hair climbing out over his undone buttons as if trying to escape. He wore gold chains around his neck and both hands were covered in diamond-studded rings and gold bracelets. The one digit without decoration was his wedding finger. Everything was on show except his eyes, which remained concealed behind his over-sized sunglasses. Like his fellow countryman, he was an incessant talker. He felt obliged to tell the rest of the table about his personal life: as a businessman ("I own several mid-cap Tech companies."); as a poker player ("I've had a pretty good year. Two million dollars in winnings so far."); and as a Lothario ("Y'all should've seen the hard body I had in my suite last night."). As the show-off talked, Charlie observed him closely, absorbing every tell.

He wasn't sure how old the Show-Off was; anywhere between mid-thirties and late forties, he guessed, though he was in no doubt when the flashy Yank was lying. His glasses couldn't conceal everything.

His opponents did seem to have one thing in common – something Charlie wished he shared at that moment –

they all seemed to have enough money to lose.

'Action is on you, sir,' the dealer was speaking to Charlie. 'Ten thousand dollars to call.'

Charlie was holding Pocket Rockets and there was another ace in the Flop. He was left of the dealer button and had been first to bet after the first three cards had been turned over. He decided to check to see if anyone around the table fancied their hand. The Quiet European on his left and the Texan Cowboy were both clearly happy to see the next card for free. The Show-Off, probably assuming no one was holding anything of value, pushed $10,000-worth of chips into the middle to try and steal the blinds – now at $5,000 and $10,000 apiece. The Skinny Arab folded and it was Charlie's turn to play.

'Difficult to compete with two aces in the hole,' said the Show-Off. 'I would fold like the Mute if I were you, Limey.'

Charlie knew he was bluffing. He wasn't holding two aces. There were only four in the pack and Charlie had two in his hand. The Show-Off had revealed another basic tell. Charlie looked at his own cards and waited for a few seconds, pretending he was doing some mental arithmetic or deliberating whether to call or fold.

'Raise,' said Charlie, matching the Show-Off's $10,000 bet and pushing $10,000 more into the pot.

The Quiet European folded.

'The Limey's got nothing,' said the Texan in a slow and defeated drawl. 'But I ain't either,' he folded his hand and beckoned the waitress over for another drink.

Now the Show-Off looked at his cards. Charlie knew what was coming next. He'd been hoping the guy would match his raise but the Show-Off wasn't that reckless. He folded in silence.

The size of the pot was $80,000. Charlie now had a large stack of chips; more than double what was in front of the Arab and the European. It was only a matter of time before they'd be out of the game, he thought, but he wanted the Show-Off to leave the table next.

Card 18

Heads Up: Playing against a single opponent.

Las Vegas, 11 July 2009
CHARLIE'S HAND

'You're the big blind, sir,' said the dealer. 'Ten thousand dollars.'

Charlie's attention was elsewhere. He was looking in the corner of the room, where a young man with an arm in a sling was pointing in his direction as he talked to two large, official-looking casino employees.

'Please excuse me, gentlemen,' Charlie said. Without looking at his cards, he pushed $10,000 over the line, folded his hand, stood up and left the table.

'What's up, Limey? Had enough already?' the Show-Off demanded.

'I hear the Brits have weak bladders, just like black men can't swim. It's genetic,' drawled the Texan.

Charlie marched towards the table where Mr. Yin was sitting and subtly handed over two objects from his jacket. He whispered something in Mr. Yin's ear and marched back.

'What the hell are you doing?' Jack called out as Charlie brushed past without saying a word. He didn't have time to explain.

'Sir, I'm going to have to ask you to come with us for a moment,' one of the casino employees addressed Charlie as he returned to his seat at the card table.

'I'm in the middle of a game here. Can't it wait?' Charlie noted the plastic earpiece in one of the men's eardrums.

'No, sir. We need to speak with you in private, now.'

Charlie stood up compliantly.

'Before I leave with these two polite gentlemen, may I request that someone replace me at the table?' Charlie asked the dealer calmly, eying the four remaining players and hoping they might show some leniency.

'I'm afraid the house rules state that you can only be replaced by another player if everyone at the table is in agreement,' said the dealer, swinging his attention from Charlie to the others. There was silence. Charlie noted from the players' expressions that they were enjoying the interruption.

'Personally, I'll be glad to see the back of him. He's taken half my chips,' said the Texan.

The Quiet European and Skinny Arab looked up at Charlie, back toward the dealer, and then nodded in agreement. He detected a hint of disappointment on their faces, as if they were losing an ally.

'Three out of four,' said the dealer. All eyes were now on the Show-Off, who was rolling a $500 chip around the knuckles of his decorated hand.

He grinned deviously. 'I'll agree, Limey, but on two conditions – one, you give me that $10,000 you just won from me and two, you can't come back.'

'Agreed,' Charlie said without delay. He stacked up $10,000 in chips, asked the dealer to pass it to the Show-Off, and left the table. He strode over to Jack and Tom.

'What the hell is going on?' Jack asked angrily. He looked tense and anxious.

'You're up, JD. I'm tagging you in. I need to accompany these gentlemen from security for a moment. Good luck and don't forget what's at stake.'

Before Jack had time to respond, Charlie had marched off, flanked by the two very large men.

'Would you care to tell me what this is all about?' he asked as he was ushered out of the room.

'We've received a complaint from one of the guests – Mr. Williams,' said one of the men. 'He said you assaulted him. Hotel policy is to treat all complaints seriously, Mr. Preston. Irrespective of the status of our guests. I'm sure you understand.'

'I'm afraid, gentlemen, there's been a misunderstanding,' Charlie said confidently. 'I can sort this out with one brief phone call, if you'll allow it.'

'You'll have your chance,' the other man said. 'We just need you to stay calm and follow us, without making a scene.'

Charlie's accuser, Mr. Williams, followed several paces behind them, trying to keep up with the longer strides of the three taller men. It was only after the four of them filed into the elevator, halfway down the lavish red-and-gold-carpeted corridor, that the size difference became obvious. The casino employees were at least 6'6" tall and built like professional wrestlers. They had short marine-style haircuts and wore black suits that had clearly been tailored for their above-average dimensions. Charlie glanced at their hotel name badges: Harry and Larry. *Unlikely,* he thought.

Mr. Williams stood silently, facing away from them. Charlie watched his face in the elevator mirror; he had the smug expression of someone in complete control – like a cowardly owner of two intimidating dogs.

Sandwiched between the two men, Charlie was by no means intimidated, despite their two-inch height advantage. He knew how to handle himself and he'd fought bigger men in his life; men who had been trained to kill, not just to fight.

When the elevator reached the lower ground floor, they ushered Charlie out and advanced down the corridor toward an ominous-looking door marked "Security Personnel Only". Harry punched in a code and crossed the threshold into a small room.

'This way please,' Larry said unnecessarily.

Charlie's blue eyes absorbed every detail of the room. Not that there was much to take in. It was cold and bare, with no windows, poor lighting, and a heavy smell of iodine. A table was bolted to the concrete floor and two metal chairs rested either side. He noticed a surveillance camera suspended in the corner and couldn't tell whether it was switched on. He suspected it wasn't.

'Take a seat,' Harry directed them both.

Mr. Williams sat in the seat facing the door. Charlie sat in front of him and studied him intently. The young man with the bruised face was a younger version of someone he used to know – a hawkish face from his past. He appeared to be enjoying himself, his "dogs" completely under control and ready to attack at his command. He met Charlie's stare and grinned inanely.

'OK. As I said, we've received a complaint from Mr. Williams here. He said you assaulted him and his friends and then stole his watch,' said Larry to Charlie.

'Where is it?' Williams snapped. 'My dad gave me that Rolex for my twenty-first birthday, butt.'

Charlie frowned, trying to convey confusion. He recognized Mr. Williams from the encounter in the airport lounge and then again outside the hotel earlier that afternoon. Aside from each having a black eye, the two men couldn't have looked more different. The Welshman wore jeans and a white Adidas tracksuit top with three black stripes running down the arms, while Charlie looked distinguished in his high-collared white shirt and double-breasted navy suit with gold buttons – his blue-and-red silk RMP pocket square hinting at his military background.

'And as I told you, there appears to be some confusion, gentlemen,' Charlie spoke his finest English, choosing his words carefully in an effort to undermine. 'I've never seen this young boy in my life and I have no idea about the incident you have just described. Perhaps he has mistaken me for someone else?'

'He claims you jumped him from behind while he was walking back to the hotel with his friends. He's going to make a formal complaint to the police and his friends are willing to testify,' said Larry with a perfunctory tone.

'But we understand you are staying in the Presidential Suite and so before we alert the authorities it's hotel policy to try and resolve this sensibly; give you an opportunity to explain yourself and return the stolen watch,' added Harry.

Charlie appeared unfazed. 'I don't much care for flashy Rolexes, I'm afraid. I prefer this sort of thing,' he said, tapping the face of his black G-Shock. 'Nearly twenty years old and it does the job perfectly. No need for another. It's served two tours of Afghanistan with me, it's incredibly robust. Doesn't break easily.'

Charlie stared at Harry and Larry.

'Listen here, you English prick,' Williams snarled. 'I don't give a shit how many tours you've been on. Tell me where my Rolex is, you thieving bastard.'

Charlie allowed the young man's words to hang in the air for several seconds before turning to Harry and asking calmly, 'May I use your cell to make a brief call, sir? I assure you this is a misunderstanding.'

The two men exchanged glances, shrugged, and then nodded in agreement.

'Thank you,' Charlie said as he took Harry's phone. 'Let me set the record straight.'

He punched in a number from memory and stared into Williams' eyes as he waited for an answer.

'It's Captain Preston,' he said after a brief delay.

Two seconds later, he handed the phone to Williams and whispered quietly, 'Your daddy wants a word.'

'Dad?' said the young man in disbelief as he pressed the phone to his ear.

'But I'm with the English prick that jumped me. He needs a serious kicking, like. I'm gonna break his bloody arm.'

Charlie looked across at Harry who moved his weight from one foot to the other.

'But he broke my arm,' Williams protested. 'We can't let him get away with that. You always taught me—'

There was silence as Williams froze. Before Charlie's eyes, his face crumpled in a mixture of fear, anger and confusion.

'OK. OK. I get it, Dad. I'm sorry.'

It was Charlie's turn to grin.

Card 19

Under The Gun: The player who is 'under the gun' must act first on the first round of betting.

Las Vegas, 11 July 2009
MR. YIN'S HAND

Shortly after Charlie had been escorted from the poker table, Mr. Yin stood up and advanced towards the bar at the back of the room.

'Excuse me, sir. Mr. Williams, isn't it?' he said as he approached an elderly man perched on a bar stool. 'May I speak with you privately? It's about your son.'

Gethin Williams turned around slowly and stared at Mr. Yin, taking in the black suit and white shirt. 'I've already spoken to you lot about the mugging. He's come all this way from Wales for his bachelor's party – as you boyos like to call it – the last thing I expected was some English twat to have jumped him and nicked his watch. What else is there to say, like?'

'If you'd like to come with me, sir. My two colleagues are questioning someone now. We think we've found the watch in his hotel room but we need you to come and verify it before we can remove it. This is just precautionary,' said Mr. Yin, holding out his hand. Gethin grunted and waved him away, dismissing the gesture with a look of contempt.

'I'm fine, butt. Do I look like I need a walking stick?' he said before necking the remainder of his Long Island Iced Tea and climbing down from the bar stool.

'I gave him that watch for his birthday, butt. It's a Rolex – rare one. Worth a lot of money. But Geraint means the world to me, see?'

Mr. Yin led the old man out of the room and towards the hotel's elevators.

Gethin Williams carried all the hallmarks of a life lived on the rough side. His large shiny head had more scars than hair. His neck was as thick as a prop forward's and his nose had clearly suffered numerous fights. He looked to be in his late seventies; from an older generation of criminal, Mr. Yin thought, his face and behavior now proof of his brutality. He wore his scars and broken nose proudly, though, like badges of his criminal service. The man was a walking advertisement of a life of crime and violence.

Mr. Yin and the 14K were a different breed altogether. They prided themselves on subtlety, preferring to operate in the shadows rather than broadcast their business to the public.

No one forgets a distinctive face, thought Mr. Yin, *and, more importantly, no one remembers an unremarkable one.*

***

MR. YIN'S HAND

Gethin Williams sat on the end of the bed in Mr. Yin and Mr. Yang's twin hotel room.

'So, I understand the watch you gave your son was not

yours to give,' said Mr. Yin.

Gethin didn't reply. His hawkish face was lined with anger.

'Let me explain something to you, Mr. Williams. We work for a man called Mr. Lee, Mr. Harald Lee. You may or you may not know who he is but by the look on your face right now, I suspect you've heard of him and our organization.'

Gethin nodded slowly. His blotchy red face and aged yellow irises revealed a look of fear.

'Good – it makes my job a lot easier if the person we're threatening knows exactly who they're dealing with. It's more convenient, less time-consuming, and a lot less messy, when the mention of a name has the same effect as the use of violence, don't you think?' Mr. Yin asked the question rhetorically, half turning towards Mr. Yang, who stood behind him, eating a banana while pointing his Beretta at Gethin's bald head.

Mr. Yin turned back towards Gethin, pulled the Rolex from his pocket and held it up so the old man could see its distinctive red-and-blue face.

'You stole this watch from a client of Mr. Lee's. A client who owes a considerable sum of money to Mr. Lee. This watch is now collateral for that debt. Do you understand what that means?' Mr. Yin looked at him steadily.

'The watch belongs to Mr. Lee now,' Mr. Yang added through a mouthful of banana.

Gethin nodded. The scar running from the back of his bald scalp toward the top of his eye had become a miniature aqueduct, transporting sweat to his sallow face. Before Gethin had a chance to respond, a phone rang from inside Mr. Yin's pocket. He answered it and then pressed the speakerphone button.

'It's for you, Mr. Williams. Your son wants a word,' he said, holding the phone close to Gethin's fear-soaked face.

'Geraint?' Gethin said, finding his voice.

'Dad?'

'Listen, son. There's been a mistake, OK? That watch isn't yours anymore. I'll buy you a new one.'

'But I'm with the English prick that jumped me. He needs a serious kicking, like. I'm gonna break his arm.'

Mr. Yang pushed the Beretta up against Gethin's left eye and shook his head slowly.

'Drop it, Geraint. Let's just carry on with the rest of your stag weekend as if none of this happened, OK?'

'But he broke my arm. We can't let him get away with that. You always taught me—'

'And I'll break your other arm if you don't do as I say,' Gethin roared down the phone, causing Mr. Yang to tighten his grip on the Beretta. 'Get this into your thick skull. We're not going to do nothing. This stops right now. There are forces much bigger than us at play here. Do you still want to tie the knot, son? Because if you do, you'll just drop it and forget about this whole nonsense,' he barked, though Mr. Yin could sense the wavering sound of panic in his gravelly voice.

There was a moment of silence before his son replied.

'OK. OK. I get it, Dad. I'm sorry.'

Card 20

The Bad Beat: *To lose a hand despite being considerably ahead of the eventual winning hand before the final card is drawn.*

Las Vegas, 1 July 2009
CHARLIE'S HAND

'Where the hell have you been?' Tom said to Charlie as he sat down beside him.

'Let's just say there was a case of mistaken identity,' Charlie said, looking across at the action. 'How's JD getting on?'

'Well, he's still there. Dallas Cowboy and the flathead left about ten minutes ago. I hope to God JD doesn't screw this up,' Tom finished the last few drops of his bourbon. He looked around the room in search of the waitress.

Charlie stood up and turned to leave.

'Hold on,' Tom called out with enough volume to turn a few heads. 'I've got your phone – some Chinese bloke gave it to me. At least, he said it was yours. He musta been hotel staff or something.'

'Thanks.' Charlie took the iPhone from Tom, slipped it

into his pocket and advanced toward the poker game. He could see that the Show-Off was chip leading and the Skinny Arab was short-stacked. The big blinds had now risen to $30,000 and all three players were too engrossed in the game to even notice him.

'Call,' said the Show-Off. He pushed $100,000 of chips across the table and chewed his gum slowly.

The Skinny Arab looked at his cards and looked at the Flop. The ten of spades, jack of diamonds and queen of hearts lay neatly next to one another on the dark green felt. Charlie could see that the Arab had just enough chips to call as well. If he had half-decent pocket cards, he would obviously go all in, otherwise the blinds on the next hand would wipe out his remaining chips.

Sure enough, the Skinny Arab pushed the pile of chips in front of him onto the table.

'All in,' the dealer spoke for him.

'Show us the Turn,' said the Show-Off, eager to continue the betting. Charlie sensed he had a decent hand. He just hoped Jack had a better one. He wished he was still in the game.

The dealer burnt a card and placed the Turn on the green felt, neatly next to the queen of hearts. It was a ten of diamonds.

Jack checked, applying pressure to the Show-Off, who was now chewing his gum frantically and staring down at the four cards on the table. 'One hundred thousand,' the Show-Off said after a brief pause.

Charlie couldn't see Jack's face. He had no idea what he was thinking, no idea what cards he held, and no idea what he was going to do. Charlie was a helpless spectator, hoping that Jack knew what he was doing.

'Call,' said Jack. He counted out $100,000 of chips and pushed them over the line in front of him.

The dealer burnt a card from the top of the pack and placed the River card on the table; a seven of diamonds.

Charlie glanced at the Show-Off, trying to gauge his reaction to the final card. As he half-cradled his pocket cards and turned up the ends with his thumb, Charlie noticed he'd stopped chewing his gum.

It was amateur behavior, Charlie thought; something novices did when they forgot the suits of their pocket cards. Then it dawned on him. The Show-Off had just made a Flush on the last card. There were three diamonds on the table and the guy must have another two in his hand.

'All in,' Jack said without delay.

Charlie felt a cold sweat come on. He swallowed hard as Jack pushed all of his remaining chips out in front of him.

'Call. Let's see what you've got, Limey Number Two.'

The Arab turned over his cards first: a pair of jacks.

'Full House. Jacks over tens,' announced the dealer.

Jack flipped over his cards confidently: a pair of queens.

'Full House. Queens over tens,' said the dealer.

The Arab shook his head, stood up, and slipped quietly away from the table.

All eyes were now on the Show-Off as he took off his dark glasses, dropped them into the breast pocket of his burgundy shirt and smiled. Then he revealed his pocket cards: a nine and an eight of diamonds.

Jack stayed in his seat, staring at the cards in front of him for a moment, then his head slumped forward.

'Straight Flush beats a Full House. Congratulations, sir. You're the winner – $850,000 dollars is all yours,' the dealer announced with the professionalism he had maintained all night.

The Show-Off didn't utter a word; he didn't need to. His face couldn't disguise his smug sense of entitlement.

Jack sat, motionless, for a while longer. Then he stood up and walked listlessly away. His face was ashen as he passed Charlie, seemingly oblivious to everything and everyone around him. Charlie didn't offer any words of support or reassurance. He couldn't. He too was stunned by what he'd just witnessed. An unusual wave of emotion began to rise inside him. Feelings of failure and helplessness swelled. He felt his throat tighten and swallowed hard.

We're running out of time.

***

MR. YIN'S HAND

Mr. Yin and Mr. Yang sat around the glass-topped table in their twin hotel room on the 24th floor of Caesars Palace. The watch lay on the table next to the room's phone. It was 11pm.

'Hold on,' Mr. Yang said as Mr. Yin held the receiver to his ear. 'Maybe we don't call the Black Octopus just yet. Think about it, he won't be happy that we've lost the asset, will he?'

'*We* didn't lose him, *you* did,' said Mr. Yin curtly as he put the receiver down. 'He was under your watch last night. Anyway, he'll be less impressed if we don't tell him what's happened. Remember our instructions?' He didn't bother waiting for an answer. 'To keep our eyes on the asset at all times and to report back anything out of the ordinary.'

'But what if he hasn't been kidnapped or his friends pay the ransom and get him back? Maybe we just wait a few days and see what happens. No harm, no foul.'

'No,' snapped Mr. Yin. 'That's not an option.'

'But he'll blame us. Can't you see? There's no way we'll get another chance. We'll get some shitty assignment again.'

'You need to earn your opportunities in this

organization. We've been over this before. Prove yourself first then reap the rewards. You need to be patient if you want to succeed.'

Mr. Yang shuffled in his seat. 'Come on, Yin. We didn't swear the oath for this bullshit. We wanted action. Don't tell me you joined the 14K to follow a bum around for half a year like some glorified babysitter.'

Mr. Yin shook his head in disappointment. 'We don't know the full story with the asset. At this level, you never do. That's the way it has to be. This assignment may seem trivial to you but I'm sure it's all part of a bigger plan. You'd do well to remember that.'

Mr. Yin had made up his mind. He reached for the receiver and dialed his boss. 'Dragon Master, sir. We have an unexpected problem,' said Mr. Yin, trying to remain calm. 'The asset appears to have ... gone missing.'

A customary silence extended across the line.

Mr. Yin took a deep breath and continued, 'We lost track of him last night on the Las Vegas Boulevard. He didn't return to the hotel with the others. It seems he's been ... kidnapped.'

Still no answer. Mr. Yin eyed Mr. Yang and carried on. 'We don't know which gang, if any, is involved, but we do know they've demanded a ransom. We found out from Captain Preston. He confronted us ... thought we were involved.'

Silence.

Mr. Lee was famous for extracting things: money, services, teeth, but his specialty was information. As the Dragon Master of the 14K, he made a living out of extortion. He understood that, in a world of noise, silence was a powerful tool. Deployed correctly, it was capable of delivering exactly the information he needed.

'The ransom is half a million dollars, Dragon Master. Not a significant sum, all things considered, and we suspect his friends have enough to cover it, at least. They seem to have plenty of funds at their disposal.'

Mr. Yin picked up the watch from the glass table and examined it.

'We also have the asset's watch. A rare Rolex, apparently … it looks expensive. It's a goodwill gesture from Captain Preston. He said we could keep it as collateral for the debt.'

He turned the watch around in his hand. 'It has "Happy Birthday Son" engraved on the back.'

'Make sure the asset stay alive,' Mr. Lee said finally. 'At all cost. He valuable. Worth more alive – you understand, right?' He spoke in broken English, his voice high-pitched. 'Bring back watch. May need in future. And be careful. Captain Preston not to be trusted. Keep eye on him, but remember Piers main focus. Once they pay ransom, don't let him out of sight again, OK?'

Mr. Yin opened his mouth to reply but the Dragon Master had already hung up.

Mr. Yang got up from his chair and patted his stomach. 'Talking to the Black Octopus always makes me hungry.'

'You're always hungry,' snapped Mr. Yin. 'Anyway, I didn't hear you do any of the talking.' He slipped the watch inside his jacket pocket and the two of them left their hotel room, Mr. Yang debating the best place to go for dinner.

Card 21

Blind Steal: A raise from a late position with a
weak hand when all other players have folded, with
the intention of winning the blinds and antes.

Las Vegas, 11 July 2009
APRIL'S HAND

'I don't know, April. It ain't like any other scam we've
pulled,' Danny said as he picked at an old scab on his
knuckle.

April's older brother Kyle was as hard as nails but her
other brother was a whole toolbox harder. Danny Parker
was thirty-seven but looked years older. Like a
sensational autobiography, his face told the story of his
incarceration in the Michigan State prison system.

He had six distinct scars on his face and neck, each a
different size and shape, all competing for attention
should anyone be brave enough to stare at him for longer
than a few seconds. Each scar marked a chapter in the
"book of Danny", though they reminded him of events
he'd far rather forget. Teardrops were etched
permanently under his left eye and a tattoo crawled up
his neck. The overcast look in his eyes told of violence
and abuse. But it was the scars which no one could see

that were the most shocking of all.

The prison system had broken him, then picked him up and glued him back together, but he was left damaged and insecure.

Unlike April, whose bewitching good looks were her most valuable asset, Danny's once handsome features had become a liability. Prison rape was a harsh reality in Detroit, especially for good-looking first-timers with no connections inside. During his first stretch, sexual and physical abuse made his punishment seem far longer than a six-month sentence. Eighteen months later, when he was arrested for credit card fraud and banged up for another two years, he joined a gang to avoid the same abuse. It worked but there was a price to pay and the ink and scars on his face were testament to his gang-related activities; symbols of solidarity, loyalty and violence.

'Look, it'll be fine, Danny,' April explained, brimming with her usual confidence, her smile as bright and enticing as a casino floor. 'This is the big one – the stakes are high but it's an easy score. There's only two of them and they're lightweight, middle-aged tourists with more money than sense. They'll just hand over the cash in return for the mark. It's a straight-up exchange. No different than we've ever done before.'

'But we ain't never kidnapped anyone before and we've never asked for this much money,' Danny said, still scratching at his scab.

'You know how it is, sis. Bigger the job, bigger the risk. What if they run to the Feds? What if they bring guns?' Kyle said, echoing his brother's concerns.

'Kyle's right. What if it doesn't go to plan? I ain't goin' inside again. Not for some punk-ass tourists. You know I'll be locked up for good if we get caught,' said Danny.

'Listen. No one is gonna get hurt, I promise. And none of us gonna do any time over this. Trust me,' April flashed her winning smile. 'This is the big one, y'all.

Think about it, will you? Gonna be the easiest half a million we'll ever make. Maybe the last time we ever need to pull a scam. With money like this, we could start all over. Look, these guys are good for it. I looked them in the eyes. They're weak. They ain't a threat. They'll do what we say. No one's callin' the Feds, OK? It'll be like taking candy from a baby, honestly. Just like it always is.'

Kyle and Danny looked at each other and then back at their younger sister.

'Sure is a big score, bro,' Kyle said, lifting the peak of his New York Yankees baseball cap. 'We could get that Airstream we've been wanting. Get outta here, man. See where the road takes us.'

'Kyle's right. This could be a new dawn for us. And anyway, have I ever let y'all down before?' April said, staring at her two brothers. 'Hey, if you're worried about them callin' the cops, Kyle can head down to Caesars tonight – after we make the call – make sure nothing goes down. Keep an eye out, yeah?'

'Sure can,' Kyle replied. 'It's a good idea, sis.'

A moment passed while Danny stared at his sister. His dark eyes narrowed.

'OK,' he said eventually, with a grin. 'I could do with gettin' out of Dodge, I reckon it's 'bout time we cashed in anyway.'

Card 22

Out of the Money: Competing in a tournament without winning a prize.

Las Vegas, 11 July 2009
JACK'S HAND

Back in their hotel suite it was nearly midnight and Jack, Charlie and Tom looked physically and emotionally exhausted. Tom had poured himself another cognac and was standing by the Steinway, staring down at his feet.

Jack was slumped on the cream leather couch. 'I can't believe that lucky Yank hit the seven of diamonds on the last card.'

'I can't believe you lost half a million dollars' worth of chips in less than an hour,' said Charlie curtly.

'Half a million!' shouted Tom.

'Come on guys, that's not fair. I didn't think I was going to be playing tonight. You dropped me in it at the last minute. I was half-cut by then,' Jack shot Charlie a look. 'Where the hell did you go, anyway?'

'Some guest got assaulted and they thought I had something to do with it. It was just a misunderstanding.'

'What are we going to do now?' Tom slurred.

The huge room fell silent, but for the clinking of ice in Tom's crystal glass. He swayed from side to side like cigarette paper in the breeze. 'Maybe we should try and call his mother? If the stories he told us are true and she really is minted, she'll be able to pay the ransom, right?' Tom said, spilling half his cognac on the Persian rug underneath the piano.

'I think you've probably had enough to drink, Patto,' said Charlie.

'Whatever,' Tom spat out the words, knocking back the dregs left in his glass.

'How do we even get hold of Mrs. Upwell, anyway?' Jack asked.

'It'll be difficult if she's so rich and powerful that I can't even find her online. I told you, I've tried, but there are no mining dynasties in the name of Upwell,' Tom shouted, staring at the Persian rug beneath his feet.

Charlie didn't say a word.

'You know these old things are like ancient message boards. The patterns are supposed to have hidden meanings...' Tom had managed to completely distract himself. 'I wonder what this giant rug is trying to say?'

'It's probably trying to tell you that you've had enough to drink,' Jack said under his breath.

'Drink?' Tom asked, lifting his head up again. 'Yes, please, Jack. Good idea. I'll take another Ricky Martin, thank you very much,' he muttered to himself as he stumbled towards the bar.

'Patto, seriously. I reckon Charlie was right, you've probably had enough for one night, don't you think? Remember what they say: at the third cup, wine drinks the man.'

'Bite me, JD. You can't judge me. Not after what you've done.'

Tom clattered around the bar, as if he was deliberately trying to make as much noise as possible, while he fixed himself another cognac. 'If Piers dies,' he slurred, 'because we don't turn up tomorrow with the ransom, whose fault will that be? The kidnappers' ... or yours, JD?'

'Enough already,' shouted Charlie. 'Piers is not going to die. I'm not going to let that happen.'

'Exactly. It's not over 'til it's over,' Jack said. 'We'll figure something out. Let's not start turning on each other, OK?'

Jack felt less anxious than the others. He was gutted he'd passed up the chance to be the hero at the poker table but he knew exactly what the solution was. He had one last trick up his sleeve but he needed to be careful how he played it. Withdrawing money from his own account and giving it away to the kidnappers was a simple solution but it was definitely a last resort and he was having difficulty reconciling it in his own mind. He knew questions would be asked, and he wasn't sure he was ready to answer them.

The phone rang. Charlie sprung up to answer it. He turned to the others, placed his finger over his lips, and pressed the speakerphone button. 'Hello.'

'Listen up,' a male voice commanded. 'We're gonna meet you tomorrow at ten in the morning at Martin Luther King Park. Bring half a million dollars in cash and we'll return your precious friend in one piece. No funny business or all bets are off and y'all end up searching for his dead body in the Nevada Desert instead. You know this ain't no game, yeah?'

'We've got the cash,' Charlie said quickly. 'Put Piers on the line so we know he's still OK.'

'He's fine. 10am. In the parking lot. Don't go tryin' to be the heroes, yo. And make sure you come alone. No Feds.'

The line went dead.

'Shit!' Charlie slammed down the receiver. Tom and

Jack exchanged looks. It was the first time Jack had ever heard Charlie raise his voice in anger, let alone swear.

They searched on the internet for the meeting place and discovered that Martin Luther King Park was in Sunrise Manor, near a rough-looking trailer park and clusters of old buildings that looked long past their best. A poor area where municipal funds had been spent in vain on regeneration. Online images of the place looked depressing. Apart from some dry-looking grass park where they were scheduled to meet, the whole area was barren and dilapidated, with badly neglected industrial parks, scrap yards and rusty trailer homes.

'How much money can we scrape together from our own savings?' Charlie asked. He was sounding desperate now.

'JD?' he said, filling the silence.

'I don't know, I guess I could probably access, perhaps like, $100,000,' Jack said, avoiding Charlie's gaze.

'That's a start. I have £75,000 in my current account. So that'd be $120,000. Tom, what about you?'

Jack felt a twinge of irritation.

'Tom?' Charlie asked again. 'How much have you got in the bank?'

A few seconds passed before Tom replied, slurring as he spoke, 'Hold on, you've just given me an idea.'

He pulled out his cell phone and stumbled out of the atrium towards his bedroom suite.

***

TOM'S HAND

'You know I like you, Tommy, but have you any idea how ridiculous you sound? You want me to wire you half a million dollars to pay a ransom because some long-lost friend, called Piers, has been kidnapped in Las Vegas?'

It was only when Jonny said the words out loud that it slowly dawned on Tom how stupid his request must have sounded.

'But it's true – honestly – no word of a lie. He's been taken—'

'You're in Vegas with your mates. Probably high or playing a stupid prank or something – what time is it over there, anyway? What would you do if you were me, huh? Send the money no questions asked?'

'Damn it, Jonny. I'm not high. I may be drunk, but I'm not making this shit up, OK?' said Tom desperately. 'If I were you, I'd take my word for it and send the money in good faith.'

'If this is your way of asking for a handout, it's pretty bloody extreme. I didn't think things were that bad, mate.'

'Things are bad! Piers has been kidnapped. He needs the money, not me. You've got enough of the bloody stuff, you tight bastard, think of it as temporary loan. His mother can pay you back. She's a billionaire.'

'Look, pal. You're out of work. You're on the other side of the pond and you've deserted your new wife, for God's sake. She doesn't even know if you're coming home. She's worried about you, Tommy, and I'm beginning to think maybe she should be. You sound drunk and delusional – who put you up to this nonsense you're spurting?'

Tom ignored the question. 'Why is she worried? I've only been gone a few days and I told her I was interviewing with your bank, anyway.'

'She knows you've been lying to her. She thinks you're trying to hide from your problems.'

Tom's ears were burning. He could feel his chest heaving as his heart pumped the blood to his brain. A sudden rush of fluid to his head weakened the rest of his body.

'I'm not hiding from anything,' he said quietly as he dropped his phone and was violently sick on the floor next to his bed. The long and fraught day, the non-stop drinking and the home truths from Jonny all caught up with Tom in a resounding punch to the gut. As he lay on the floor staring up at the white ceiling, it was the effect of the betrayal, not the alcohol, that he blamed for his wretched condition.

***

CHARLIE'S HAND

'For God's sake,' said Charlie as he strode into Tom's bedroom. 'Jack, come and give me a hand. Patto's thrown up everywhere.'

Tom was curled up in the fetal position with his back facing them so they couldn't see the anguish on his face. A pool of vomit lay on the floor next to him.

'Jesus. It's like we're back at Talybont in the '90s,' said Jack as he rushed in.

'At the risk of sounding insensitive, Tom, did you have any luck getting hold of some money?' Charlie asked calmly.

'I've got nothing. I've got nothing, OK?' he wailed drunkenly. His intonation was erratic, like a foreign student reading English out loud for the first time. 'He's got everything and I've got nothing, left of the dealer, small blind sir, you are the small bloody blind, as a bat, should have seen this coming,' Tom rambled. His words were barely audible, though the pain was loud and clear.

'Come on, Patto,' said Jack. 'Don't worry about any of that. Let's get you to bed, OK? We'll sort out a plan for Piers, don't worry. Just concentrate on getting some rest. We'll need you sober in the morning, OK, big man?'

Charlie stepped closer, carefully avoiding the vomit.

He picked Tom up and carried him across to the couch at the foot of the bed. Jack took off his mate's shoes and socks and Tom gradually disappeared, swallowed up by a pile of oversized cushions.

'Hey, remember Wednesdays in the Taf? Extra Cheeky Vimto night? You drank ten one night and still managed to pull Bethan Matthews. Times really have changed haven't they, mate?' Jack was trying his best to make light of the situation. 'Let's get you out of these clothes and into bed, so you can sleep this off, OK? I'll get housekeeping to come and clean the mess up in the morning.'

'Housekeeping – she'll keep the house – keeping – no way – not fair – not him – slick – creeping – running – laughing – both of them – all the way to the bank, Jonny fucking Banks! He's already got everything!' Tom's voice was jumpy, like someone was adjusting his tuning. He shook his head frantically as he spoke and, although his eyes were closed, tears streamed down his alcohol-reddened cheeks.

Charlie and Jack exchanged looks, shrugged and carried on stripping him down to his boxer shorts, then lifted him into his giant bed. By the time they left he was already asleep, snoring angrily.

Charlie turned to Jack as they sat back down in the main atrium. 'OK. T-minus eleven hours before we show up at Martin Luther King Park with the ransom. Tom doesn't look like he's going to be much use,' he said, setting a timer on his G-Shock. 'If we pool our savings together we'll have $220,000, right? Can we borrow the rest?'

'Where would we find that kind of money at this time of night?'

'The hotel might lend it to us. We're in Vegas, after all – it's not unusual for the big casinos to lend money to their guests.'

'If you say so,' Jack said, pausing for a few seconds. 'And I guess, if we do borrow the money, we could ask Piers or his family to pay us back? I mean, don't get me wrong, I like the guy; he's an old friend and he's been incredibly generous to us in the past, but I do expect to be paid back, don't you?'

Charlie eyed Jack, but said nothing.

'What's that look for?' Jack shifted in his seat. 'You're doing that thing you used to do at university, you're trying to get a read on me or something.'

'I know as much about his family as you do, but I would assume they're good for the money, especially if they're as rich as he says,' Charlie said flatly.

'Well, I guess if you believe he's the heir to billions – he's a triple A-rated credit, right? Nothing safer.'

Charlie studied his friend's face and shrugged. 'If you say so.'

'I'm going downstairs to get some fresh air. The smell of Tom's vomit is making me feel sick,' Jack said as he walked toward the private elevator and pressed the gold button. 'Do you want anything?'

'Find out how we can get hold of our savings at this hour and whether the hotel will lend us the rest.'

Jack stepped inside, turned back to face Charlie, then nodded slowly as the elevator door slid shut in front of him.

Card 23

Staking: The act of one person putting up cash for a poker player, in the hope that the player wins.

Las Vegas, 11 July 2009
MR. YIN'S HAND

Mr. Yin resumed his position in the lobby at Caesars Palace. He sat facing the main entrance, both the elevators and the front desk within sight. He had just relieved Mr. Yang, who had rushed off to the food court to fill his stomach with ramen and braised pork belly before his favorite restaurant closed.

Mr. Yin was concerned about the asset's disappearance but he was more worried about what Mr. Lee would do if they couldn't find him. His boss was a ruthless, violent sociopath. Mr. Yin had once witnessed him cave in an employee's face with a hole-punch and then imprint a message on his bare chest with a staple gun. The victim was one of the 14K's accountants, who had made a simple bookkeeping error. Twice. The blood-soaked message was *"chéng qián bì hòu"*. A Chinese proverb that means: "Learn from past mistakes to avoid future ones".

Mr. Yin didn't want to let down the 14K and he

certainly didn't want to be on the receiving end of one of Mr. Lee's infamous messages.

There were still a lot of unanswered questions and Mr. Yin felt exposed. His primary objective was to keep track of the asset at all times, following him around without being seen and reporting anything unusual to the Dragon Master.

He had managed the assignment with ease over the last six months. It had been a relatively simple and boring task, watching from a distance and keeping a low profile, but Mr. Yin felt his associate had become sloppy.

Mr. Yin was beginning to question whether the asset had really been kidnapped. Or had Captain Preston spun an elaborate lie to keep them off the trail? The phone call to his boss had focused his mind and reminded him that, in his line of work, no one could be trusted.

With a renewed purpose, he scanned the opulent gold lobby, looking out for anything unusual. *Hang on a second.* Mr. Yin saw one of the asset's friends step out of the private elevator alone. He checked his watch. It was 11.45 pm. He watched him walk over to the concierge's desk. Five minutes later, he noticed a suspicious-looking man heading towards him. The man was wearing a New York Yankees baseball cap with the logo embroidered on the front in white stitching. Mr. Yin noticed the cap was pulled down lower than normal, hiding his unshaven face. He had a phone pressed against his ear. Mr. Yin was just close enough to hear his side of the conversation.

'We're on. This is actually happening. There's no sign of the Feds and I just heard some Brit ask the concierge for half a million dollars. He looks a lightweight, too. There's nothing to worry about here. You were right, this is going to be easy, sis. Like taking candy from a baby.'

Mr. Yin smiled to himself as he overheard the man describe what he had just seen. He waited for him to walk past then stood and followed him out of the hotel.

***

JACK'S HAND

Jack knew what he had to do. They were short-stacked and the game was coming to an end. Now was his chance to play his best card and go all in. He breathed deeply, stepped out of the elevator, and walked towards a young, spotty-faced concierge at the front desk in the hotel lobby.

'I have a small predicament, sir,' he said, leaning in and deploying heartfelt British deference. 'My name is Jack Davidson. I'm staying in the Presidential Suite, Forum Tower, and I need to withdraw some money rather urgently.'

'Of course, sir,' the concierge replied. 'We have teller machines just over there where you can—'

'I'm afraid I need to withdraw quite a significant amount,' Jack interrupted. 'I need half a million dollars. Tonight, if possible.' He lowered his voice, trying his best not to draw attention to himself.

'Oh. I see, sir. Well, in that case, I'll need to speak with the manager. Please excuse me.'

The concierge walked off and stood by a man who was helping a guest with directions. His black hair was greasy and scraped back into a ponytail, and he sported a short, neat mustache. As the concierge relayed the request, Jack observed the expression on the manager's face; incredulity mixed with intrigue.

The manager strolled confidently towards him and thrust out his hand. 'Good evening, Mr. Davidson. My name is Carlos Hayman, I am one of the managers at Caesars Palace,' he said proudly. His serious face softened as he spoke, revealing what seemed like avuncular warmth. 'I understand you need half a million dollars, yes?' Carlos Hayman was now smiling broadly, his expressive face lit up.

Jack half-smiled and nodded. He noticed the manager's gold name badge was much shinier than that of the young concierge and wondered which of them was new: the name badge or Carlos Hayman.

'Before I take this further, Mr. Davidson, yes. You should know that it's hotel policy to carry out a few basic checks first, yes?'

'I would expect nothing less,' Jack said, relieved that getting half a million dollars in cash at this hour was at least a possibility.

'If you would like to follow me, Mr. Davidson.' More grinning. More teeth. 'We can discuss this further in private, yes?' Carlos smiled a smile that was brighter than a Christmas tree with glittering baubles.

Only in Vegas, thought Jack as he followed Carlos Hayman into the manager's office.

Card 24

Full Tilt: A state of mental or emotional confusion or frustration in which a player adopts a less than optimal strategy.

Las Vegas, 11 July 2009
JACK'S HAND

The Mad House oozed the sweet smell of skin and seduction. This was Sin City's newest gentleman's club and it was enchanting. Jack had read that it was the reinvention of a former club that had struggled to keep afloat. Now the place had a freshness about it; inside and out, everything looked new and untouched – which was certainly desirable in a lap-dancing club. The Mad House was obviously still launching a charm offensive to impress and entice new customers, and the effect was working – the place was busy; full of people and steeped in vice.

It was close to 1am when Jack, Tom and Piers arrived. Jack had reserved a table in the High Roller section of the club, overlooking the largest stage, with a perfect view of the topless dancers. Their mirrored table was covered by ice buckets, alcohol and champagne flutes, and surrounded by a bounty of girls wearing smiles and skimpy lingerie.

'Can I get y'all more drinks?' asked their Hispanic-looking waitress.

Piers and Tom were too busy chatting to a group of dancers who had congregated around them.

'We'll take another bottle of bourbon, some more mixers and a magnum of Dom Pérignon this time,' Jack said, smiling in an effort to appear less drunk than he actually was. The waitress smiled back and Jack found himself staring at the gap between her two front teeth – it was big enough to slot a coin through.

'Sure thing, and y'all know if there's anything else you want – on or off the menu – be sure to holler, baby,' the waitress whispered in Jack's ear before she turned to leave.

Jack guessed she was no older than nineteen. He followed her caramel-brown body with his eyes as she navigated her way skillfully across the endless shiny black floor of the club but he lost her amongst the sea of gorgeous women. The waitresses, dancers, bar girls and even a few female customers seemed implausibly beautiful. Everywhere Jack turned there was a scantily dressed girl with round breasts and big hair. As soon as his attention was drawn to one sexy blonde, his eyes would refocus on another almost straightaway: a pale red-head with green eyes, balancing a tray of champagne flutes; a skinny brunette chatting playfully to someone at the bar, her firm body on full display through her black lace chemise; a peroxide blonde, covered in colorful tattoos, swinging expertly around a pole on the stage, her eyes seemingly fixed on Jack as she did the box splits suspended in mid-air.

Jack turned back to the table and looked at Tom, who had honed in on one of the girls. She was draped all over him and as he talked excitedly, she laughed, her breasts undulating gently, and stroked his face with the back of her hand. Jack noticed that her toenails were a different color to her fingernails.

'Let me pour you another drink, Tom,' she said loudly over the thumping music. She reached across, brushing his cheek with her breasts, as she picked up the bottle of Jack Daniels from the mirrored table. She whispered in his ear as she filled the glass and Tom smiled like an embarrassed teenager.

'You look like the pussy that got the cream,' Jack said, leaning over and pouring himself another glass of Dom Pérignon. 'Or should it be the other way around?' he said with a smile.

'I'm going for a dance with Kitty,' Tom replied. He grinned at Jack and walked off hand in hand with his new feline friend.

Jack had been to plenty of strip clubs back in London. Buttering up corporate male clients was part of his job. It never seemed to matter whether they were single, married or had children; faced with the temptation of gorgeous girls flattering them, pampering them and offering a private audience, their response was always the same. Jack wasn't a fool. He knew it was strictly business. The oldest type of business, in fact. The women were only interested in making money. They were hustling. Using their looks and bodies to take advantage of men's inherent weakness. But it was just a charade and, as with all forms of commerce, one thing was simply being traded for another.

'Excuse me,' Jack called out, catching the attention of the languorously attractive blonde in front of him. 'If you're going to drink my champagne, you could at least come over and talk to me. I promise I won't bite. What's your name, sweetheart?'

'Sindy,' the blonde replied with an equable smile. 'Sindy with an "S".'

Of course it is, Jack thought. He knew that wasn't her real name, just as he was sure that her gravity-defying physique was unlikely to be her own, either. He returned the smile and held out his hand.

'So what's your name, mister?' Sindy asked as she took his hand and, without invitation, straddled his lap.

He paused as he considered "Ken". Too predictable, he thought, and anyway he couldn't be sure if Ken was Sindy's boyfriend or Barbie's. He was meticulous, even when making a joke with a stripper. 'Jack with a "J",' he said in the end.

'As in Union Jack?' Sindy said, still smiling, showing off her perfect, straight, white teeth. 'I love your accent, Jack. Are you from Lon-don?' she asked, doing her best to mimic the Queen's English.

'I am, as a matter of fact.'

'What line of work are you in, Jack?'

'I'm a partner at an international law firm.'

'Oh really, which one?'

'Spear, Collier & Horn,' he said, humoring her.

'Wow. That's a big firm, Jack. Didn't you guys act for Microsoft in their patent lawsuit against Apple last year? You must work long hours. Do the lawyers in London have the same targets as New York?'

Jack shrugged. 'Much the same,' he said, feigning aloofness. He was impressed that she'd even heard of his firm, let alone knew any of its business.

It turned out Sindy had planned to become a lawyer. Majoring in law at Cornell University, she'd only moved to Vegas to get work experience in her uncle's real estate practice while she studied for the California Bar Exam. But after Bear Stearns and Lehman Brothers collapsed, her uncle had gone out of business and she'd ended up working at the Mad House to keep on top of her student debt.

Jack couldn't tell whether her story was true or a work

of fiction conjured up to endear herself to wealthy punters. He gave it no more than a moment's thought, though; in a place like the Mad House, a lie was almost always more intriguing than the truth.

'Shall we have a dance, Sindy with an "S"?' he said, interrupting her conversation mid-flow.

She took his hand and led him away, out of the High Roller section and towards the private rooms at the back of the club.

***

HONEY'S HAND

The music in the Mad House was loud and relentless; a regular beat for the girls to move their lust-inducing bodies to. It was also functional; serving as a shield to block out the misery of banal conversations repeated night after night. *What's your real name? Do you enjoy your job? Does your daddy know you do this? How much for sex?*

For the novice or less confident girls at the Mad House, the music was something to hide behind, shielding them from the real world outside, allowing them to lose themselves in melodies and lyrics. But for the club's experienced hustlers, like Honey, the music was a tool in their armory; a cloak of noise that could conceal their true intentions.

Honey had been with Piers all night. As he talked, animated by alcohol, she leaned in and out of his personal space, smiling and giggling encouragingly. She was an expert and he was her mark.

She kept leading him off for private dances; linking his arm, like a naughty school girl leading him round the back of the bike sheds. His eyes were bloodshot and his pupils dilated. He had been drinking bourbon and champagne all night like it was water and Honey knew that the only reason he hadn't collapsed on the floor was because of the cocaine racing through his bloodstream.

'What time do you finish?' he shouted, the words leaving his mouth quickly as if they were in a hurry to escape. 'Why don't you come back to ours? We're in the Presidential Suite at Caesars. There's plenty of room. The place is massive.'

Jackpot. They must be high rollers, Honey thought to herself. She pulled the lollipop from her mouth and smiled at him. 'You're sweet, baby, but look, I've got another couple of hours before Franco will let me go for the night, I'm doin' the late shift today,' she said, placing the lollipop in his mouth and stroking his jaw.

'Franco?' Piers mumbled.

'Don't worry, baby. He's just the Scottish guy who owns this place. He's harmless enough. A lot nicer than some of the other club owners in this city.'

'I don't want you to dance for anyone else but me,' Piers said.

'You know what, baby? Why don't we go somewhere private for my last two hours? It ain't cheap, but you know I'm worth it, and hey, if you're staying in the Presidential Suite I know you can afford me. I got a special room, real discreet. Just you and me. It's a thousand dollars for half an hour, but because I like you, Piers, we could spend the rest of my shift there, just the two of us, for thirty-nine hundred? What do you say? I'll show you a good time, I promise.'

She reached over and, with one hand behind his neck and the other on his groin, caressed him gently.

'It's real private,' she whispered as she kissed his earlobe.

***

PIERS' HAND

Away from the crowds upstairs in the club, Honey and Piers sat in a private room, drinking Dom Pérignon on a Louis XIV-inspired chaise longue. The "French Suite" was exclusive, with Baroque-style, heavy gilded plaster moldings and Bordeaux-colored walls. A malodorous waft of cheap perfume hung in the air, masking any sense of real elegance, but Piers was too preoccupied to notice.

Honey stood in front of him, writhing slowly to the music, rolling her hips in time with the distant beat, and Piers was transfixed. She was wearing a tartan mini-skirt so short that it revealed her white lace knickers, long white socks pulled up just below the knee and a white shirt, unbuttoned and tied below her large breasts, leaving nothing to the imagination.

Piers was well and truly under her spell and as she danced in front of him he was drawn to her milk-chocolate eyes. When she spoke, he was hypnotized by the languid movement of her pillow-soft lips. Everything about her was mesmerizing. Her petite figure, perfect curves and firm tummy were eye-catching, but Piers was drawn to her face. It was perfectly formed, unblemished and subtly tanned – framed by wavy, shoulder-length brown hair that had a slight caramel hue.

'So tell me, Honey. How does a beautiful girl like you end up working in a place like this?' Piers said, handing Honey the rolled-up fifty-dollar bill.

'I don't normally do this,' she said, bending down to the line of coke on the glass-topped table.

'It's perfectly fine, honestly. I've been doing it all night. It's good quality stuff.'

Honey flicked her long brown hair to one side and deftly snorted the white powder up her left nostril.

'I mean, I don't normally talk to people about that

kinda stuff, you know? But I like you, Piers. I feel safe around you.'

'Tell you what, Honey. Let's play a game. You tell me a secret and I'll tell you one back. It's good to open up to people. Supposed to cleanse your soul.'

'Sure.'

'But it has to be the truth or there's no point playing, OK?'

'We'll see,' she said with a grin. 'You start.'

Piers held her gaze. 'I've never met my dad. I don't even know his name.'

'Me too,' Honey said quickly. 'I mean, I guess I met him at some point, but I don't remember. He left when I was a baby. Creep didn't want anything to do with us. Just left my poor mom to fend for herself with me and my two older brothers. Deserted us in the middle of the night without saying a word.'

'Have you ever tried to find him?'

'No. Why would I? I've hated him for so long I can't see the point, you know?'

'I guess I feel the same. If he never bothered to make contact, why should I? At least you had your mum to look after you. Mine deserted me when I was little. Sent me to a boarding school in another country and never came to visit. Now that I'm grown up, and need her more than anything right now, she doesn't even want to speak to me.'

'My mom's dead,' Honey said quietly. 'Died of an overdose on my seventh birthday.'

'Oh Jesus, I'm so terribly sorry.'

'I found her body on the bathroom floor beside an empty bottle of pills.'

There was a brief pause while Piers wondered how best to respond.

'That must have been awful. How did you manage?' he said eventually.

'Spent a few years as a ward of the state but in the end they gave my two brothers custody. It was tough, you know, coming from a broken home in Detroit, life was never gonna be easy. My brothers turned to crime to make ends meet and keep us together; shoplifting, pickpocketing, innocent misdemeanors, that kinda thing. Soon, they got me involved. I helped them with their scams and confidence tricks back home in Michigan.'

'And that's how you wound up here? Working in a club like this is just one big con, right?' Piers said.

'Pretty much,' Honey said with a smile. 'But what else can a girl do? I ain't got no prospects, and dancing in a place like this or running a scam with my brothers allows me to be someone else, someone other than me, for just a brief moment. It allows me to escape, if you know what I mean?'

'But don't you feel bad for your victims?'

'What, dirty old men who should know better? No chance.'

'Is that what you think of me? Am I just another dirty old man who should know better?'

'I wouldn't be telling you any of this if I didn't think you were different, would I?' She smiled at him mischievously. 'Come on. It's your turn, why don't you tell me why you and your buddies are in Vegas?' Her brown eyes were wide with genuine interest. 'Y'all here on business or pleasure?'

Piers picked up his gold Amex and started cutting up the heap of powder that was still on the glass table.

'How about we do another line, Honey, and I'll tell you everything? It's quite some story.'

Card 25

Backdoor: A different hand to that which the player was intending to make.

Las Vegas, 11 July 2009
PIERS' HAND

'It's all gone I'm afraid. I'm really sorry, dear boy. The market really turned on us. No one could have possibly seen this coming. It's no consolation I'm sure, but you're not the only one. I've lost nearly two million of my own savings. All of our clients – anyone exposed to the MBS market – they're all carrying huge losses. I'm frightfully sorry, but there was nothing we could have done.'

'But you said it was a sure thing, Leonard. You promised me my money was safe with Sterling Securities. You told me it was invested in bricks and mortar. "Safe as houses" is what you said.'

'Ironically, that was the very problem, old bean. The whole property market in the US has crashed and burned. Look, this really is unprecedented. It's never happened in my lifetime. Blame the rating agencies or the mortgage brokers if you need to blame anyone.'

'I blame you, Leonard. You conniving snake. You sold

me those goddamn products. What am I going to do now? I've lost everything.'

'Look, I advised you of the risks. You're a big boy. You knew the dangers of investing. I told you that past performance wasn't a guide to the future. You made the decision to invest the money yourself. I've got to call the rest of my clients now and then my wife – you are not the only one suffering here, Piers. We're going to have to take the boys out of Eton. This is a complete disaster.'

Piers bolted awake in a cold sweat, his heart beating like a carnival drum. The dream always left him feeling angry and panicked. But on this occasion, those feelings were overshadowed by a sharp pain he felt from behind his eyes. He lifted his throbbing head from the sweat-drenched pillow and took in the unfamiliar surroundings. He was completely naked, lying in a bed in what appeared to be an anodyne motel room.

He was confused. This wasn't the Presidential Suite. The neurotransmitters in his brain were having difficulty conveying simple messages. His drowsy eyes could just about register lifeless shapes of furniture. He had no idea where he was. He peeled the thin bed sheets from his clammy frame while scanning the room with squinting eyes, looking for clues that might jog his absent memory. *Where on earth am I?*

The headache was worse than usual. He closed his eyes and tried to remember where he was and how he'd got there. He felt like he was coming out of a coma, rather than waking from a bad dream. *Have I been in an accident? Am I in hospital? Perhaps I'm still dreaming? Where the hell are the others?* He had no answers to the panicky questions that were darting around his fragile brain.

The thumping headache worsened. His skin itched. He opened his eyes again, took several deep breaths, and waited for the pain to subside.

He noticed his clothes strewn on the floor beside a basic-looking wooden table and chair. He could just make out the shape of his wallet in the pocket of his pants. A black digital clock on the table revealed that it was 13:42. The two flashing red dots between the three and four seemed to speed up, like they were trying to warn him about something.

He rubbed his eyes and stood up wearily from the damp bed but almost immediately felt a sudden pain in his nose, like all the hairs had been plucked from his nostrils at once. *Bloody hell.* Now he remembered something. A long white line of regret, he thought as he tried to keep his balance. Normally, he hated himself the morning after the night before, but this time he was too confused to feel any guilt or self-loathing. He picked up his pants and checked his wallet. There was no money left but all his cards appeared to be there. As he reached down for his shirt, he noticed a blue condom wrapper lying under the bed on the cheap linoleum floor. He had no idea whether it was his. He still didn't know where he was and however hard he tried to search his memory, he was lost and felt helpless. The lack of recall made him feel sick.

The linoleum seemed to oscillate beneath him as he pulled on his pants and shirt, struggling with the small buttons in his clammy hands. He heard the rattle of keys from behind the motel-room door and a fresh wave of nausea mixed with adrenaline surged through his feeble body. His instincts told him to shout for help. But why, exactly? Better to wait and see who was behind the door first. The rattling stopped. Then he panicked again – what if his voice was too hoarse and tongue too swollen for anyone to hear if he did need to shout?

The door swung open, finally, and sunlight poured in, unlocking the floodgates of his memory and bringing with it a very different wave of sickness.

How could I forget someone like you? he thought as a young woman floated into the room.

'You don't look like you slept too well, baby. Here – get some coffee in you – black medicine, I like to call it,' she said with a smile as she handed him one of the Styrofoam cups she was holding. 'You'll feel better soon, I promise.'

She perched on the end of the wooden table, her legs crossed at the ankles, knee-high black patent leather boots with six-inch heels swinging gently above the linoleum. With a nod of her head, she invited Piers to sit in the chair in front of her. He sipped his coffee, unsure whether it was still too hot to drink, and took a seat willingly. His head was at the same level as her belt but his eyes remained fixated on her face. She was wearing a long, dark green raincoat tied at the waist, covering her body and thighs. Her caramel-brown hair was tied back in a neat ponytail, emphasizing her beautiful features.

As she fidgeted on top of the table, he noticed her belt was beginning to loosen. He took another sip of coffee and felt a rush of blood to his groin. The top of her thigh was now on show. He glimpsed her black lace garter suspenders.

'Thanks for last night, by the way,' she said, smiling, while her coat parted at the waist to reveal a light pink satin boudoir corset with a skirt of black lace. 'It was a lot of fun. It got real crazy. I mean, we really connected, don't you think? Stuff we shared, you know, the things we said? The things we did together.' She paused and smiled mischievously. Then her face changed, her hazelnut eyes grew more tender, putting him at his ease, and she reached out and gently took hold of his clammy hand. He felt an instant connection.

'Look. I want you to know that, sure, I'm no angel, but I don't usually do what we did last night. I mean that. I've never really connected like that with anyone else. So this is all kinda new for me, baby. I haven't really felt this way before. It sounds silly, I know, but I'm real excited about our future. We've got lots to discuss.'

Piers rubbed his eyes. What was going on? Was he still dreaming? In front of him sat the prettiest girl he had ever laid eyes on and she was talking about a future with him. *If only I could remember what happened last night. Why is she so taken by me? What kind of line did I spin her? Or was it just the lines of cocaine? Maybe I should get some more?* He gulped the coffee, put the cup on the table and stood up. Moving towards her, he slipped his hands around her petite waist and kissed her forehead.

'You're frightfully beautiful. I can't quite believe any of this is real. It feels like the most extraordinary dream. Like I'm going to wake up any minute with nothing but this awfully embarrassing erection,' he smiled at her as he eyed his groin.

She giggled playfully. 'Why don't you take a shower first, baby, and then we can pick up where we left off last night. We've so much to talk about,' she said, as she slowly took off her coat and draped it over the back of the chair.

His eyes were drawn to her cleavage, where the cups of her corset were struggling to contain her ample breasts. *If only I could remember her bloody name.*

'I'm dying to get out of these clothes. You have no idea how hot I am.'

'Oh I do, honey. I most definitely do,' he said, beaming, as he shed the clothes he had struggled to put on only minutes earlier.

***

PIERS' HAND

Piers hummed happily as he washed himself in the

motel-room shower, the water splashing off his shoulders onto the terracotta tiles beneath his feet. But, just as a seedling eventually germinates, given the right amount of water, his recollection of last night's conversations was beginning to return. *Oh no,* he thought, as snatches of memories flashed through his mind. *Shit. What have I done?*

All of a sudden his heart rate slowed. The water droplets from the shower began to feel like boulders crashing against his sore head. He couldn't stand the pressure and was struggling to draw breath. Within a matter of seconds, he lost consciousness and collapsed on the floor of the shower.

Card 26

Suck Out: A situation when a hand heavily favored to win loses to an inferior hand after all the cards are dealt. The winning hand is said to have 'sucked out'.

Las Vegas, 11 July 2009
APRIL'S HAND

April Parker knew when someone was lying to her. It happened every night at the Mad House. A strip club is a melting pot of liars, deviants and cheats so she'd had plenty of practice and, by now, she was an expert at reading the signs.

Most people avoided eye contact or looked up and to the left when they were lying, or they might over-compensate by staring directly at her. Alternatively, they might unwittingly shrug a shoulder or shake their head when answering "yes". She could pick out a genuine punter and April had little doubt that, despite his state of intoxication, Piers had been telling her the God's-honest truth.

She pulled on her raincoat, making sure the belt was tightly fastened at the waist this time. She lifted the plastic lid of Piers' coffee cup and checked how much was left.

Any time now.

Picking up the Styrofoam cup, she strode confidently into the motel bathroom, her six-inch heels clicking noisily on the tiled flooring. Piers was humming away happily with his back to her. He didn't see her pour the remnants of the coffee into the washbasin.

The humming stopped and, after a moment or two, she saw him wobble. She advanced toward the shower cubicle and just caught his head before it hit the metal valve as he slumped to the floor. Good catch, she thought, as she cradled him in her arms and turned off the shower.

'Or are you the good catch?' she said out loud, knowing full well he couldn't hear her.

April waited a few seconds to catch her breath. Her adrenaline was always high when she was running a scam but she felt especially charged on this occasion. Could she be making a mistake? The guy's honesty had disarmed her and she had also shared with him things which she'd never told anyone else before. She lifted his head up gently and slid her arm out, before placing him in the recovery position. As she carefully stepped over him she caught a glimpse of herself in the cheap, rectangular bathroom mirror. When her hair was scraped back in a ponytail she looked much like her mom did in the few old photos she still had. Her mom had been about the same age when she'd taken her own life. The photographs were all she had left, the memories faded a long time ago.

As she stared into the mirror, the steam from the shower slowly eroded her reflection. She couldn't help but wonder how her life might have turned out if her dad hadn't abandoned them and her mom hadn't swallowed those pills. *Will today be the start of a new life for me? A new identity?*

Her mind jolted back to her very first mark: Mr. Harris Nicholson.

Since moving to Vegas with her brothers, all their scams had turned a tidy profit. They seemed to be on a winning streak. It had been April's idea to extort money from punters at the Mad House, using information gleaned from a few hours of seduction. Their most profitable trick was demanding cash in exchange for photos of marks in compromising situations. Young men on bachelor weekends, enjoying their last acts of freedom. Student travelers stopping over for a night in Sin City before returning home to study. Businessmen with no business being in certain parts of the city. Different kinds of victim, who shared the same desperate need to comply with their demands. At first, she had been surprised how easily people handed over their money to keep a secret, stop an anonymous call to a loved one, or prevent an incriminating photo landing on their employer's desk. But she quickly realized that people with something to lose were always willing to pay. Those who had the most at stake always paid the quickest.

Ironically, it had begun with a selfless act of civic duty. At the end of one of her shifts at the Mad House, April had come across a wallet tucked inside one of the leather seats in a private room. It was full of the usual stuff: cash, credit cards, a driver's license and a family photo of a wife and young daughter. April had lifted the cash but decided to track down the owner, Mr. Harris Nicholson, and return the wallet. The girl in the photo looked sweet and innocent and there was something about the wife that reminded April of her own mom. After sifting through the receipts and making a few calls, she found the hotel where Mr. Nicholson had been staying and asked to be put through to his suite.

April could remember, as if it was yesterday, his flustered voice as he lied to his wife. "It's no one, darling. Nothing for you to worry about!"

He'd begged April to leave his wallet at the front desk of his hotel but she'd insisted she would only return it to him in person, or wait for his wife or daughter in the lobby and hand it to one of them instead. "How much do you want?" Harris Nicholson had asked in a frantic whisper. "I'm guessing this is about money, right?"

April looked back at the steamed-up mirror. Her face had vanished completely.

A gentle knock on the motel-room door brought her back into the present. *Stick to the plan,* she thought, as she crossed the threshold from the bathroom back into the bedroom, leaving Piers' naked body behind her on the tiled floor.

'That didn't take long,' Kyle said loudly as he walked into the motel room, carrying a tanned leather holdall. Danny followed him in, closed the door gently then locked it.

'He still had some of the sedative in his body from last night. I'm surprised he even made it to the shower, to be honest,' April said.

Kyle placed the holdall on top of the wooden table before walking into the bathroom. 'Danny, get a load of this, bro. He's still got a boner,' Kyle shouted.

'Shut up,' Danny whispered manically as he peered into the bathroom. 'How many times have I gotta say it? Call me Elvis when we're working, you dumbass.'

'Just bring him in here, and be careful with his head,' April said, realizing how stupid that sounded in the light of what they were planning to do next.

Card 27

Underdog: A person or hand not mathematically favored to win a pot.

Las Vegas, 11 July 2009
PIERS' HAND

Piers woke up again with another pounding headache. He opened his eyes slowly but the room was too dark to see. He could feel a cold sweat dripping down his forehead and onto the bridge of his nose. He was disorientated and confused. His eyes tried to focus whilst his brain struggled to engage with his surroundings. He thought of shouting out for help but registered the tape over his mouth. He tried to reach for it, to pull it off, but his hands were tied behind his back. Panic set in when he realized he was bound to a chair in a darkened room. He had no idea what was going on.

He wriggled around, frantically trying to loosen the binding on his hands and feet, shouting for help at the same time. Though the noise inside his head was loud and immediate, the only actual sound he seemed to be making was a muffled hum. In a panic, he shook himself from side to side until the chair toppled over and crashed to the floor. Now his face was pressed against the dusty concrete; a sense of hopelessness washed over him.

His body started to shake and he began to cry. His tears slid across the cold sweat on his face, forming a mixture that rolled into his right eye as he lay on his side, helpless and unable to move. His eye started to sting and he blinked hard but couldn't stop the flow. He lay there, bewildered, abandoned and helpless. Seconds later, a door in the corner of the room opened, letting in a flood of yellow light. He registered two pairs of legs before the door closed and the darkness returned.

A male voice said, 'Can't you just sit here quietly?' Its tone was chilling.

A light flashed in his eyes and he felt someone reach down and lift him up with such ease that he could only be some sort of giant.

'Listen up,' the voice came again, 'there's no need to panic. I ain't gonna hurt you. But if we don't get paid, hell, I can get all sorts of nasty. I've been inside, so I know what to do to preppies like you.'

Jesus, Piers hummed as the masking tape was ripped from his mouth.

'Now drink this,' added a second voice.

Cold water was pouring into his mouth. It eased the pain and he drank without pause, blinking back in silent appreciation.

'What do you want? How much do you want?' Piers said faintly, his vocal chords raw from the muffled shouting. He felt tepid, tobacco-laced breath brush his face as the chilling voice whispered in his ear.

'You're worth half a million dollars. Ain't that something?'

Card 28

Sleight of Hand: Hand methods and dealing techniques used by cheats to manipulate shuffling and dealing cards or to steal chips from opponents' stacks without them noticing.

Las Vegas, 11 July 2009
PIERS' HAND

After an hour, Piers' eyes slowly began to adjust to the darkness. Despite his fragile state, his body was urgently responding to his surroundings – a natural survival mechanism was kicking in. His pupils were fighting against the poor light. His senses were enhanced. He could still smell the rancid breath and body odor of his captors.

Every little sound was amplified by his ears and now there was another voice coming from outside the room. One he thought he recognized. There was a sudden burst of activity in his brain as incomplete thoughts darted around his head. Fragments of information hurtled around at light speed. His brain's chemistry was still imbalanced. Flashbacks of a dream, a nightmare, an encounter; conversations with someone pretty important; important conversations with someone pretty. He wasn't sure. He tried to rationalize and process messages from his brain but nothing seemed to make sense. He couldn't separate reality from illusion.

Piers closed his eyes and tried to concentrate but his mind just threw out another piece of the confusing puzzle before he had a chance to catch the last. Then his brain stalled and a single word flashed before his eyes.

Honey.

The door to the room swung open again and Piers braced himself, his weak body tensed and his heart rate quickened. His pupils were fully dilated and there was just enough light from the opening of the door for him to make out the shapes of three people entering.

A familiar smell: cheap perfume filled the air and had a calming effect on his heart rate. Although he was tied to a chair with masking tape over his mouth, in a dark and dusty room with no idea where he was or what was happening, for some reason he suddenly felt less vulnerable. As the woman approached, the scent of her perfume became stronger and the sound of her heels on the concrete floor grew louder until she was right in front of him.

'Sorry, Piers. Honey's not always good for you,' her familiar voice announced.

Before Piers could grasp what she meant, she punched him in the face. Her fist was decorated with rings and he felt each one penetrate his clammy, cold skin. Stars danced in front of his eyes like someone had pulled a sequined hood over his head.

He felt the warmth of blood inside his nostrils and at the back of his mouth. It tasted metallic. In his privileged upbringing he'd never been punched before, his only encounters with violence were being slapped round the back of the head by Father Arnold at Eton for being late to choir practice and being held in a headlock by a Welsh psychopath in the Dragon's Den casino. This was an entirely new experience and he didn't much like it. The sequins still danced but they were starting to fade. He braced himself for another blow. There was nothing. The heels turned and walked away, the cheap fragrance lingering for a while.

'Let's be clear,' a thundering male voice barked. 'Our sister ain't interested in you or your fantasies. You're nothing but a means to an end. D'you understand?'

Piers felt a cold metal sphere pressing hard against his forehead. Now he could taste fear at the back of his throat.

'I've used my piece before on marks just as dumb as you, and I'll use it again if your buddies don't show with the ransom tomorrow. And if they go contacting the Feds or trying anything funny, I'm gonna stick it in your mouth and pull the trigger, you hear me?'

The two men left the room and Piers was alone once more. He was in pain and in total shock, adrenaline pumping through his veins. He couldn't think properly so he concentrated on his breathing, slowly inhaling and exhaling through his blood-filled nostrils, returning a degree of calm to his body.

Several minutes passed before the door swung open once more and the noise of heavy footsteps broke the silence. In a split second, two dark silhouettes towered over him.

'Your buddies seem to think this is some kind of hoax,' the chilling voice whispered. 'They want to speak with you to be sure we ain't playin' games. Let them know we're serious and don't say nothing stupid or y'all regret it.'

The tape was ripped from his mouth again and a phone thrust toward his face. Piers sensed a cue to speak.

'It's me ... Piers. Please just do as they say and get me out of here. They aren't messing around. They're bloody mental. They've got weapons. They'll kill me if you don't do exactly what—'

'I think they've heard enough. Tape him back up so he doesn't start screaming again. Not that anyone can hear you down here. This ain't exactly a Neighborhood Watch area.'

In an instant, the tape had been refastened, the heavy footsteps had retreated, and the light from outside had washed in and then drained away, leaving Piers alone in the room, wondering when the next wave would hit him.

Card 29

Variance: A measure of the up-and-down swings your bankroll goes through. Variance is not necessarily a measure of how well you play. However, the higher your variance, the wider the swings you'll see in your bankroll.

Las Vegas, 12 July 2009
CHARLIE'S HAND

Charlie stood up, walked to the bar and poured a large glass of Woodford Reserve. He knew what he had to do but the thought of phoning his dad filled him with dread. It was an acknowledgement of defeat in his mind. An admission of failure.

He hadn't needed his dad's help in nearly two decades and he hated asking for it but now he didn't know what else to do. His dad would be disappointed, Charlie knew that much. He wouldn't say it, of course; he didn't need to.

Charlie downed the bourbon and poured himself another without thinking. He walked past the Steinway and observed the starkly contrasting black and white keys. He slid open the glass door and stepped outside onto the large balcony that overlooked the city.

The fresh air caught him by surprise. It was windy and he felt a little uneasy on his feet as he looked out across the bright Las Vegas skyline. It was a clear night and the view was spectacular; a vibrant mix of dazzling colors against a heavy curtain of darkness. The electric lights of the casinos, hotels, water displays and giant signs seemed alive with energy and allure, against the black backdrop of nothingness. Vegas looked too awake ever to sleep, too preoccupied to rest. Charlie was much the same – too distracted by Piers' kidnapping to get any meaningful rest.

Between the four of them, they had only managed a few hours' sleep since they had arrived and Charlie sensed that it was beginning to take its toll. Tom was clearly suffering from the alcohol overload and God knew what else besides. Jack had shown poor judgment at the poker table but with all the alcohol and the sleep deprivation, it was hardly surprising. Charlie knew if he were to have any chance of getting Piers back, he needed to be well rested in the morning. What was it his commanding officer used to say at Sandhurst? Sleep is every bit as important as cleaning your service weapon.

He checked the twinkling skyline, its dazzling lights and attention-grabbing signs, and imagined how tired Piers must be feeling at that moment. How could things have gone so wrong since university that he'd ended up in debt to the Triads? Charlie's dad once told him that everything in life needed the right balance between darkness and light; good and bad. He thought about the grand piano, how its black and white keys complemented each other, and sensed that Sin City's bright lights were clearly overcompensating. The artificial neon signs of the Strip were trying to make amends for a natural dark side. The imbalance unsettled him.

He looked down at his whisky glass and poured what was left of it over the balcony, vowing not to drink again until Piers was safely back with them. Then he dialed his dad's private line.

'Dad? It's me, Charles. Piers has been kidnapped. I need money urgently to pay the ransom. Call me as soon as you get this message. I'm serious; this isn't a hoax. I wouldn't be calling if I could handle this on my own. I really need your help.'

***

JACK'S HAND

Jack tottered slowly down the corridor towards their suite. He glanced at his watch. It was 12.30 am.

The walls around him were dressed in a luxurious cream-and-white striped wallpaper. Imposing gold chandeliers hung ostentatiously from the ceiling. Underneath, the thick-pile red-and-gold carpet revealed delicate, leaf-like patterns. Four over-excited guests brushed against him as they barreled past. But Jack wasn't paying attention, he was too engrossed in his own thoughts. He was focused on the money; the crisp $100 bills in stacks of $10,000 that he had seen the manager take from a safe and place neatly into a black canvas bag. The bag he was now holding firmly in his right hand.

He reflected on how few questions the hotel manager had asked before handing over half a million dollars from the hotel's petty cash. *Only in Vegas,* he thought.

All the manager had seemed to care about was how the money would be repaid; not what it would be used for, or why it was needed so urgently. Jack had simply logged into his Coutts account using the computer in the manager's office and revealed his bank balance: £659,823.43. The figure had given Jack a sense of pride as well as shame. With the manager looking over his shoulder, he executed the transfer and wired half a million dollars into Caesars Palace's loan account.

That was it.

He pressed the gold button on the elevator at the end of the corridor and looked down at the black canvas bag as he waited. He could picture the virtuous expression of Benjamin Franklin staring up at him from the top of each ten-thousand-dollar stack. The irony was not lost on him.

In his mind, Jack wrestled with the imaginary charges he might face and he tried in vain to justify his actions. He came up with well-worn arguments, defending himself with mitigating circumstances. But the verdict would be damning and he knew it – he was already sentenced to a dark chasm of shame and failure too wide to avoid and too deep to escape.

Sudden raucous cheers of excitement careering down the corridor brought him back into the moment. Jack knew exactly what they signaled: someone had beaten the House. He paused and thought for a brief while, sensing an opportunity to save himself.

When the elevator doors opened, Jack wasn't there. He was pacing back down the corridor towards the casino.

Time for a new plan.

Card 30

Collusion: When two or more players conspire to
cheat in a poker game.

Las Vegas, 12 July 2009
MR. YIN'S HAND

Mr. Yin sat in his rental car, a jet-black Dodge Avenger.
He was closely monitoring the front door to a
dilapidated souvenir shop on Industrial Road, opposite
Boulder Casino. He'd watched a man wearing a New
York Yankees baseball cap enter that same doorway an
hour earlier.

'Any movement?' Mr. Yang asked from the other end
of the line.

'No sign of the asset but I'm positive he's holed up
here. There are no other exits, just a few small windows
that haven't been boarded up. So far, three people have
passed through. The man from the hotel, another guy
with tattoos on his neck, and a young woman. I'm
staking the place out. If I stay close to these guys, I'm
positive the asset will surface. What's the status your
end?'

'Mr. Davidson is standing at the roulette table in the

Forum Casino.'

'Don't tell me he's gambling with the ransom.'

'I'm not sure. He just walked into the casino, carrying a bag, and wandered around for a while. He looked on edge. After about ten minutes, he went to the cashier and exchanged a load of money for chips. Now he's just standing at the roulette table, surrounded by other guests.'

'Stay close to him and make sure he doesn't do anything stupid.'

**

PIERS' HAND

'Byron, it's all gone. Everything we invested has gone. It turns out the property market in the US was built on sand. I'm really sorry. There was nothing I could do. It's just plain bad luck.'

'Bad luck? It's got nothing to do with luck and everything to do with stupidity. How much did you lose?'

'We've lost everything.'

'How much have you lost, Piers?'

'All of it. Twenty-five million ... and all my own savings.'

'Holy shit.'

'I'm awfully sorry, no one saw this coming.'

'Mum is going to be beside herself. This might even kill her. You know she's not been well. She'll never forgive us for this. You've really messed up this time. This was our last chance. You know I couldn't tell her about the Madoff scheme. I thought we'd recover our losses with your friend's firm. You promised returns of 50%. You said we'd make the money back by the end of the year. You said it was a sure thing, Piers. Christ. What are we going to do now? Oh dear God...'

Piers emerged from the dream into his latest living nightmare. He could smell the cheap scent again but this time it hung over him like an acrid cloud.

'How's your face?' a familiar voice whispered as she pulled the masking tape lightly from his chapped lips.

He felt dreadful. His injuries, lack of sleep, and a three-day hangover were making him delirious. Before he had a chance to marshal his thoughts, the hushed voice spoke again: 'I'm sorry, baby. I had to do it. Believe me, I didn't want to hurt you, but I had to make it look authentic, you know? We need to convince your friends, and my brothers. It's the only way this con is going to work.'

Piers' head was still spinning. 'I don't know what the hell you're talking about,' he pleaded. His chain of memory was still missing several critical links. 'You didn't mention anything about being drugged, tied up or threatened, goddamn it. My mind is a bloody mess. I don't know what's real and what isn't anymore. I have no idea what's going on. I thought those goons were actually going to kill me. They're not, are they? I swear the scary-looking one threatened to rape me, for Christ's sake.'

'Calm down, baby. My brothers will do exactly what I say. But listen, if this is going to work, if we are really going to pull this off, we have to do it like this. It's the only way. As far as they're concerned, they think you're the one being conned, not them, remember? If they find out what's really going on, they'll go mental. They'll kill me. They'll kill us both. That's why we need to do this my way. Understand?'

Piers shrugged. He was sore and tired but she'd made him feel a little better.

As he finished the bottle of water she'd brought him, she parted his greasy, lank hair and kissed his forehead before gently sticking the tape back over his mouth. 'Now try and get some rest, baby. Just remember, in less than six hours' time all our problems will be solved. We'll have enough money to escape this hellhole and start afresh,' she said quietly. Then she left him alone again in the cold, dark room.

He was still confused, struggling to get a grip on reality. He couldn't remember whose idea it had been or what the idea was in the first place but it didn't matter anymore. The cards had been dealt and his hands were literally tied.

***

TOM'S HAND

It was 5am when Tom woke from his broken sleep. He staggered into the enormous bathroom suite and purged a clear stream of vomit into the toilet. His inflamed stomach ached as he retched.

Crawling back to the bedroom on all fours, he noticed his phone on the floor. It was flashing. He picked it up and looked at it suspiciously, with blurry eyes. He had eleven missed calls: nine from his wife and two from his best friend. The voicemail icon was showing on the home screen of his iPhone. He pulled himself up into the plumped-up luxury of his over-sized bed, curled into a ball and listened to the voicemail.

'Tom, it's Victoria. I've spoken with Jonny.' There was an uncomfortable pause. 'Just call me when you get this message. We need to talk. I – er – I'm – er – just call me back, OK? This is really important ... we need to talk.'

Tom instantly felt sick again. He knew he had to speak to his wife, but he couldn't bear the thought of what she might say.

Card 31

Intuition: A natural ability or power that guides a
player to act in a certain way during a poker game.

Las Vegas, 12 July 2009
CHARLIE'S HAND

'Well howdy, sir. How was Serendipity? Did you find
what you were looking for?' Malik S. Ahmed said as the
doors to his yellow taxi slid shut.

Charlie didn't acknowledge the driver's questions,
instead he gave instructions. 'Martin Luther King Park,
East Carey Avenue, please. If you can drop us off, circle
round and then pick us up, we'll give you a big tip for
your trouble.'

'You bet I can, mister. Not the nicest part of town,
though. Sure you're going to the right place? Not much
to see around there for tourists.'

'We don't intend to stay very long. We're picking
someone up at 10am. We'll be no more than twenty
minutes,' said Jack before turning to Charlie and
muttering under his breath, 'hopefully.'

'Sure thing. If that's what you want, folks, that's fine
by me,' Malik S. Ahmed replied cheerily then pulled out
of the taxi rank, leaving the splendor of Caesars Palace

behind them.

Charlie and Jack sat on the back seat of the taxi. The black canvas bag was wedged between them. The money was all there; they had counted it together earlier that morning, but Charlie was sensing something didn't quite add up.

He studied Jack's tired but calm face in the wing mirror and wondered where the half-million dollars had really come from. Jack obviously hadn't won it gambling his own money at the roulette table, as he'd claimed when he'd returned to the suite. Charlie was confident of that.

He could usually tell when his friend was lying. Sitting across the table from him for hundreds of hands of poker while they were at uni meant that Charlie had picked up most of Jack's tells. The same tells, magnified by the effects of stress and alcohol, had been jumping out at Charlie early that morning, whenever he mentioned the money. Charlie knew he would find out the truth at some stage but for now all that mattered was getting Piers back safely.

'So how's this going to work, exactly? I mean, what's the procedure for paying a ransom?' Jack asked quietly as he stared out of the taxi window.

Charlie wasn't sure exactly. But he knew that when you're buying something illicit on the street or trading on the black market, you should see what you're getting before you pay for it. Check the goods are not damaged or faulty first. And, importantly, you should try to keep your leverage until the last moment. As soon as that leverage is lost, the terms of an agreement are at risk. Similar principles applied, he assumed, when paying a ransom in exchange for a hostage.

'Kidnappers don't honor agreements like your corporate clients do, JD. They don't play by the same rules. We need to maintain our bargaining position for as long as humanly possible.'

Jack eyed him blankly.

'That means you let me do the talking and don't do anything unless I tell you to.'

Eventually, Malik S. Ahmed pulled into the gray, dusty parking lot at Martin Luther King Park. It was empty. Eerily empty.

'You guys be careful, OK? This may look like a peaceful space with a nice name, but hey, looks and names can be deceptive, right? It's got a bad reputation. All sorts of things go on down here. There was a spate of murders over there last year. Some kinda turf war,' Malik cautioned, pointing at the playground. 'I'll be back in twenty but if you're not here, I ain't waiting around.'

'We'll be here,' Charlie said as he handed over a fifty-dollar bill. 'Just make sure you come back.'

Charlie stepped out of the taxi and surveyed the area quickly. There was only one entrance from East Carey Avenue, no CCTV cameras or tall buildings overlooking the parking lot. *A black spot,* he thought; *the ideal place for criminal activity.*

They stood in the middle of the empty parking lot and waited, the black canvas bag resting against Jack's leg. The bright morning sunlight cast long shadows across the floor in front of them. Charlie's shadow was enormous. The fine film of light gray dust that covered the ground beneath them reminded him of Afghanistan: desert terrain.

'Did you bring a gun?' Jack asked. 'I thought it might be a good idea in case, you know, things go a little south.' He hesitated then unzipped the bag and pulled out a small handgun.

With lightning speed, Charlie snatched the weapon, disengaged the safety mechanism and dislodged the magazine to check if it was loaded. It was a Glock 26 pistol: slimline, compact, and favored by women for its size and weight. It looked like a toy gun in Charlie's spade-like hands.

'The magazine's full. Ten rounds,' Jack said. 'I got it last night. I was surprised how easy it is to—'

'Christ, JD,' Charlie snapped, 'what were you thinking?' He slipped the weapon carefully into the back of his pants, hidden behind the side-vents of his navy-blue corduroy jacket.

'I was thinking,' Jack said defensively, 'we might need it. I wasn't sure if you were going to be prepared.'

Charlie didn't respond. He now had two guns concealed on his person, and a steak knife. He had no intention of using them or mentioning them to Jack, but he was always prepared. Compliance was the order of the day. Hand over the money and get Piers back. A straightforward exchange. No guns. No bloodshed. No heroes.

'Funny, isn't it?' Jack said, trying to change the subject. 'You realize we were due at the range today? We were going to let off steam firing Uzis at targets dressed as Arabs. I booked the VIP package at the Gun Store. We could've fired Tommy Guns, AK-47s, MP5s – even a grenade launcher. How cool would that be?'

'There's nothing funny about our situation,' Charlie said abruptly. He could see nothing cool about gun ranges, either. Especially Las Vegas gun ranges. They were crass and irresponsible. The world would be a lot less messed up, Charlie thought, if some people didn't glamorize weapons.

A minute passed in silence before a battered-looking SUV crawled along East Carey Avenue and turned into the parking lot. It came to a standstill twenty meters in front of them. It was only 10.05 am but the low sunlight reflecting off the windshield made it difficult to see into the vehicle ahead.

'Remember what I told you earlier,' Charlie said

calmly. 'Let me do the talking and follow my lead. Don't make any sudden movements. Just observe. Try and take in as much information as possible. We might need the intel afterwards.'

There was no response. Charlie turned to see Jack's face had completely drained of color. He was staring straight ahead, eyes squinting, eyebrows caved in, emphasizing the creases in his sweaty forehead. His body was perfectly still but both hands were shaking and a look of utter disbelief hung on his face.

'JD, are you, OK?' Charlie said. 'I need you to stay calm, mate.'

'What the hell!' Jack said, in a high-pitched squeak. 'Is that... is that... can you see what I'm seeing, Charlie...? That looks like... is that... Michael Jackson?'

Card 32

Showdown: A reference to two or more players who are in a poker hand all the way to the end, at which point a winner must be determined.

Las Vegas, 12 July 2009
APRIL'S HAND

As the stolen Chevrolet Trailblazer turned into Martin Luther King Park, April examined the two men standing in the parking lot with a black bag in front of them.

'Hold on, Danny. Slow up just a second. I don't recognize the big one,' April said, her voice faltering as she spoke. 'He wasn't with them at the club. I would have noticed him for sure.'

Danny applied the brakes and swung round from the wheel. 'If they've called the Feds, I'll ice you right now,' he snarled, pressing his gun to Piers' forehead. April quickly pulled down the blindfold and ripped the masking tape from Piers' mouth.

'Who's the heavy?' Kyle shouted, spraying Piers with tobacco-laced spittle.

Piers blinked several times and peered into the light. 'Don't shoot. Please don't shoot. That's a friend. He's one of us. That's Charlie. He wasn't with us the other night, but he's not police,' he replied breathlessly, his body trembling as the words tumbled from his mouth.

'You better not be lying, punk. If our money ain't in the bag, I swear I'll end all three of you in broad daylight,' Danny snapped. He turned back to the steering wheel, put the gearstick into neutral and pulled up the handbrake.

'Let's do this,' his tone was calmer now. 'Just stick to the plan and remember – no names, OK?'

The SUV's engine continued to tick over as Kyle reached into the foot well and lifted up two life-like plastic masks. He handed one of them to his brother and grinned. 'Sure thing, Elvis.'

They pulled the masks over their heads, opened the doors of the SUV and stepped onto the dusty parking lot.

'Be careful,' April said quietly as the doors slammed behind them.

No one would imagine that behind Elvis's youthful good looks lurked a face so decorated with scars and tattoos. The Michael Jackson mask had been chosen by Kyle himself; he was an unapologetic fan. Its light skin tone and curly hair represented Jackson during the *Bad* years, back in 1987, when the singer was at his best musically and aesthetically – according to Kyle at least – and before everything took a turn for the worse. But April had always suspected his love for the period had more to do with their mom being alive back then. The last time they'd truly been a family.

By the time of his death, of course, Jackson's appearance was very different. The world media had delighted in reflecting his changing image. It seemed almost as if their intrusive camera lenses were projecting some deadly compound onto his skin. In fact, Kyle was convinced it was overexposure to the limelight that had caused the star's skin cells to whiten and mutate, and nothing to do with plastic surgery. April smiled at her brother's stupidity and watched as the two dead kings of pop walked smartly away from her, guns at the ready.

***

CHARLIE'S HAND

The two masked men rushed towards Charlie and Jack, waving pistols in the air. Elvis Presley headed straight for Charlie, thrusting his gun within an inch of Charlie's face.

'Who the hell are you, punk?' Elvis shouted. 'I said no Feds.'

Charlie saw Jack's shadow recede as he took several steps back, surrendering control of their invisible border and giving precious inches of psychological advantage to the kidnapper in the Michael Jackson mask.

Within seconds of observing the men, Charlie had digested a feast of essential intel: their body shapes; height; weight; gait; the clothes and shoes they were wearing. He picked up as many tells as he could and jotted them down on his mental notepad. It was a skill that came naturally. Growing up, he had always been inquisitive and suspicious; he'd learned from his dad but his time with the RMP had taught him that attention to detail and the ability to pick up subtle signs in a fleeting moment could be the difference between success and failure. Life and death.

Elvis, the taller and heavier of the two, seemed older. He was in charge. Charlie figured that from the way he walked, the tone of his voice, the fact he had been driving the SUV and had addressed him first. And despite the distortion of the voice through the plastic mask, Charlie recognized his tone from the phone calls from the day before.

Their clothing was nondescript and dark but Charlie registered a flash of color from a well-worn belt buckle. The faint red, white and blue shades of what looked like the bottom of a basketball were briefly exposed when Michael Jackson pushed his M1911 pistol in the direction of Jack's face.

Charlie and Jack raised their hands above their heads.

'Relax, we spoke on the phone. I'm Piers' friend,' Charlie said calmly, emphasizing his English accent. 'Do I sound like a Federal Agent to you? The money is all there.' He nudged the bag forward with his left foot while keeping his hands up high. As he spoke, he fixed Elvis with his eyes. 'We've just come to get our friend back. No funny business. Like you said on the phone, remember?'

Michael Jackson reached across and picked up the bag. He unzipped it and rummaged through the neat stacks of $100 bills with one hand while his other waved his gun carelessly in Jack's direction.

'Looks like it's all here, Danny ... shit, I mean Elvis. We're rich, we're finally rich, bro,' he said excitedly.

Charlie jotted down the gratuitous tells. *Elvis is Danny. Danny is in charge. Michael Jackson is a liability. Sounds like they could be brothers.*

'We've upheld our side of the deal,' Charlie said carefully, 'now where's Piers?'

'Get the mark,' Elvis said irritably.

As Michael Jackson picked up the black canvas bag, hurried back to the SUV and opened the rear passenger door, Elvis was retreating slowly, keeping his pistol pointed at Charlie. Jackson threw the bag into the back seat and pulled Piers out by his arm. He was blindfolded, his hands were tied, and masking tape covered his mouth. But finally there he was, standing before them on wobbly legs, looking rather sad and pathetic.

'Elvis is leaving the building,' Danny said, cackling to himself as he stepped into the SUV.

'Who's bad?' Michael Jackson added, with a shake of his head and a high kick vaguely resembling a dance move. He joined in with the cackling laughter as he climbed into the front of the SUV, still waving his gun in front of him.

Amateurs, Charlie tutted to himself.

Within seconds, the doors closed and the SUV sped around, leaving Charlie, Jack and Piers standing in the middle of the parking lot, in a cloud of dust.

***

MR. YIN'S HAND

A kilometer away, on the outskirts of a ramshackle trailer park, Mr. Yin sat in his jet-black Dodge Avenger. He was pleased with himself. His instincts had been right about the man with the Yankees baseball cap. He was glad he'd followed him to the dilapidated souvenir shop.

Earlier that morning, after a sleepless night in his car, he had finally caught a glimpse of the asset. Blindfolded and with his hands bound together, a young woman and two large men had escorted him to a rusty-looking Chevrolet Trailblazer. Mr. Yin recognized Piers' skinny frame instantly – he'd been following the asset for the last six months, after all – and was relieved to see that he was still alive. He'd reported back to Mr. Yang and then cautiously tailed the SUV to the trailer park in Sunrise Manor, which was close enough to Martin Luther King Park for him to observe the exchange through the lenses of his binoculars.

Mr. Yin watched as the SUV turned off East Carey Avenue and onto Betty Lane then he picked up his phone to update Mr. Yang.

'The handover has just gone ahead. Without incident.

189

The asset is safe. It looks like they just paid the ransom. No heroics from Captain Preston. The whole thing was over in less than five minutes.'

'Good. There's still no sign of Mr. Patterson. I think he's still in the hotel room. No sign of him at the breakfast buffet this morning. I had some more of those red velvet pancakes. You need to try them out tomorrow, they're so good. Are you following the asset back to the hotel? I assume they'll be coming back here.'

'I'm going to do some shopping first,' Mr. Yin said.

'What?'

'I'm going to follow the kidnappers. Find out a bit more. Something's bugging me, something feels wrong about this whole thing. They aren't a professional outfit, that's for sure. Plus, they've got half a million dollars that doesn't belong to them. All that time I spent last night staring at a dilapidated souvenir shop got me thinking – what would the Dragon Master say if we brought him back a little souvenir from Vegas?'

Mr. Yin hung up before Mr. Yang had a chance to respond. Then he pulled out of the trailer park onto Betty Lane, resuming his pursuit of the rusty SUV, this time with a very different purpose in mind.

***

CHARLIE'S HAND

Charlie rushed over to Piers, pulled off his blindfold and hugged his skinny frame. His hair was a tangle and he had a cut on his nose and light swelling under his eyes.

'Christ, Piers, are you OK?' Charlie ripped the masking tape from his friend's mouth and with the steak knife cut free his hands. 'Are you hurt? What happened? Did you see their faces? Can you identify them? Where were they keeping you? How many were involved?'

Piers stared blankly into the middle distance, avoiding eye contact. He blinked, adjusting to the morning sunlight, and focused on the dust particles still hanging in the air. He didn't respond.

Jack looked to still be in shock as he walked towards them but the color in his face was slowly returning to normal as the dust in the parking lot began to settle. He placed an arm around Piers' shoulders and squeezed gently as he offered his own words of comfort: 'Well, that was all a bit weird, wasn't it? First Michael Jackson dies and we get a million pounds, then he comes back from the afterlife and takes half a million dollars back. He looked good though, didn't he, even if he was a bit out of practice?'

Charlie examined Piers' face cautiously. Maybe he wasn't ready to appreciate a joke. After a few seconds, though, he smiled broadly. Then he began to giggle. The nervous giggle gave way to a chuckle, which was quickly overtaken by a fit of laughter that made his whole body shake. Soon, tears were flowing down his face. The floodgates of relief had burst open.

'Everything's going to be alright, mate. You're a lucky man. Always have been,' Jack said with a chuckle, as if Piers had infected him with his laughter.

'I'm so sorry. I've ruined everything,' Piers said between bursts of laughter which belied his sincerity. 'You must all hate me. I really am sorry.'

Charlie wasn't at all amused but he knew shock affected people in different ways. 'Listen, there's nothing to be sorry about, Piers. None of this was your fault. It all worked out in the end and no one got hurt, so don't apologize. The main thing is, you're safe. We can discuss everything else later. Let's just get you back to the hotel first. Get you cleaned up.' Charlie spoke with the deadpan expression of a poker player studying his opponent for clues.

Card 33

Down to the Green: Down to the felt; having no chips remaining at the table; busted out; broke.

Las Vegas, 12 July 2009
CHARLIE'S HAND

The ride back to Caesars Palace was a silent one. Malik S. Ahmed had tried to make conversation but it was obvious no one was in the mood.

'Thank you for coming back for us, Malik,' Charlie said as the taxi finally pulled up outside their hotel. He paid the fare, handing over a crisp $100 bill.

Malik's eyes lit up and he replied gratefully, 'No. Thank you, sir. Listen, anytime. Here, take my card, just in case you need another ride during your stay. I work around the clock so feel free to call me whenever you like. I'll be happy to oblige, sir.'

Charlie smiled and, out of politeness, took the card and slipped it into the pocket of his corduroy jacket next to the steak knife. As he walked back to join the others, he checked his cell. He had a voicemail. It had been made in the early hours of the morning.

Dad.

He'd forgotten about his distress call. The urgent panic

about getting the money had disappeared when Jack returned with a bag full of cash and a far-fetched story about making a sequence of lucky bets on the roulette table with what was left of the kitty. The battery on his phone was low but he had enough time to listen to the message before it cut out.

'Charles. I got your voicemail. I'll cut to the chase. I know where you can find Piers. He's in Vegas, Nevada. He's at a location on Industrial Road in Winchester, near Boulder Casino. Call me as soon as you get this and I will give you more information, but I'm sorry, there's absolutely no way I can help with the ransom. There are some family issues you're probably not aware of. I'll explain everything when we speak. Call me back.'

Charlie was surprised and confused. *How does Dad know where Piers is being held? I hadn't even mentioned we were in Vegas. And what did he mean about not being able to get the money together? What family issues?* Half a million dollars to Piers' family was surely non-material; nothing more than a small blind in a low-stakes game of poker?

Time for some answers.

Charlie jogged through the busy hotel lobby and joined Jack and Piers, waiting for their private elevator.

'You OK, mate?' Jack asked as the doors opened. 'You don't look well. Are you feeling alright?'

'It's nothing. Sorry. I had to make a call, but my battery's died again. I hate these new iPhones. They can't seem to hold a charge for longer than a day.'

The three of them filed into the elevator. Jack swiped his hotel card and pressed the button for the Presidential Suite. Piers stood quietly, staring at himself in the elevator mirror as he moved his fingers gingerly over his bruised and clammy face.

'I seem to be the only one here who hasn't been punched in the face,' said Jack as he studied himself in the mirror. 'Mind you, with these bags under my eyes it looks like I've got a couple of shiners anyway.'

'I bet you can't wait to get out of those clothes and clean yourself up,' Charlie said to Piers.

'I could do with a stiff drink as well,' Piers replied huskily. It was the first thing he'd said since they'd left the parking lot.

'Let's hope there's some left,' Jack said, 'Tom got through a lot of it last night. He was completely smashed. We had to put the poor sod to bed in the end. We left him behind this morning to sleep it off. Now you're back, Piers, and hopefully Tom's feeling better, maybe we can start this trip all over again. Try and forget about everything and just head down to the Strip later. Remember, boys: Today is the shadow of tomorrow. Onwards and upwards, as they say.'

The elevator doors opened on their luxurious suite but all was not as it should have been.

'Don't move,' Charlie ordered, extending his arm in front of his friends protectively.

Jack and Piers froze as they looked over Charlie's shoulder. Face-down on the Persian rug, next to the Steinway, lay a body with a dark band of blood circling its head.

'Wait here,' Charlie ordered as he moved across the floor cautiously, avoiding the shards of glass scattered all over the bloodied rug. In an instant, he had drawn his two weapons and his arms were out-stretched, rigid like the hands of a clock. The Glock 26 in his left hand was pointing towards eleven, while the Browning nine-millimeter in his right was aiming at two.

His head and eyes darted from left to right, surveying the room quickly as he glided across the floor, arms swinging round the clock face as he adjusted to the different angles and objects in each room. Charlie's military instincts were as sharp as ever. He needed to secure the area first so he checked each room methodically for danger.

'All clear,' he shouted after sweeping the entire suite in less than sixty seconds. It was empty.

Now the percussion of crashing doors had stopped, there was nothing but a tense silence hanging uncomfortably in the air. Jack and Piers stood next to one another in front of the elevator, still frozen and in total shock at the sight of the body, the blood, and the broken glass.

As he returned one gun to the back of his pants and slipped the other into his jacket pocket, Charlie studied his two friends' faces. While Jack looked shocked and bewildered, Piers seemed petrified and guilty. There was a genuine look of fear on his pallid face; a strange mixture of distress and remorse.

'We need an ambulance. Call downstairs and tell the concierge it's an emergency,' Charlie shouted as he marched towards the lifeless body. One arm was stretched out and Charlie recognized the watch instantly – an IWC Portuguese...

'Now,' barked Charlie, startling Jack and finally setting him free from his trance. 'We haven't got much time.'

Card 34

Equity: Your 'rightful' share of a pot. If the pot contains $100, and you have a 50% chance of winning it, you have $50 equity in the pot.

Las Vegas, 12 July 2009
APRIL'S HAND

April and her brothers were sitting around the white plastic table closest to the window in the In-N-Out Burger restaurant just off the North Vegas Boulevard. They looked on edge but pleased with themselves, like truanting school kids bunking off for the first time. Underneath the table, flanked by Danny's size twelve feet, was the black canvas bag. In between bites of greasy fast food they looked up and around anxiously, scanning the restaurant for any sign of trouble.

'I say we get outta here right now. Find somewhere out of State to hole up for a while. I've got some connections in Cali who owe me a solid,' Danny said, picking up his milkshake. His cheeks pinched inwards as he sucked it up through the collapsed straw.

'I dunno, bro,' Kyle said. 'I was thinking we lay low at the office for a day or two, make sure there's no heat first, then buy that Airstream we've been looking at and head home to Detroit.' Kyle held his brother's gaze. 'I've been thinkin' about this, Danny. We need to stop runnin'. Go back home and start over. This is our chance, man. We've enough money to go legit. We'd be stupid not to. What d'you think, sis?'

Danny shook his head and took a chunk out of his double cheeseburger. A mixture of grease and ketchup dripped onto his scarred hands. 'We sure as hell need to get out of this dump,' he said, spraying the table with morsels of food.

April was staring out of the window, watching a little girl run between the picnic tables outside, screaming with either joy or panic – it was hard to say which – as two older boys chased her.

'I agree with y'all. We need a fresh start,' she said, turning back round to face them. 'But we need to bide our time. We can't be rushin' things or we'll make mistakes. We need to be certain the money is clean, which means working it through the cycle like we always do. Play it safe, yeah? I've already reached out to Franco. It'll take a while but it's important we get it right, you see? We sure as hell don't want any of this getting back to us, or we'll be lookin' over our shoulders for the rest of our lives.'

'What about going back home?' Kyle asked.

'We can go anywhere with this money and you talkin' shit about headin' back to Michigan?' Danny grunted. 'I thought you hated that place as much as me, Kyle? Too many bad memories.' He shoved a fistful of fries into his mouth.

'Look, bro. I think we should finish on a high. Cash in everything. Leave all the hustlin' behind us in Vegas. A clean break. Think about it, man. You and me could go work for Uncle Jimmy in the repair shop or somethin'. Buy a house together, just the three of us, somewhere off Sycamore Street or near where we used to live as kids, you know, before...' He looked down at his tray of untouched food. 'Before Mom...' Kyle paused for a heartbeat, 'April, you could work at the Anchor for a while, take some evening classes. You always wanted to teach kids and—'

'Sounds like you got it all mapped out,' Danny said with his mouth half full. 'But I ain't goin' back to Detroit. I ain't working for Uncle-fuckin'-Jimmy and I sure as hell ain't playin' happy families. I'd sooner slit my wrists.'

'The main thing is, we stay cool. We need to focus on the here and now, OK?' April said, looking from Danny to Kyle and back again. 'Which means we ride out the rest of the week without attracting attention. I'll meet up with Franco tonight after work and tomorrow we can talk more about what we do next. But for now, I say we head back to the office and ditch the SUV before someone calls it in, can we at least agree on that?'

A young waitress walked by and they stopped talking and looked down at their food. Danny, dragging on his milkshake, glanced around to check she was out of earshot and then said under his breath, 'D'you really trust that Jock? I know he's come good in the past, but we've never asked him to wash this kinda money. He might try to play us or triple his take.'

'I already thought this through,' replied April, 'I'm gonna ask him to wash a little at a time, just ten grand to start with. And there's my tips from the club and the tables at Boulder Casino. Crawford owes me for organizing the girls for his party last month. If I work double shifts, with plenty of ghost dances and we each play small and win big at the Boulder this week, we can clean all of this money by next Saturday.'

'Always one step ahead of us, that's what I love about you, sis,' Kyle said. 'Sounds like a plan to me.'

'There is one thing you're forgetting though,' Danny

said, keeping his voice low and leaning in. 'The mark. That greasy Brit might try and track us down and take back what he thinks is his. If he fesses up to his friends, comes clean and admits that the kidnapping was made up between the two of you and not by some proper gang, they might try and retaliate, come find you at the club or contact the Feds. He's a loose end.'

'Danny's right, man,' Kyle conceded. 'Just think how pissed he's gonna be. We didn't just fleece his friends, you double-crossed him and probably broke his heart as well. He'll be after revenge, for sure.'

'Don't worry about the mark,' April said, looking back towards the kids running around the picnic tables outside. 'He ain't gonna talk to his friends or the Feds any time soon. But y'all right. He will come looking for Honey...'

'Huh?' grunted Kyle.

'Let me put it another way,' April said, turning to face them both. 'He still thinks he's got skin in the game.' She paused and studied her brothers' faces. 'I ain't broken his heart just yet ...'

Card 35

Rounders: Card players who hustle for a living.

Las Vegas, 12 July 2009
CHARLIE'S HAND

'The medics are on their way,' Jack called out, 'they'll be here in less than eight minutes.'

Charlie was kneeling down assessing Tom's injuries. The large wound to his forehead was now sealed by a congealed crust of blood so dark it was almost black.

'His natural defenses have kicked in and stemmed the flow of blood,' Charlie said. 'But you've got to be careful with a trauma to the brain. I've seen innocuous bangs to the head, which hardly show any damage at all, kill a man. Then again, in Afghanistan some soldiers with severe lacerations and what looked like extreme blood loss survived with just a few stitches. Hopefully Tom's injuries are on the low end of the scale.'

A cloying stench of alcohol hung off the motionless body, strong enough to make Charlie want to vomit as he moved Tom carefully into the recovery position.

'Is he still breathing?' Piers asked.

'Yes, but he's unconscious and he's lost a lot of blood. It's difficult to tell how long he's been like this. God only knows how much alcohol he's had,' Charlie replied.

'So he wasn't shot or beaten up, then? This is self-inflicted, you think?' Piers asked hesitantly.

Jack spread a blanket over Tom's body. 'It doesn't take Sherlock to work out what's happened here. He's obviously gone on another bender, tripped, hit his head on the side of the piano and passed out,' he said as he tucked the blanket around his friend.

'We've got to get him to hospital. He needs blood quickly. Where the hell is that ambulance?' Charlie said.

Several minutes later, three paramedics, dressed in white shirts and black pants, finally stormed into the suite.

'He's unconscious. We found him ten minutes ago. We suspect he banged his head and passed out. He's got a two-and-a-half-inch laceration above his left eye.' Charlie spoke quickly and clearly as the paramedics placed Tom on a stretcher and checked his vitals.

'Thank you, sir,' one of them said while he placed an oxygen mask over Tom's airways. 'He's lost a lot of blood. We need to get him to the Trauma Unit at UMC as quickly as possible. Can you ride with us? We're gonna need some information and I'm assuming this man is known to you?'

'Yes, he's a friend. He's one of our best friends,' Jack answered, following the paramedics as they hurried out of the suite.

Charlie and Piers followed closely behind and joined the paramedics and Jack in the large, steel-clad service elevator at the end of the corridor. They were soon on the ground floor and sprinting towards the ambulance parked out front.

A swarm of tourists buzzing around the hotel lobby were soon rubbernecking, gawking and gasping with excitement as they witnessed a man on a stretcher being rushed out of the building. There was a burst of camera flashes as they captured the events unfolding frame by frame, as if it was some sort of macabre Las Vegas show.

***

PIERS' HAND

In all the commotion, Piers felt someone grab his upper arm and pull him away. He swerved to one side and the tourist swarm that was following the stretcher whirred through the lobby without him.

'I'm sorry to approach you like this, Mr. Upwell, but I wasn't sure when I might see you again.'

'What's all this about?' Piers protested. 'Who are you?'

'I'm sorry, forgive me. My name is Carlos Hayman, I'm the hotel manager. I received a call earlier,' he began, his face devoid of expression. 'A woman told me to pass a message to you personally – she said it was extremely confidential and very urgent – asked me to give you this without delay. What with the emergency and everything, I didn't have the chance. Well, anyway – here you go, sir.'

Piers looked around nervously as he took a white envelope from the hotel manager's hand and opened it.

Through the swarm of tourists he heard the sound of screeching tires and caught a glimpse of the back of the ambulance as it swung around and sped off out of sight.

'And sir, I am sorry about your friend. Mr. Patterson, wasn't it? He's in very safe hands. You know the hospital is only a few minutes away? You can meet your friends there in no time at all. Shall I arrange for a cab?'

Piers was too distracted to respond. He was staring down at a sheet of Caesars Palace imperial headed paper. The hotel's name jumped from the page in embossed gold lettering but Piers' attention was drawn to the middle of the paper where, scribbled in blue biro, was the name of a location, the words "5pm", and a single letter - "H".

He put the paper back in the envelope, slipped it into the pocket of his pants, and walked toward the private elevator.

***

APRIL'S HAND

After leaving the burger bar, the Parkers had set off back to Winchester, keeping to the speed limit all the way. They'd abandoned the rusty Chevrolet Trailblazer in the neighboring parking lot, where Kyle had hot-wired it earlier that day, and crossed the road to the dilapidated souvenir shop they called "the office".

The shop, like most of the commercial premises in the area, including Boulder Casino, was owned by a local businessman called Ely Crawford.

Ely had allowed the Parkers use of the building until a new tenant was found but since the global financial crisis had hit there had been no takers for a retail shop in a rundown part of town. The Parkers had been there for seven months now. Occasionally, Crawford would call on Danny and Kyle to carry out "solids" – as he liked to call them – in lieu of rent. The jobs often involved intimidating ex-employees or punters from his casinos who had got on the wrong side of him. Sometimes he just asked them to ride with him to business meetings or collect money from a difficult tenant.

They rarely asked questions and were happy enough to oblige. More often than not, they played non-speaking bit-parts in Crawford's seedy dramas. Just the sight of Danny – his sheer size and tattooed face – was usually enough to ensure the job would be carried out successfully. Crawford was well connected and every so often he would give them an angle on someone, pass on damning information, which they could exploit for one of their scams.

The souvenir shop had a cavernous basement. The previous tenant had used it for storage but it had become the Parkers' makeshift office. Cardboard boxes were piled high in the dusty room. Inside were relics from a happier time: keyrings, shot-glasses, T-shirts and fridge magnets; all souvenirs of the city, with the words "Las Vegas" emblazoned on the side to prove it.

The space was equipped with basic furniture, including a rickety coffee table and a large mahogany desk. A three-seater couch pushed up against the wall closest to the stairs was so old that the brown leather had started to discolor and peel away. Since the last of the strip lights had recently blown, the only light came from the glare of a wall-mounted TV so the old metal safe in a shadowy corner of the room, behind four dusty boxes, was difficult to spot.

'How are you so sure he's gonna show?' Danny said.

'He'll be there at five o'clock,' Honey replied, tucking stacks of $100 bills neatly inside the safe. 'If I know anything about this mark – and, well, men in general, I suppose – I know they're weak. They think with their dicks and they're greedy. Present company excluded, of course. So he'll be there, Danny, don't worry about that. He'll want his share.'

April left the last five stacks of bills in the bag, pushed the safe door shut, turned the combination lock, then dragged the three boxes of unwanted souvenirs in front of it, concealing it from sight.

She strolled over and sat in between her brothers on the leather couch, the bag underneath her feet.

'Right, so here's the plan – I'll give this to Franco after my shift tonight and start the wash.' She placed a neat $10,000-stack on the coffee table in front of her. 'You take twenty thousand each.'

She placed two stacks in front of her brothers. 'Danny, after you've dealt with the mark, you go see Crawford. By then I'll have sorted when we can start playin' on his tables. Twenty thousand will be a sweetener, OK?'

'Let me deal with Ely,' Danny said. 'He trusts me.'

Honey shrugged. 'Sure, but I don't want him to think we're moving in on his patch or nothing.'

Danny grunted and scratched at the arm of the couch. 'I've been in this game longer than you, don't forget. I can handle Crawford.'

'And my twenty – what's that for?' Kyle interrupted as he picked up his share.

'After you help Danny get rid of the mark, I want you to head down to the Mad House and pay for some special dances.' She winked at Kyle. 'Be generous, won't you?'

Kyle grinned broadly. 'Sure thing, sis. It'll be my pleasure.'

***

MR. YIN'S HAND

According to the clock on the dashboard of the Dodge Avenger, it was 4.15 pm. Mr. Yin was back watching the souvenir shop and the kidnappers hadn't surfaced for close to two hours.

His phone vibrated.

'Mr. Patterson has just been rushed to hospital,' Mr. Yang said quickly. 'No idea why,' he continued without waiting for a response. 'Captain Preston and Mr. Davidson were with him. They're heading to the University Medical Centre on West Charleston Boulevard.'

'And the asset?' Mr. Yin said abruptly.

'I saw the manager give him an envelope in the lobby.

Ten minutes later, he'd changed his clothes and was at the front desk asking for his passport. He's on the move now. I'm tailing him in a taxi.'

'What's he up to?'

'No idea, but he's definitely not heading to the hospital. We've hit the lights on East Flamingo Road. What's your status? I could do with some relief here, I haven't eaten since breakfast.'

'Listen. Don't lose him again or the next time you eat it'll be through a straw – sounds like he's trying to escape. Hold on a second...' Mr. Yin froze and lowered his voice. 'I've got eyes on two of the kidnappers. They're leaving the shop with the black bag and getting into a car. It looks like they're on the move with the ransom. But there's no sign of the girl yet.'

'What's your location?' Mr. Yang asked.

'I'm still in the parking lot across the road. They've just turned north onto South Lamb Boulevard. They're in a dark blue Lincoln Continental with Michigan plates.'

'What are you going to do?'

'I'm going to follow the money. You stay with the asset. Whatever you do, don't let him out of your sight this time.'

Card 36

Drawing Dead: A drawing hand that will lose
even if it improves.

Las Vegas, 12 July 2009
JACK'S HAND

In the back of the ambulance, Charlie and Jack could do
very little. They watched helplessly as the paramedics
tended to Tom. It seemed he was in a critical state, much
worse than Jack had originally thought.

As the paramedics busied themselves trying to
stabilize their patient and prepare him for the
emergency room at UMC, they asked Jack and Charlie a
number of routine questions.

Yes, Tom was their friend. No, neither of them were
his next of kin, his wife presumably was: Victoria
Patterson. Jack was impressed that Charlie had
remembered her name. No, they didn't know his blood
type. Who does know their friends' blood group? Jack
had asked. No, they didn't know his date of birth, but he
had to be thirty-six or thirty-seven, or was he thirty-
eight? They struggled to remember even the month –
whilst Piers had always made a great deal of every
birthday at Cardiff, Tom hadn't been one for

celebrations. Yes, he was insured. Jack had arranged the policy himself. No, he wasn't allergic to anything, as far as they were aware.

Yes, Tom had been drinking. Most of yesterday and, by the smell of it, earlier that morning as well. Although, Jack quickly qualified his response by saying that it was merely his opinion and he couldn't claim it to be a fact. He then added that he had not personally witnessed Tom drink any alcohol that day. No, they didn't think he had taken any drugs although again, Jack could not state that as a fact.

In the end, the paramedic stopped what he was doing and angrily asked Jack whether he was some kind of ambulance-chasing lawyer or a friend of the patient. The L-word propelled from the paramedic's mouth like an obscenity and for once Jack felt a sense of shame instead of pride as he admitted that he was indeed a lawyer.

The paramedic reminded him that it was his job to save Tom's life. He wasn't interested in bringing a case against Jack, or anyone else, for that matter. What Tom could really use right now was a supportive friend, he snapped, and not some slippery defense attorney.

Jack thought about apologizing, explaining about their trip and that they hadn't seen one another for over a decade, but in the end he just withdrew in silence. He wondered whether he would ever get the chance to be a proper friend to Tom. He should have known Tom's age, he thought. He hoped that one day they could celebrate his birthday together back in London; he might even get to know Tom's wife and maybe one day they'd all be able to look back on this trip and laugh about it. A sudden feeling of guilt clouded Jack's thoughts. Tom had clearly been in distress. How had he missed the obvious signs? The truth was, he'd been too self-involved to worry about anyone else's problems.

It was 4.20 pm when the ambulance pulled up in front

of UMC. The journey had taken a little under seven minutes. As soon as the doors were opened, Tom was rolled down an aluminum ramp and rushed towards the Trauma Unit. A noisy cluster of green-and-white-clad hospital staff surrounded the stretcher, shouting a conversation that could have been a foreign language. Each of them had their own distinct tasks but they shared a common goal: to save Tom's life. Charlie and Jack followed the routine chaos through several swinging doors, until they were intercepted at the entrance to the Emergency Room and ushered to one side by a large, elderly black woman.

'If you would just take a seat over here,' the woman said quietly but firmly as she led them to the waiting area. Her almost hypnotic Southern drawl and neat, graying Afro afforded her an instant respect. The badge on her big, flowery blouse identified her as Marlowe D. Robson, an administrator at UMC.

'The doctors and nurses are doing all they can,' she said calmly.

'When can we see him?' Jack asked as he sat down on a green plastic chair. He noticed a gold cross hanging on a chain around her neck. Is he going to be alright?'

'I'm afraid I don't know just now. He's suffered severe bleeding but he's receiving urgent attention and is in safe hands. Our Trauma Unit is the best in the State.' Marlowe's calm words had a soothing effect. 'As soon as I know any more, I'll come get you but until then, try not to worry. If you could fill out these forms, it will speed up the process. I'm guessing the patient is a friend?'

'Yes,' Jack said with a sigh. His shoulders slumped as he took the clipboard Marlowe handed him. 'He's one of our best friends.'

Marlowe D. Robson smiled gently and placed a hand on Jack's shoulder. 'I'll come back in a while to get these and take you through to the hospital room where your friend will be staying after the surgery. The restrooms are just there and if you follow the signs for the food hall you can get a coffee and a slice of pie,' she said with a nod of her head. Then she swept out of the room before either of them had a chance to ask anything else.

'Shit. This trip is a disaster. I bloody hope Tom makes it. He looked so bad, didn't he? Christ knows what I'll do if anything happens to him. It's my bloody fault we're here in the first place. I'll never be able to forgive myself.'

Charlie was looking anxiously at the entrance to the hospital. 'I thought Piers was right behind us?'

'What about his wife?' Jack continued almost to himself. 'Do you think I should call her? I don't have her number ... but if we can get his phone we could contact her, right? Or maybe Piers knows it. Shouldn't he be here by now?'

'I'm worried about him,' Charlie said, still looking towards the entrance.

'Me too. He definitely hasn't been straight with us. I should have spotted the signs sooner. Maybe it's to do with his marriage?'

'No. I meant Piers. I'm still worried about Piers. He's not right, either. I'm thinking he's hiding something, too—'

'He's just been kidnapped, for Christ's sake, I reckon even you might be acting strangely if you'd been through what he just has. He'll be fine, though, Charlie – he's like a cat with nine lives, that one. How many times did he get into trouble at Cardiff? He always came through in the end. Though, thinking about it, that was mostly thanks to you.'

Charlie looked down at his G-Shock and didn't respond.

Jack carried on regardless. 'You know, for a long time, Tom and I thought you were infatuated with Piers. I mean, like, romantically. It was the way you used to follow him around and then always somehow rescue him, like you were his knight in shining armor. It was all a bit creepy and, if I'm being honest, Charlie, you're doing it again now. It's Tom's life hanging in the balance and you're still obsessing over Piers. We've just paid half a million dollars to rescue the guy. He's hardly going to get kidnapped again, is he? He probably got caught in traffic or decided to take a long hot shower.'

Several seconds of awkward silence passed before Charlie spoke. 'I'm going back to the hotel to check if he's still there. Something doesn't feel right to me.' The plastic chair creaked as he stood up.

'What, so you're just going to leave me here?' Jack said, looking up from the clipboard. 'Don't you think we should all be here when Tom wakes up? He could use the support of all of his friends right now. Piers will be fine.'

'I agree something's not right with Tom, either,' said Charlie stiffly. 'I can tell he's hiding something, JD. He's had a drink in his hand from the moment we landed. He's obviously unhappy. I've seen it often enough with soldiers who hit the bottle to escape the horror of war.'

'We should have said something to him. Maybe we could have prevented this—'

'Look, JD, there's no point looking back and saying we should have done this or we should have said that. None of this is your doing so don't beat yourself up about it.'

'I guess you're right.'

'When he gets out of here, you can help him get better. We can both help him get better. But right now, there's nothing we can do for him. He's with doctors, they're the ones who can help him.'

Charlie looked at his G-Shock again. 'But Piers is AWOL. And God only knows what trouble he might still be in. I need to find him, JD. He should've been here by now. Can I use your phone?' he asked urgently.

Jack patted himself down with one hand and then held

out his cell while he continued to stare at the questionnaire.

'Always on some kind of mission, aren't you, Captain Preston?'

Charlie took the phone, reached into his pocket and pulled out Malik S. Ahmed's business card. Then he called for a ride.

Card 37

Splashing the Pot: Putting chips or money directly into the pot, rather than on the edge of the pot in front of you; especially by throwing the chips or money so that they scatter. Splashing the pot is considered bad poker etiquette.

Las Vegas, 12 July 2009
CHARLIE'S HAND

'Well, howdy, sir. You OK? You'd be surprised by the number of tourists I've picked up from this place,' Malik said loudly through the open window. 'You sounded in a hurry on the phone.'

Charlie jumped in and closed the taxi door behind him. 'Yes, yes, but I've lost something important. I need to get back to the hotel to check if it's still there.'

'Sure thing, sir,' Malik said as he stepped on the gas and screeched away from the hospital taxi rank.

'Sorry to ask, but do you have a cell phone I could use? My battery is dead and I need to make an urgent call.' Charlie took a fifty-dollar bill from his wallet and waved it at Malik.

'Sure can, mister. Hell, for that kind of money, you can

call Australia if you need to,' Malik joked as he swapped the fifty-dollar bill for his five-year-old Motorola.

Charlie punched in his dad's number, hoping he'd pick up this time. He was in luck.

'Peter Preston,' his dad answered.

'Dad, it's me. I got your message. I have no idea how you managed to track down Piers before but I need you to do it again.'

'OK. OK. Slow down, son. Tell me what's happened. Is Piers OK?'

'I'm not sure. I think he's still in trouble. The kidnappers weren't exactly what I was expecting and I'm worried he's somehow mixed up in their plans. It sounds ridiculous, I know—'

'But you managed to pull together the half-million?'

'Yes. It's a long story and I don't even know the full details myself. But we paid the ransom to a couple of amateurs this morning. Now I'm worried about Piers' frame of mind. He doesn't look well, he's acting weird, and he's in serious debt to a dangerous mobster. I just need to find him before he gets himself into more trouble.'

'Or causes any more trouble,' Charlie's dad replied, frustration in his voice. 'You won't have heard, Charles, but he's been responsible for all manner of problems at home. He's got a gambling habit. His mum has been so sick with worry she's been bedridden for the best part of this year – won't see anyone but her doctors, the family lawyer and me. She won't even see Byron. Some of the papers are reporting she's died and the business is on the brink of bankruptcy. I couldn't tell her about the kidnapping, it might have been the death of her. She still loves Piers in spite of everything he's done; she only ever wanted him to lead a normal life. I couldn't tell her he'd been kidnapped. It would've destroyed her. It's what she's feared all his life.'

'Why did she always think he'd be kidnapped?'

Charlie's dad coughed nervously. 'She got menacing letters and phone calls back when she was pregnant with him, threatening the life of her unborn child or suggesting he'd be kidnapped at the very least. It's one of the reasons she sent him to England with a new surname. She wanted him to get away from the media circus that followed the family around Australia, too.' He paused for several seconds to catch his breath. 'Needless to say, I was responsible for neutralizing the threats.'

'You never told me about any threats.'

'Well, I suppose I didn't tell you everything, Charles, because I didn't want you to worry. I convinced Mrs. Clayton-Hill that you were the right person for the job, because I knew you wanted to join the army. You were practically the same age as Piers and a better solution than a real bodyguard, who would have stuck out like a sore thumb. The family had someone they knew would protect Piers without him knowing and you got first-hand experience of covert ops. Plus, the family saved money on round-the-clock surveillance and protection and I saved money on your education. It was win-win.'

'But it could have been lose-lose. You should have told me, Dad. I might have acted differently.'

'It doesn't matter now, Charles. He wasn't kidnapped back then. And luckily, when he was kidnapped, you were there to take care of things ... there's a sense of irony about this all, really. All these years after the threats on Piers' life, now it's Piers himself who's the real threat to the family.'

'I don't follow.'

'I guess he didn't tell you about the Ponzi scheme he persuaded Byron to join or the fact he lost tens of millions of dollars trading dodgy securities trying to recover his losses?'

Charlie was stunned.

'There's a black hole in the company's finances, Charles. The share price is trading in the twenties, hundreds of employees have been made redundant and there's a group of shareholders becoming hostile. The CFO was removed from the board last month. It's a disaster back here, son. The recession and Piers' investments have decimated the business and driven a coach and horses through the family.'

'I guess that explains a few things,' Charlie finally said, 'but right now I need to stop him from making any more mistakes. Can you help me, Dad? I need to track him down again.'

Several seconds extended into a full minute, with nothing but silence on the other end of the line. Finally, his dad gave him an address. Charlie thanked him, promised to keep him updated, and hung up.

'Change of destination,' Charlie said, passing the Motorola back to Malik. 'Take me to Martin Luther King Park.'

Card 38

*Dead Money: Refers to money in the pot other
than that contributed by players who remain active in
the hand (e.g. money put in by players who have since
folded). The term can also refer to an inexperienced
player who has little chance of winning.*

Las Vegas, 12 July 2009
PIERS' HAND

Piers sat in the back of his taxi, reflecting. He had lost
millions of dollars of family money and been ex-
communicated as a result; his mother had stopped
returning his calls, his brother had told him that she
never wanted to see him again. No one else in the family
seemed even remotely interested in lending a hand.

His Old Etonian network had dried up as soon as they
discovered how badly the Bernard Madoff scandal and
his exposure to the US sub-prime market had crippled
him financially. That charlatan, Leonard Hartley-
Warren of Sterling Securities, had a big mouth and took
great pleasure in disclosing information about his clients
to anyone who would listen. Piers became a popular
talking point in the dining rooms of the Garrick Club and

the RAC in London. His problems made everyone else's seem trivial in comparison and, as his debts mounted, the rumors spread – out of all proportion.

You remember Upwell from Eton, don't you? Son of an Australian billionaire. You'll never guess... He's lost everything... He's living rough in Paris... He's destitute and selling stories about his family to make ends meet... He's bankrupt, his family have disowned him... He lost his mother's fortune and now he's a drug-addict, selling his body to sex tourists in Bangkok to feed his habit. Such a shame. Used to think he had it all!

Whether or not the rumors were true hardly mattered. The net result was the same. None of his rich school friends wanted to know him anymore. He was no longer one of them but just another leech trying to hold onto their expensive coattails. A pathetic loser.

Borrowing money from Mr. Harald Lee had seemed like the only way out. Piers had been convinced he would be able to gamble his way out of the bind he was in but matters only got worse. When Michael Jackson died and he had contacted Jack, he'd been convinced it was a sign. A new start with old friends, who hadn't heard the rumors or didn't know about his dire situation. He could escape to happier times, enjoy an all-expenses paid vacation to Sin City and forget about his family troubles.

But then he met Honey and realized that she was the new start he had been waiting for. The one person who had been missing from his life. She was beautiful but she was ambitious, too. She was the one who'd finally come up with a plan to save him.

Honey really seemed to care about him. She'd been fascinated by his life, concerned about his worries; the perfect ending to his story. He so wanted her to be genuine. She'd convinced him that the half-million was mostly his anyway; far better to use it to right a wrong than simply squander it on booze and poker chips. Piers had readily agreed with her. He knew he was about to run out of money. He wouldn't be able to pay the interest on the loan from Mr. Lee and then his life really would be in danger.

Honey knew a thing or two about the Triads. She told him about their reputation for brutal violence and kneecappings and said they thought nothing of cutting off a finger when someone failed to honor even a small a debt.

He'd believed Honey when she'd told him that her brothers had to be handled with care. It was a dangerous game she was playing and confidence was the most important element of any scam, but they would both win in the end. Piers would save her from her brothers, and she would save him from the Triads by using the money to pay down his debt. Together, they were a perfect match. His friends and family would forgive him over time and his mother would grow to like his new girlfriend. Piers was quite sure of it.

The taxi pulled up to the address Honey had given him. He was two minutes early. He paid the driver, stepped out of the cab, and closed the door. The driver sped off quickly, leaving Piers alone in the gray, dusty parking lot, looking around for Honey and wondering what she had planned for him next.

It never crossed his mind that she might not be there.

Card 39

Driving Seat: A player in the 'Driving Seat' is the one taking the initiative in all the betting.

Las Vegas, 12 July 2009
KYLE'S HAND

Kyle and Danny sat in their Lincoln Continental, parked up on East Carey Avenue opposite the entrance to the parking lot at Martin Luther King Park, waiting for Piers to arrive.

'So what we gonna do with his body, then?' Kyle asked as he checked the magazine of his pistol. 'I don't know 'bout you, bro, but I got me some ideas.'

Danny turned to Kyle. 'Oh yeah?' He sounded surprised. 'What were you thinking?'

'Well, we could drive it out to Reno and bury it in the desert where no one will ever find it. Or we could chop it up somehow and put the pieces through a wood chipper. You know Crawford's got a rental company? They'll be sure to have equipment like that. Or we could even—'

'Hold up, Kyle. D'you really think we're gonna just kill the mark in cold blood, right here in MLK?' Danny shot back with a look of disgust on his face. 'Hell no, you idiot,' he added loudly before Kyle had a chance to speak.

'But he's a risk,' Kyle replied. 'You heard April. She said we needed to take care of it. Get rid of the problem once and for all. You said yourself, he's a loose end, remember?'

'He is, you fool. But we're not gonna kill him, for fuck's sake.' Danny pulled out his own pistol. 'We're just gonna scare the hell out of the little punk. Remember, he's gonna turn up thinkin' Honey'll be here with his share of the score and that they're gonna run off together into the sunset or somethin'. But when we show instead, we'll be breakin' his heart... Hell, I might get to break a few bones as well. But we ain't gonna—'

'But April said—'

'Damn it, Kyle – you'd do anythin' she said, would you?' Danny grunted. 'Even kill a tourist in broad-goddamn-daylight.'

Kyle kept quiet and glanced down at his watch. It was now 4.57 pm.

No loose ends, he thought.

***

PIERS' HAND

'Piers... Piers. Over here.'

Piers spun around and saw Honey's beautiful face peering out from the side of a rundown shop. She looked like a rose among the thorns. She was looking around nervously as she called out his name in a half-shout, half-whisper.

He felt a rush of blood to his heart. Each time he laid eyes on her he was struck by her beauty, like he was seeing it for the first time. He couldn't quite believe he had slept with her. He may not be able to remember any of it but that didn't matter. There would be plenty of other opportunities. He walked towards her briskly, suddenly light on his feet, unburdened by his past and excited by the future.

'Are you OK, baby? How's your eye?' Honey asked sympathetically as Piers stepped close, her voice still a whisper.

'It's fine. A small price to pay,' he said.

They hugged and her distinctive fragrance wrapped around him as tightly as her embrace.

'I'm so glad you're here,' she said. 'Come on, follow me.' She held Piers by the hand and led him through the battered front door of the dilapidated souvenir shop and down a creaky set of wooden stairs into a dimly-lit basement. 'Welcome to my office,' she said sarcastically, 'take a seat.'

Piers felt a strange sense of déjà vu as he sat down on the brown leather couch and put his feet up on the coffee table. He looked around the room and noticed dozens of dusty cardboard boxes.

'I wasn't sure if you'd show. I was worried you wouldn't get the message in time or you might have changed your mind.' She paused, looked at him and offered a shy smile, 'But you still want to do this, right?'

'I am never going to desert you, my precious little petal. I haven't stopped thinking about you since this morning. I feel so alive when I'm with you. You're my savior. If I hadn't met you, I don't know how I would be able to get my life back.'

Honey picked up an olive-green rucksack that was resting behind the desk. 'Speaking of which, it's all in there. Well, almost all of it. I had to give forty thousand dollars to my brothers as a kind of severance package.'

The thought of Honey's brothers put Piers on edge. 'Where are they, anyway?'

'They've gone to meet you,' Honey said as she put down the rucksack next to the coffee table. 'I sent them on a little errand, so we don't have long. We'll need to leave soon, just in case they come back early.'

Piers stood up quickly. Suddenly, he felt vulnerable. 'Well, I've got my passport, that's all I need. Let's get the hell out of here now. We've got the money – what else are we waiting for?'

'Let me just get my stuff from upstairs,' Honey said. 'I don't have a passport but there's a few personal things I want to take with me.'

She kissed his forehead quickly and started to climb the creaky stairs, 'Relax, sit down and keep an eye on the money. I'll be back soon and then we'll get the hell out of Dodge, OK?'

Before Piers had a chance to respond, she was gone. He wished she hadn't left him. He felt uneasy. He scanned the dark room but the sight of the towers of boxes made it worse. What was inside them? His instincts told him he was being watched. Someone could be hiding in one of the larger boxes, ready to jump out like a human jack-in-the-box. *Get a grip, Piers.* He breathed deeply and told himself that the only thing that mattered was what was inside the olive-green rucksack.

But he couldn't brush off his paranoia so easily. It seeped into his mind, polluting the portrait of Honey that hung there. He felt a twinge of infidelity as he unzipped the rucksack and looked inside to check its contents.

Card 40

The Bubble: *The period just before the money is reached in a tournament. The period itself — when just one or a few players need to be eliminated before reaching the cash — is referred to as the 'bubble'.*

Las Vegas, 12 July 2009
CHARLIE'S HAND

As Malik S. Ahmed's yellow taxi turned onto East Carey Avenue, Charlie peered out of the window and surveyed the surrounds. His eyes analyzed the area while his mind was preoccupied with questions. *Why would Piers come back to Martin Luther King Park? Am I too late?* The conversation with his dad had ended before he'd had the chance to ask about his source but he was beginning to wonder if the intelligence was being delayed. He had been with Piers in the parking lot earlier that day but Piers didn't appear to be there now. If there had been a time lag, Piers could be anywhere by now.

'Slow down, please?' Charlie asked. His voice was calm, disguising his concern.

Malik dropped into second gear and crawled along East Carey Avenue at fifteen miles per hour. Charlie kept staring through the window, absorbing every detail. The parking lot was empty. Six guys in their late teens/early twenties were playing a pick-up game on the adjacent basketball court. Three people were walking dogs. A teenager, smoking a cigarette, rocked on a swing in the children's play area. Charlie glanced to his left quickly as the taxi rolled past a stationary dark blue Lincoln Continental, two men sitting in the front. The driver had a tattoo running up his neck and the passenger was wearing a baseball cap. There was no sign of Piers.

Charlie asked Malik to turn onto the street that ran beside the basketball court, where a line of cars was parked. The taxi turned right, onto North Bledsloe Lane, as one of the cars started up its engine and peeled away from the others. It was a black Dodge Avenger.

As the car drove past, Charlie instantly recognized the driver. At least, it had to be one of two people. Mr. Yin or Mr. Yang.

'Malik, in fifty meters I want you to turn around slowly,' Charlie said as he watched the Dodge Avenger in the taxi's wing mirror, 'then follow that black car behind us. Don't let it get away, OK?'

Malik hesitated for a half-second, checked his mirror, and grinned broadly. 'I've always wanted someone to say that.'

By the time Malik had executed a slow U-turn and got back onto East Carey Avenue, Charlie noticed the dark blue Lincoln Continental had gone.

***

KYLE'S HAND

Danny frowned angrily, the lines in his head creased like a maze of skin. 'What's the time, man?'

'Nearly 5.20,' replied Kyle.

'Something's not right. We've been here for nearly half an hour already and the mark ain't turned up.'

'April was sure he'd come. Let's give her a call. See if there's been a change of plan.'

Danny pulled out his cell phone and called his sister. There was no answer. He tried the Mad House. After a few rings, a woman picked up.

'Bella. This is Danny Parker. Is Honey at the club already?'

'Oh hey, Danny. No. She's not clocked in yet, but she's on the early shift, so she should be here by now.'

Danny hung up and shot Kyle a wild look. The tattoos and scars on his face looked darker than usual. 'She ain't at the club. I don't like this, Kyle. It don't feel right.'

'Relax, man. Maybe the Brit got spooked?'

'Nah. There's something else. I got that feelin' inside, you know, like when you're being played.'

'Come on, Danny. There's probably a simple explanation.'

'There better be, or else I'm gonna lose my shit. If she's conned us, I'm gonna rip her apart with my bare hands. Sister or no sister,' Danny said through gritted teeth. He spat the words from his lips like venom and gripped the steering wheel so hard his knuckles whitened.

'Call Argyll. I wanna know if she's been in contact,' he snapped before turning on the Lincoln's engine.

'You need to chill out, bro. So what if the mark ain't here? That don't mean April's been playin' us. She's our blood, man. She ain't gonna do nothin' like that. We brought her up, we're all she's got, bro,' Kyle said, shaking his head.

'I don't give a shit. Call that Scottish freak-show and find out if he knows anythin' about our score. If he ain't heard from her, we'll know she's been lyin'.'

Danny tossed his cell to his brother and swung the

Lincoln around.

Kyle quickly found Franco Argyll's number. It rang three times before there was an answer.

'Mr. Argyll. Hey, this is Kyle, April's brother. Have you spoken to her recently?'

'Who?'

Kyle swallowed hard. 'April Parker. She dances in one of your clubs ... the Mad House. Uses the name Honey. This is her brother, Kyle.'

'Honey? No, I haven't spoken to her in over a month. She in trouble? She's one of my best girls. The lass better not be leaving me.'

Kyle hesitated. 'OK, great. That's good to know. Thanks, Mr. Argyll... No. No. There's no change of plan.'

Kyle hung up before Franco had the chance to respond.

'Everything's fine,' Kyle said nervously. Sweat beginning to surface on his forehead. 'She's meeting him tonight.'

Danny grunted.

'Where we goin'?' Kyle said, glancing over at Danny.

'Back to the office. I shouldn't have left her alone with all that cash,' Danny growled as he pushed the Lincoln into third gear and accelerated into the turn onto Betty Lane.

They were both too distracted to notice the two cars following them.

Card 41

*Dead Man's Hand: A Two Pair poker hand
consisting of the black aces and black eights. Along
with an unknown 'hole' card, these were the cards
reportedly held by Old West folk hero, lawman and
gunfighter Wild Bill Hickok when he was shot dead
during a poker game.*

Las Vegas, 12 July 2009
PIERS' HAND

Piers had been alone in the dark and dusty basement for
nearly ten minutes. He just wanted to get out of there,
leave Las Vegas, and start a new life with Honey. A creak
from the wooden staircase made him jump. As he
watched Honey cautiously descending the stairs towards
him, his heart began to race.

There was an arm around her neck and it belonged to
a man he didn't recognize.

Piers stared in disbelief at the dark-suited Chinese
man with black leather gloves on his hands.

'Trying to escape, are we?' said Mr. Yang, his left arm
tightly wrapped around Honey. In his right hand he held
a gun and it was pointing directly at her. The basement

appeared darker as Piers registered the fear on Honey's angelic face.

'I've been ordered not to let you out of my sight until you've settled your debt to Mr. Lee. But it looks like you're trying to run away with this pretty thing without honoring your agreement,' Mr. Yang said, pushing the gun into Honey's cheek.

A single tear dropped from her eye onto the black aluminum barrel of the gun's suppressor.

'Don't hurt us. We've got the money. We can pay you. All of it. Just let us go,' Honey pleaded, her voice distorted by the forearm pressing against her throat.

'So you want to pay all of your debt, do you?'

'Yes,' shouted Piers, surprising himself with his confidence. 'Please don't hurt Honey. I love her. I'll give you all the money but you've got to promise that afterwards you'll leave us alone. No more interest payments, no more threats of violence, no more following me. This is it, OK?'

'Where's the money?' Mr. Yang asked as he stepped toward Piers. Honey was still firmly in his grip, her body rigid with fear. Before Piers had a chance to respond, she called out once again in a strangled voice, 'It's in the safe, in the corner, behind the boxes. I'll get it for you.'

'I don't think so,' Mr. Yang grunted. 'You're staying right here with me.' He looked at Piers, 'You get the money.' He directed him towards the boxes with a sharp tilt of the head.

Piers shot Honey a baffled glance. Her face was illuminated briefly by the glare of the TV. It looked forlorn. As usual, he had no idea what she was thinking.

'Just do it, Piers,' she pleaded. 'It's the only way. 0829 1958. That's the combination.'

'You show me the money first. Then we'll discuss settlement terms with Mr. Lee,' Mr. Yang said as Piers scurried across the basement floor toward the tower blocks of dusty boxes, 'but any surprises and this pretty thing gets a bullet straight through her face.'

Moving a stack of cardboard boxes to one side, Piers could see a tall brown, rusty safe in the shady corner of the basement. It was nearly seven feet high, with a black combination lock at its center. The white numbers were barely visible in the darkness. It quickly occurred to him that he would have no chance of opening the safe without more light. What the hell was she thinking? His stomach tightened as he repeated the combination over and over in his head. He didn't want to forget the sequence. 0829 1958 ... 0829 1958 ... 0829...

Then he noticed that the safe door was already ajar. He glanced behind him to see if he was being watched but the stack of boxes was shielding him from view. He gently pulled the door open and looked inside. At first, the safe appeared completely empty, but then Piers noticed a single object lying on the bottom shelf.

A small black pistol.

***

DANNY'S HAND

'April!' Danny bellowed as he bounded down the wooden staircase, taking two steps at a time. 'Why aren't you picking up your goddamn phone?'

Pfft. Pfft. Pfft.

Splinters of wood and chunks of masonry flew into the air indiscriminately. Danny dropped down low and then sprung back up the stairs as quickly as he had charged down them.

'What the fuck?' he shouted as he ran straight into Kyle at the top of the stairs.

'Who the hell is shooting at you?' Kyle said, his voice close to panic.

Tapping himself down, checking for injuries, Danny hissed back manically, 'Christ knows. I couldn't see shit. But whoever's down there is armed with a goddamn silencer and is shooting to kill.'

The two brothers pulled out their handguns and exchanged nervous glances.

'Franco?' suggested Danny.

'Crawford?' Kyle said.

'The mark?' they chorused.

The anger on Danny's creased face was now warped by confusion.

'Could be any of them,' Kyle whispered. 'I just hope to God it ain't our sister down there trying to kill us.'

'Hold on,' Danny said, fear in his voice. 'Did you hear that?'

Kyle shook his head and cocked his M1911.

'I swear there was a noise outside. Shit. Our cash is in the Lincoln,' Danny whispered sharply. 'Get outside and check we don't have a problem.'

'What you gonna do?'

'It's my constitutional right to protect my property, Kyle ... I'm gonna kill the sonofabitch who's broken into our office.'

Kyle's face fell. 'Hang on. What if it's April?'

Danny checked his magazine, racked the slide and then turned away, squatting at the top of the staircase.

'I don't care. If she's down there and shooting at us ... she deserves to die.'

Card 42

Deadwood: A collection of discarded, burned, folded, or fouled cards.

Las Vegas, 12 July 2009
CHARLIE'S HAND

Malik S. Ahmed had been tailing the jet-black Dodge Avenger for fifteen minutes before coming to a stop on South Lamb Boulevard. Malik and Charlie could only watch as the rear of the car jumped the red light, narrowly missing the vehicles which were turning at the intersection. As the road in front of them quickly filled up with a mayhem of cars and trucks, they lost sight of the vehicle completely.

'Damn it! I've lost him,' Malik said, slamming his hands on the steering wheel.

'How long will these lights take?'

'We're gonna be here for ages I'm afraid, sir. Worst intersection in the city.'

'I'll be quicker on foot,' Charlie said as he threw another fifty-dollar note onto the seat next to Malik and sprung out of the taxi.

'Good luck,' shouted Malik as the door slammed shut. 'I hope you find whatever it is you're looking for.'

Charlie traversed the choked lanes of the boulevard to a chorus of tooting horns, arriving safely on the sidewalk and continuing the pursuit. Jogging past the traffic at the intersection, he scanned the streets for his prey.

Although it was a warm summer's afternoon, with not a single cloud in the sky, Charlie was still wearing his corduroy jacket which concealed his two weapons.

His mind raced back to his two grueling tours of Afghanistan; days on patrol in the dry, dusty heat of the desert. The Vegas heat paled in comparison to Helmand Province yet the sweat was still pouring down his face and neck as he searched in vain for the black car.

At the next intersection, he eased into a jog and had to decide in a split second whether to continue running straight or veer off to the right or left. He couldn't see the black car anywhere. After a few minutes of sprinting, dodging the occasional pedestrian, he began to question whether keeping to the boulevard had been the right call. Had he missed the car turning down one of the side streets?

At the next junction, he noticed a huge emerald-green sign with flashing lights, on the other side of the street. He stopped and stared at it. The Boulder Casino. The name seemed familiar. He combed his memory quickly, remembering his dad's voicemail.

'He's being held at a location on Industrial Road in Winchester, near Boulder Casino.'

Charlie's eyes darted across to the left. A sign ahead gave the name of the next street: Industrial Road. Instinctively, he crossed over and started to jog down it, catching a glimpse of the rear end of a black car some distance away. Breaking into a sprint, he saw that it was a Dodge Avenger, parked up. As Charlie neared, he observed that the driver's door was wide open. Looking both ways along the road, he noted that no one was around; the place was empty and, apart from the low thrum of the boulevard traffic, it was quiet. He drew his Browning and reached for the hood of the car. The engine was hot.

There was another vehicle in the parking lot, directly in front of a run-down souvenir shop. He recognized the dark blue Lincoln Continental instantly. It had been at Martin Luther King Park, only twenty minutes earlier. He hadn't registered them at the time but he could now see the car's Michigan plates. He thumbed again through his mental notebook:

Two kidnappers. Both large men. Faint red, white and blue shades of a basketball on the kidnapper's belt buckle ... the Detroit Pistons, possibly. He had seen two men in the Lincoln. Could they have been Piers' kidnappers? Charlie was almost convinced they were. It also occurred to him that if the Triads were in the vicinity, Piers would probably be close by as well.

Pfft. Pfft. Pfft.

Charlie flinched as the inimitable sound of suppressed gunshots rang out from the dilapidated shop and cascaded through the parking lot.

Squatting low behind the front of the black car, his Browning in his right hand, he surveyed the neglected shop, hoping he wasn't too late. Then he noticed a silhouette against the wall next to the entrance. The figure was barely visible, camouflaged by the colorful graffiti and fly posters that decorated the boarded-up shop front. Yin or Yang, he thought.

Blang. Blang. Blang. Blang.

Four gunshots rang out, louder this time, and closer.

***

PIERS' HAND

Piers was shaking uncontrollably as he picked up the gun from the bottom of the safe. He had some experience shooting pheasants, with a twenty-bore shotgun, in the English countryside but he had never fired a weapon like this before. He took a deep breath. *Pull yourself together, Piers. Stay calm.* The shaking abated but did not stop completely. He struggled to suppress the sensation that he was about to hyperventilate.

Holding the gun in his right hand, he checked it was loaded. There was a rectangular button on the side of the pistol grip, close to the trigger, which he slid across to release the magazine into his trembling left hand. He could see a single gold bullet at the top of the magazine. There might be one in the chamber as well. That was at least two. How many rounds should there be in the magazine? Nine? Thirteen? *How many do I actually need? Just one, if I'm accurate... Christ, Piers. What do you think you're going to do with this thing?*

His nervousness was making the heat unbearable. Sweat gathered under his armpits and his thoughts darted all over the place. He knew that, if he was going to save Honey, he didn't have any time for self-doubt. Sliding the magazine back into position as quietly as he could, he swiveled around carefully and bent down behind the dusty stack of boxes. Then he heard the chilling sound of one of Honey's brothers and he froze.

'April! Why aren't you picking up your goddamn phone?'

Pfft. Pfft. Pfft.

What the fuck? Piers sprung backwards, squeezing himself into the metal safe as the suppressed gunshots rang out. His heart rate spiked. Instinctively, he pulled the safe door shut to protect himself. He hoped to God that Honey hadn't been caught in the gunfire. *If that Chinese bastard has done anything to hurt her, I'm going to kill him!* He could just stand up in the safe. He tried to stop his quivering legs from rattling against its metal walls.

Gun in hand and shaking spine pressed up against the back of the safe, he listened for any signs of movement. All he could hear was his own heart pounding loudly and his right foot tapping against the floor.

Twenty seconds passed before Piers plucked up the courage to investigate. He pushed open the safe door noiselessly. Keeping his head down, he moved forward and lowered himself onto the filthy floor. Lying on his stomach, he gently parted two of the cardboard boxes, creating a crack large enough to see through. He peered out nervously. Under the faint glow of the muttering TV, he saw her – lying face-down on the floor.

His stomach clenched and bile rose in his throat. The rage was volcanic. A magma of pain and anguish bubbled beneath the surface. *Oh God, please no. Not Honey. Not my precious Honey. I'm going to kill that sonofabitch.* He tensed his grip on the gun and tried to stay quiet but he was struggling to control the growing urge inside; he needed to scream.

A flash of white light blinded his vision and the accompanying gunshots stopped him dead.

Blang. Blang. Blang. Blang.

Reality booted him in the jaw. The gunfire was almost deafening this time, piercing his eardrums. *If Honey is dead, I'll be next.* He needed to protect himself. With a shaking hand, he pointed the gun through the crack between the boxes and lay in wait.

***

MR. YIN'S HAND

'Drop your weapon,' Mr. Yin ordered. He was outside the entrance to the dilapidated souvenir shop and the suppressor on his Beretta 92S was pointing at Kyle's temple.

Kyle instantly did as he was told. He lifted his hands slowly and placed them on top of his baseball cap.

'If I hear you so much as breathe, I'll shoot you. Do you understand?'

Kyle was frozen to the spot.

'Now tell me, quickly and quietly, how many people are in there?'

'I don't know. My brother's in the basement with at least one other person, possibly ... our sister,' Kyle whispered quickly, his voice heavy with defeat.

'Show me,' commanded Mr. Yin.

Kyle turned slowly, hands still on his head.

'Get on with it, we haven't got all day,' Mr. Yin hissed as he pushed the suppressor into the back of Kyle's neck and followed him into the dark, run-down shop.

Card 43

Short Stack: The player with the fewest chips remaining at a particular table or in a tournament.

Las Vegas, 12 July 2009
JACK'S HAND

The fluorescent strip lighting, white resin floor and metallic smell of antiseptic were unsettling Jack as he sat on a green plastic chair in the hospital room. His hands were clasped, head lowered, and his eyes were tightly closed. All the while, his lips moved, creating soundless words.

Tom lay peacefully on the hospital bed next to him, a fresh white bandage wrapped around his head. An IV was attached to his left forearm while earnest-looking tubes and colored wires connected him to an electronic device with a green-and-black flashing monitor. The machine beeped continuously, as if vying for attention.

Beep... Beep... Beep...

Jack wasn't a religious person. Apart from a few weddings, christenings, and the occasional funeral, he rarely went to church. His parents had never taken him to Sunday School when he was a kid, yet as he sat beside Tom he found himself deep in prayer. Praying to an unspecified god. He'd always believed in something but he'd never had cause to establish exactly what. At this particular moment, however, the existence of a supreme being, an omnipotent god, who had the power to listen to his prayers and offer redemption in return, was very clear in his mind. He prayed for help. Not for himself, but for his friend: he implored God to show his benevolence to Tom in his time of need.

Beep... Beep... Beep...

He hadn't prayed like this before. He wasn't sure about the protocol so he did what came naturally; he tried to negotiate. He promised he'd be a better person. No; far too vague and subjective. *Be more specific, Jack.* He promised he would tell the truth about the side pot to his friends. He promised he would never steal money again. He promised he would never gamble. Yes, this was it ... these were real concessions. He promised he'd quit the law, leave Spear, Collier & Horn and do something more fulfilling with his life. He promised he'd never drink. *Hold on, that's a bit much. I'm not sure I can actually do that.* He promised he would never knowingly abuse alcohol. Much more achievable. He promised he'd go to church more often. He promised he would do all these things to become a better person, on the one single condition that, in return, God showed mercy, saved Tom, gave him a second chance.

Marlowe D. Robson eased into the room quietly and stood at the foot of the hospital bed to check Tom's medical chart. The clipboard knocked against the metal frame, startling Jack into opening his eyes and quickly unclasping his hands.

'It helps to talk to Him, you know,' she said after a few

seconds. Her soothing Southern drawl instantly put Jack at ease. He wasn't sure who or what she meant by "Him", but he sensed it didn't really matter; he knew she was right, whoever "He" was.

Beep... Beep... Beep...

'What does the "D" stand for, Marlowe?' Jack asked after a brief delay.

'Come again?'

'It says Marlowe D. Robson on your name badge. What does the "D" stand for?'

'It stands for "D", darling.'

'Marlowe Darling Robson?'

'No darling, just the letter. It's like Sunny D or Franklin D. Roosevelt,' she said with an equable smile as she busied herself at the foot of Tom's bed.

'But Sunny D is short for Delight and the "D" in FDR stands for Delano. So which one is it, Marlowe? Delight or Delano?'

Marlowe giggled and her large stomach rippled under her flowery blouse.

'Lyndon B. Johnson. George W. Bush. Michael J. Fox ... Why do Americans obsess about middle initials? It strikes me as being a bit—'

'My mama and sisters'all called Marlowe. I guess we need initials to tell us apart.'

'Couldn't you have done that by using different names?'

She giggled softly, walked toward Tom and held his hand.

'Been like this for the last hour,' Jack said, biting his lip nervously. 'Hasn't moved at all. One of the nurses said he might not be the same when he wakes. His brain could be impaired by the trauma. Will he be OK, Marlowe? Do you think he'll survive?'

Marlowe kept her eyes on Tom and touched the gold cross she wore around her neck.

'Have you spoken to his wife yet?' she asked.

'No, not yet. I've only just got her number from the hotel. She's been trying to reach him all day. Luckily, she left her details with the front desk.'

'Don't you think you should call her? I'd want to know if my husband was in hospital. You can use the phone over there,' Marlowe pointed to the corner of the anodyne room. 'You have to dial 900 first and then your country code. Forty-four for England, right? I need to get on, but I'll check back in half an hour, Mr. Davidson.'

'It's Jack. Please call me Jack.'

Beep... Beep... Beep...

Marlowe turned to leave. 'Remember, talking really does help. Just the sound of a friendly voice can work wonders. Some people sit where you are and read to their loved ones around the clock. A familiar voice can have a healing effect. Therapeutic for both parties, you know?' she reached for the door handle then, turning back toward the room, she locked eyes with Jack. 'There's nothing wrong with a little prayer either, Jack,' she said softly. 'Even if you don't have religion.'

Marlowe left the room and Jack was alone once again with his thoughts. He sensed she was right. On both counts. For the first time in over two weeks he thought about his ex-girlfriend. He felt a sudden twinge of guilt about the way things had ended between them and wondered whether he had made the right decision. Amelia wasn't so bad, he reasoned. She might have been "the one". If he had been hospitalized, she would have flown out here at the drop of a hat, wouldn't she? At least Tom had a wife to call; a next of kin who loved him unconditionally. He imagined if the roles were reversed, who would Tom be calling? Ruth, his P.A.? His older brother, Robert?

Beep... Beep... Beep...

Jack's gaze moved from Tom's lifeless face to his IWC Portuguese watch and he was struck by a wave of guilt and emptiness. Rising from his seat, he walked to the corner of the room, picked up the phone and called the number he'd been clutching in his palm.

'Victoria Patterson speaking.' The voice on the other end of the line sounded strained.

'Oh yes, hi there, Mrs. Patterson. My name is Jack Davidson – you don't know me, but I'm an old friend of your husband's from university.'

'Oh dear God – what's happened? Is he OK? Please tell me he's OK?'

Hearing the panic in Victoria's voice, Jack found he was suddenly calm. 'The doctors assure me the operation went well. He's in—'

'The doctors? Christ Almighty, what the hell happened?'

'I'm afraid Tom fell and knocked his head pretty hard and lost a lot of blood. He was taken to hospital and they've patched him up and given him a blood transfusion. I'm by his side at the hospital right now.'

'Oh Christ. Is he going to be OK? Can I speak with him?'

Beep... Beep... Beep...

'Not just yet, I'm afraid. He's still under sedation.'

'Oh my God. I should be there with him. What if he doesn't ... Oh God. I feel sick. I feel physically sick. I can't handle this right now. I mean, what the hell happened, exactly?'

'Listen, Victoria, try not to worry. Stay calm. There is no need to fly out here. I'm sure he's going to wake up soon with nothing but a splitting headache and a hangover from hell. I'll get him to call you then, straightaway. Of course, if anything changes I will let you know. I just thought you'd want to know—'

'No. I'm sorry. Thank you. It's Jack, did you say?'

'Jack Davidson – I was a close friend of Tom's at Cardiff – I *am* a close friend, I should say. We used to live together.'

'I appreciate you calling, Jack. I've been trying to reach him for the last twenty-four hours. I was sick with worry. His best friend told me he went to Vegas with some old university friends. He'd told me he was going to New York! Why would he lie to me about that? What was going on in his head? We're only just married. He's got no job. How can he afford to go to Vegas? I just don't get it...'

'Tom said you were cool about the trip to Vegas. He told us he worked at UBG,' Jack said, unable to disguise his surprise. He glanced across at Tom; clearly he wasn't the only one keeping a secret.

Beep... Beep... Beep...

Victoria sighed. 'He was made redundant nearly three months ago, just after we got back from honeymoon. He's obviously lied to you, too.' She gasped struggling to keep her emotions in check. 'My husband's out of work, he's been lying to me and now he's in hospital on the other side of the world. On top of all that, I found out yesterday that I'm thirteen weeks pregnant.'

Beep... Beep... Beep...

Jack took a deep breath as he processed the news and

considered how to respond.

'Victoria, you need to stay calm, OK? I promise you Tom is going to be absolutely fine. He'll be out of hospital in no time and back to his usual chirpy self. And there are plenty of work opportunities for someone with his experience; it's only a matter of time until he finds the right job. Hey, and listen, he's going to be overjoyed by your wonderful news. Tom will make a great father; I know that much. You just need to stay strong right now and try not to stress, for your health as much as the baby's.'

'Thank you, Jack. It means a lot, knowing he's in good hands. Tell him I love him and make sure he calls me as soon as he wakes up.'

Beep... Beep... Beep...

Card 44

Split Pot: A pot that is divided between two or more players.

Las Vegas, 12 July 2009
PIERS' HAND

Piers stood trembling, his right arm outstretched and clutching the pistol. It felt heavy in his hand. He surveyed the carnage in front of him. A small ring of blood had pooled next to Honey's head. Danny was pressing his foot against Mr. Yang's right forearm. Yang's shoulder was bleeding and his torso was convulsing.

'Don't move or I'll shoot,' said Piers from the shadows, his voice lacking authority.

'You ain't got the cojones to pull the trigger, punk,' Danny shot back.

'Try me,' said Piers, with more volume.

'Come on now, buddy, don't do nothing stupid. Hand over the piece and I'll let you walk out of here alive,' Danny commanded.

'No chance. I'm not afraid to die. I've got nothing to live for anymore.' Piers' voice was growing stronger as he spoke.

'You think you can come to my office and steal from me?' shouted Danny. 'You're on my property, next to my safe, trying to steal my money. Hell, here in Nevada, I've a goddamn right to kill you in cold blood.'

Danny aimed his gun at Piers, who was still crouching behind the stacked boxes. But Mr. Yang wasn't finished. He groaned, seizing an opportunity, and grabbed Danny's leg with his uninjured arm, distracting him for a brief moment. Piers took his chance. In half a beat, he'd receded further into the shadows. Danny wrestled his foot away from Mr. Yang's desperate grip.

Blang.

The groaning stopped. Bloodied fragments of skin splattered onto Danny's black boots and jeans. 'Now look what you made me do, you stupid punk, I'm coming for you next,' he roared over the booming echo of the single gunshot. He moved forwards, stepping over the bloody mess of Mr. Yang's dead body.

The staircase creaked loudly and Danny stopped in his tracks. He swung his pistol around. 'Kyle, is that you, bro?'

Danny turned back toward Piers and trained his gun on the shadowy corner of the basement. 'Hey Kyle, be careful, yeah? Crazy little Brit won't play nice – he's armed and he's hiding in the shadows.'

No response.

'Kyle?' Danny shouted.

Piers was back at the safe door, using it as a shield. Tall stacks of dusty boxes surrounded him like loyal servants, offering protection. He aimed his pistol at Danny. *Honey's gone,* he thought. *He's killed the Triad. The other brother will be down here any second now. I'll be next unless I take the initiative. It's self-defense anyway, right?*

He tried hard to regulate his breathing and his thoughts, both of them jumpy and out of control. He pressed his finger gently against the metal trigger of the pistol. Danny's large torso was outlined by the soft glow of the TV. Piers had a clear shot. *You can do this, Piers.* He closed his eyes and gently squeezed the trigger.

Blang.

Pfft. Pfft. Pfft.

'Don't move,' a voice commanded.
Piers opened his eyes. *Oh Dear God,* he thought.

Card 45

Exposed Card: A card whose face has been
deliberately or accidentally revealed to players
normally not entitled to that information during the
play of the game.

Las Vegas, 12 July 2009
JACK'S HAND

Jack felt a sense of guilt, knowing about Tom's secret
and his wife's pregnancy. He rocked back on the green
plastic chair and stared at his friend's expressionless
face. The bandage covering Tom's forehead made him
look younger – more like the Tom who Jack
remembered from university.

'Remember, talking really does help.'

Jack recalled Marlowe's advice. He took a deep breath.
'You wouldn't guess, Tom, because of the work I do, but
I've got a dreadful memory. It's really selective. These
last few days hanging out with you all have been a lot of
fun; well, at least before all the drama. I've loved
listening to all the memories of Cardiff. Reminding one
another of the stuff we got up to back then. We did a lot
in those three years, didn't we? I'd forgotten about those

squaddies pepper-spraying you in Jumpin' Jacks and making Piers turn up to lectures in a Snow White costume after he lost at poker...' Jack smiled to himself. 'But when you dropped that dissected penis in that Guinness, or the first time Piers taught us how to play Texas Hold'em; those are the sorts of things that have stuck with me. Strange, isn't it? And one of my most vivid memories is of a piece of graffiti on one of the footbridges over the river Taf: "Today is the Shadow of Tomorrow". Remember that? I saw those words and thought they were meant for me somehow. It really resonated at the time. Like it was telling me not to worry about the present because what's coming next is going to be so much better. I can't remember the name of the first girl I kissed and I can't even picture any of my law lecturers but that trite piece of graffiti ... I just have to close my eyes and it's there.'

Beep... Beep... Beep...

Jack shuffled around on his chair.

'Can you believe it's been fifteen years since we left that place? Fifteen years, Tom. Why didn't we stay in touch? We were good friends, weren't we? Or is my memory failing me again? I'm quite sure you promised I'd be your best man. But we've got even more in common now than we had back then, don't you think? I hope we'll be better friends after all of this. You know, back in London. If we could hang out together, I'd love that. And your wife, Victoria; she seems lovely, by the way. I just spoke to her – told her about your accident. I thought she should know. She's upset, of course she is, but she wants you to know how much she loves you and she says she's thinking about you. She wants you to get better because...'

Jack paused for several seconds then took a deep

breath and continued his stream of consciousness. 'She told me about your redundancy, by the way. Listen, mate, I'm sorry, but it's not your fault, you know. It's just the economic climate – loads of people are losing their jobs right now. You shouldn't take it personally. Anyway, you'll be fine, Patto. You always land on your feet. And hey, you didn't need to keep it secret. We would've understood. Piers certainly would, the lucky shit, he's never had a job in his life!'

Beep... Beep... Beep...

'Anyway, mate, your wife – Victoria – said you'd told her you were going to New York for job interviews or something? I thought you said she was fine with you being here. I guess I understand. Sometimes making up a lie is easier than confronting reality – I get that, I really do. So no hard feelings, OK?'

Beep... Beep... Beep...

Jack took a steady sip of water and cleared his throat. It was almost as if the machine, with its constant beeping, was willing him to continue.

'Hey, listen we all tell white lies now and again. Even lawyers. Especially lawyers, you'd probably say. But white lies come from a good place. They're not supposed to hurt anyone. And, to be honest with you, Tom, I've told my fair share of white lies in the past, but I feel it's time I came clean with one particular ... mistruth.'

Jack hesitated, took a deep breath and carried on.

'The Famously Dead bank account. You know, I was looking after it for all these years ... And, well, I haven't exactly kept it separate from my own funds like I promised I would. It started small. I borrowed a bit and paid it back a few months later. A peccadillo, you might say. It was hardly worth noting. But then I borrowed again, and again. It gathered momentum, and then I found I couldn't stop myself. I'm so sorry, Tom. I truly am. I misappropriated funds for my own... Hell, who are you kidding, Jack? Be honest with yourself... Tom, I was stealing from you and the rest of the boys. I used the money to invest in assets, bricks and mortar, stocks and shares. Basically, I used the money as collateral so I could take investment risks ... I was gambling with the money, Tom.'

Jack let out a deep sigh and buried his head in his sweaty palms. He felt tears gathering in the corner of his eyes. He blinked them away.

'I don't know why I did it. It wasn't like I desperately needed the money. I just...'

Beep... Beep... Beep...

'It was greed, I guess. And jealousy. Everyone around me had been dealt a better hand than me – or that's how it seemed. I wanted what they had. I felt inadequate. I wanted what Piers had. I wanted what my clients had: the luxury of being able to make money or lose it again without having to worry about the consequences. I got a kick out of it, too, I'm not denying it. Just like poker. I knew it was wrong but I couldn't stop. I guess I wanted to feel that power, that excitement of doubling or tripling the money or ... losing everything.'

Beep... Beep... Beep...

'I hope that you can forgive me, Tom. I couldn't help myself. But I was lucky. I made money. And I replaced everything I took, I promise.'

Jack took another sip of water.

'You're the first person I've ever told about this. I know

you can't hear me right now and you won't remember any of this, but it feels good just getting it off my chest. It's like I've peeled off a mask.'

Jack paused. He felt a solitary teardrop trickle down his cheek.

Beep... Beep... Beep...

'The side pot was pure profit. £660,000. I felt too guilty to spend any of it and do you know what? I'm glad I didn't because now I've used the money to make amends. We've saved Piers' life and the rest is like a bonus. You'll definitely need some extra cash in six months, when your newborn arrives. I'm not sure I should be telling you about the baby, Tom, but you know, it's a reason you have to get better... A reason to live.'

Beep... Beep... Beep...

An hour passed before another nurse came in to check on Tom. She examined the beeping machine above his head and tapped at the monitor with her finger, picking up the clipboard from the end of the bed and scribbling hastily before leaving the room without uttering a word.

Beep... Beep... Beep...

Jack was barely awake, entangled in a web of dark thoughts, and still sitting on the plastic chair beside the bed, eyes closed, daydreaming about life and death and what people would say at his funeral if he were to die in Vegas.

Good dress sense. No common sense.
Very observant. Didn't see this coming.

Promising youth. Disappointing adult.
Average lawyer. Terrible human.

The imaginary epitaphs grew progressively worse as he lost control of his subconscious. He thought about his future, Tom's future, past friendships, his present life ... and felt a sense of despair, shame and disappointment – the mask of a winner worn by a loser. *I'm like a drug-cheat, who knows the winning medal doesn't belong to him.* But it wasn't too late to change course. To seek redemption. To remove his mask.

Bip.Bip.Bip.Bip.Bip.Bip.

The familiar beeping of the machine was suddenly faster; more urgent. More distressing. Jack opened his sore eyes, sprung from his chair, and scrambled out of the hospital room.

Bip.Bip.Bip.Bip.Bip.Bip.

'Nurse! Nurse!' he shouted as he opened the door and lunged into the brightly lit corridor. 'The machine. Someone get a doctor, quick, for God's sake, the machine. The machine...'
Then blackness descended and Jack collapsed onto the white resin floor.

Card 46

Three of a Kind: A hand that contains three cards
of the same rank.

Las Vegas, 12July 2009
CHARLIE'S HAND

Charlie followed Mr. Yin and Kyle into the dilapidated
souvenir shop and observed them negotiate the wooden
stairs to the basement. He stood at the top of the
staircase, his Browning in his right hand, the Glock 26 in
his left, both pointing at the back of Mr. Yin's head. Faint
voices drifted up from below. Muffled but familiar.
Charlie hoped his instincts were right, that Piers was
down there and, more importantly, he was still alive.

Blang.

A single gunshot reverberated around the basement and
whooshed up the stairs, shattering the relative quiet
outside. Charlie tensed as he watched Mr. Yin stop
momentarily then nudge Kyle, forcing him to take
another step. The staircase creaked loudly under the
weight of the two men.

Suddenly, Mr. Yin grabbed Kyle and thrust him

forward, a human shield.

Blang.

A spray of blood spattered the exposed-brick walls and Kyle's large body jolted backwards with the force of a bullet to his left shoulder. He let out an angry bark, like a dog that's been kicked, then sprung back towards Mr. Yin.

Pfft. Pfft. Pfft.

Charlie watched Mr. Yin dispatch Kyle with a single shot to the head then hide behind his large frame, firing two further shots into the darkness.

Time's running out.

Charlie knew he needed to act; he couldn't just stand by and watch. He needed to take control. Those shots could have been aimed at Piers.

'Don't move,' Charlie commanded.

Mr. Yin let go of Kyle and raised his hands as Charlie moved down the stairs towards him. Kyle's legs buckled under his weight and with a dull thud his bloody skull hit the wooden handrail and continued down the stairs, leaving a mess of brain matter, blood and skin.

'Drop your weapon,' Charlie ordered.

Obediently, Mr. Yin dropped his pistol and then returned his hands to the air.

'It's too late,' he muttered under his breath but with enough volume for Charlie to hear. 'He's dead. They've already killed him.'

Charlie felt his pulse quicken. His stomach clenched and bile rose to the back of his throat. He moved cautiously.

'Piers?' Charlie called out, scanning the poorly lit basement, all the while keeping the Browning trained on the back of Mr. Yin's head. 'Walk forward slowly,' he ordered as he tucked the Glock inside the back of his jeans.

Passing Kyle's bulky frame, Charlie glanced briefly at the mess of the exit wound on his face and followed Mr. Yin down the stairs.

He surveyed the damage. Aside from the bloody mess on the staircase, a woman and two men lay face-down on the concrete floor. Dark pools of blood were visible on the dusty floorboards and more was sprayed across the piles of cardboard boxes.

Charlie trained his weapon on Mr. Yin and picked up his Beretta. He dislodged the magazine with one hand, letting it fall to the floor, then slipped the gun into the outside pocket of his corduroy jacket.

'Piers, are you down here?' Charlie called out, keeping a close eye on Mr. Yin.

The echo of the gunshots had reduced to a hum and the only noise came from the murmuring TV. Then, 'Charlie? It's me. Don't shoot. By God, am I glad to see you.'

Piers stepped out from the shadows. 'I don't know what happened but I think I killed him. You have to help me. It was self-defense, I promise. He was going to shoot me. Oh God, am I going to jail?' He spoke hurriedly, in a panic. 'I don't think I'll cope.'

Charlie watched as a distraught-looking Piers moved towards him, his gaunt face pale with shock, still clutching a pistol in his trembling right hand.

'It's OK, Piers. Calm down. Give me the gun and let's get you out of here, OK? I promise you, you're not in danger anymore. I'm here now. Whatever you've done, we'll deal with it together, OK?'

'I killed a man, Charlie. I killed a man. There's no dealing with that. I shot him, for God's sake.' Piers stopped, held out the gun and took a shaky aim. Charlie registered a flash of white anger in his eyes.

'What are you doing, Piers?' Charlie asked.

'You. You did this,' Piers screamed, pointing his pistol in front of him. 'Your brother killed my girlfriend.'

Mr. Yin remained silent, hands still raised, his eyes focused on Mr. Yang's lifeless, blood-soaked body.

'Wait, Piers,' Charlie commanded. 'I need you to listen to me very carefully. If you shoot this man, it won't be just your life in danger but everyone's in your family, and all the people close to you. Listen, I know about your debt to Mr. Lee and trust me, Piers, he is not the type of person to show mercy if you kill one of his gang.'

'I don't care. My life's over anyway. I've got nothing left. The one chance I had...'

Piers looked down at Honey's motionless body, blood pooling on the floor beside her head, then back at Mr. Yin. His index finger hovered over the trigger of the pistol.

Card 47

Nosebleed: The highest of the high-stakes games of poker, e.g. games where the small blinds are $500 or more.

Las Vegas, 13 July 2009
JACK'S HAND

'Mr. Davidson. Mr. Davidson,' a soft female voice was calling. 'Jack. Jack.'

Jack slowly opened his heavy eyes then smiled as he registered Marlowe D. Robson's milk-chocolate face. Her gray Afro was like a halo above her head as she leaned across him, straightened the bed sheets and smiled back.

'What happened?' Jack asked, his voice hoarse as the fog began to clear.

'You came running into the corridor and collapsed. Here, drink this, darling,' she said, handing him a can of Mountain Dew. He took the can, grateful for the sugar rush, and thanked her with his eyes.

'What happened to Tom? Is he OK?' Jack felt a familiar panic. 'The heart machine was making the sort of noise you hear on TV when a patient is flat-lining.'

Marlowe smiled as she touched the gold cross around her neck. 'Your friend is fine. He's better than fine, in fact. It was an EEG machine, not a heart machine, silly – it was monitoring his brain. He's awake and talking to the doctors now. The surgery was a success –' she smiled in delight '– he'll be ready to leave soon. We'll need to keep an eye on him over night but he should be fine to be discharged in the morning.'

'Thank God,' Jack took another swig of Mountain Dew. 'I thought he was—'

'We should thank God, you know,' Marlowe said softly. 'Your friend's a lucky man. So are you, Jack.'

'I don't feel very lucky. I feel dreadful.' Jack touched his swollen nose.

'You'll be fine. You just need some sugar, a good night's sleep, and maybe lay off the alcohol for a day or two. You're lucky you didn't cause more damage when you passed out.'

'I feel like I've been punched in the face.'

You had a nosebleed. Nothing to worry about.'

Jack looked around the room and noticed familiar pictures hanging on the walls. 'Am I in Tom's old room, Marlowe?'

'A lot of these rooms look similar. But they're all slightly different,' Marlowe replied with a smile. 'Your friend is just down the corridor, would you like to go see him now?'

'Yes, please.' Jack climbed gingerly out of the hospital bed. 'Does he know I stayed with him the whole time he was here – well, till I passed out?'

'I'll let you tell him that, if you like,' Marlowe said with a giggle as she held open the door.

Card 48

Cash Out: To leave a game and convert your chips to cash.

Las Vegas, 13 July 2009
JACK'S HAND

The dazzling multi-colored lights of the slot machines winked at Jack as he breezed past them in his double-breasted Tom Ford dinner suit, freshly pressed shirt and black velvet bow tie. He was clean-shaven, doused in Dior Homme, and strode across the room in his favorite Crockett & Jones crocodile loafers. He felt exceptional as he passed, unnoticed, through the hubbub of Caesars Palace guests and eased towards the gaudy casino bar where they'd arranged to meet. *Man in the Mirror* was playing quietly in the background but Jack could hear the lyrics clearly. Tom and Charlie were in a red leather-clad booth. They smiled at him as he approached.

'Here he is. The bloody idiot whose idea it was to come to Vegas,' Tom said as Jack sidled over to the seat beside him.

Jack noticed the bottle of San Pellegrino in front of Tom. 'Come on, guys, I'm sorry. You know if I could turn back time I would.'

'I'm just playing, JD. We don't blame you for anything. None of this was seriously your fault,' Tom said, taking a sip of his sparkling water.

A large white Band-Aid replaced the hospital dressing around Tom's head. It covered eight stitches. Except for the bandage, he looked much the same as every other hotel guest milling around the casino: sleep-deprived and a little worse for wear.

Charlie and Tom wore their dinner suits, too. They had agreed to try and make the most of their last night in Vegas.

'It's certainly been a few days I won't forget,' Charlie said without a hint of emotion.

Jack glanced down at his Franck Muller watch. It was 11pm. 'Where's Piers? There's something I need to say to all of you.'

Before anyone had a chance to reply, a waiter appeared beside them. Jack ordered a magnum of Bollinger and a large bourbon on the rocks.

'Are you sure we've got enough in the kitty for that?' Charlie asked after the waiter had left the table.

'That's one of the things I need to talk to you about,' Jack said as he fiddled with his gauntlet cuffs. 'But I should probably wait until we're quorate,' he scanned the room. 'Ah, there he is.'

Piers, wearing his finest threads, was standing at one of the craps tables, amidst a sea of other players. A well-fitted white tuxedo showed off his svelte physique, though Jack thought Piers was looking a little too thin. Come to think of it, when had any of them last eaten? He couldn't remember. At Maestro's Ocean Club on the night Piers went missing? They'd ordered the Maine lobster and king crab tails.

Piers was freshly shaven and his hair neatly gelled back. He seemed immersed in the excitement of the game. A hotchpotch of guests and locals, tourists and purists, surrounded the craps table: the well-dressed and the well-fed. Vegas appeared immune from the global banking crisis but Jack suspected this was an illusion. Sin City was probably awash with desperate people, ignoring their worries or trying to gamble themselves out of trouble.

A huge cheer erupted from the table, followed by high fives and shouts of encouragement. Piers joined in with the chorus. He seemed happy. Relaxed.

'Hey, check out the girl holding onto Piers,' Jack said. 'She's stunning.'

The waiter returned with the bourbon and champagne.

'Shall we put this on your tab, sir?'

'If you don't mind,' Jack replied. 'Presidential Suite. Forum Tower. Thank you kindly.'

'We just need your signature, sir.'

Jack scrawled on the bar slip and thanked the waiter with a crisp $50 bill. He then bolted his bourbon in one and slammed the glass down on the table. The two ice cubes chimed harmoniously for the briefest of moments then slid apart in quiet resignation.

'Sorry, mate, that was a bit inconsiderate of me,' he said, turning to Tom. 'I bet you could murder a drink right now?'

'You know what? I'm fine actually, JD. I think the bang to the head has shaken me up a little. In a good way. I feel like a different person, with a different perspective. I'm going to stay sober for a while. I've got some big life decisions to make and it's much better if my head's in the right place, you know?'

'Oh God, Patto. You've not gone all spiritual on us, have you? Did you visit the pearly gates and meet an old man with a white beard while you were under?' Jack laughed but he remembered his own desperate prayers and immediately felt guilty. He'd already forgotten his bargain with God. The conditional contract he had negotiated.

His hearing focused in on the music for a moment. He heard Michael Jackson, the very man whose death had brought them all here, remind him he had to take a look at himself and make a change.

'I'm only playing, Tom,' Jack said apologetically, 'I think you're absolutely right; in fact, I'm going to cut back on the booze myself. This trip has been life-changing for me as well, you know. And I've made a decision. I'm going to leave Spear, Collier & Horn. Get out of the law while I still can. Have a go at something completely different.'

Silence extended across the table before Charlie finally spoke. 'That's a big decision, JD, are you sure you're not just letting the Vegas atmosphere cloud your judgment?'

'No,' Jack shot back confidently, 'I've been thinking about this for a while now. The last few days have really focused my mind. It's the right decision in the cold light of day and the right decision slightly drunk beneath the lights of a Vegas casino. I've made up my mind. I'm going to hand in my notice when I get back on Tuesday. I can't take having to justify every single minute of my working day, dissecting my very existence into six-minute units. I hate my clients. I dislike my colleagues and the prospect of doing what I do forever fills me with dread. It's time for a change. Time to take a punt. Today is the shadow of tomorrow, right?'

'Good on you, mate. It takes real guts to give up something you've been doing for such a long time,' Tom glanced across at the empty whisky glass in front of Jack. 'So I guess you'll be joining me in looking for a new job?'

'Hold on, what have I missed? Are you quitting your job as well?' Charlie asked.

'I don't like the word "quitting",' Jack said. 'It has such a negative connotation. Think of it more as moving on, trying something different.'

Tom took a deep breath before saying with a solemn expression, 'The truth is, guys; I haven't been telling you the truth. I don't work at UBG anymore. They made me redundant nearly three months ago.' He picked at the label on his bottle of San Pellegrino as he spoke.

Charlie responded first: 'That must have been tough, but why didn't you tell us before? Are you OK about it?'

'It's been hard; I'm not going to pretend otherwise. I was in a dark place... Newly married, not knowing what the future holds. You know? But now I feel at peace. I feel lucky ... really lucky to be alive and I realize I've only got one chance to make the most of whatever life throws at me. Who cares if I'm out of work? I never really liked the job anyway. So what if my wife is sleeping with my best friend? I'll find someone else... Life isn't supposed to be easy and I'm genuinely excited about whatever's round the corner. It's a bit like the feeling I had when I graduated back in '93. Like Jack says, today's the shadow of tomorrow and all that.'

'Hang on. What did you say?' Jack asked.

'Today is the shadow of tomorrow.'

'No. You said your wife is sleeping with your friend?'

'Typical, isn't it?' said Tom calmly. 'Jonny Banks, the man who has everything, had to take the one thing that was mine.' It was clear, despite his upbeat tone, that Tom was still brooding on the past.

'Are you sure? When did she tell you this?' Jack was finding it hard to believe. When he'd spoken to Victoria it hadn't occurred to him that her pregnancy may not be welcome news.

'Well, they haven't so much as admitted it, but I can sense it. You know, like when you feel something is wrong deep down in your stomach. The signs are obvious. It's the way they are with each other. The way he calls her Vicky. The mutual admiration. I should have seen it coming. Jonny always gets his way, in business and with women. I was surprised when Victoria chose me, to be honest. Girls usually prefer Jonny.'

Tom scratched his wiry beard and continued to pick the label of his bottle of water.

'She even pretended he made her feel uncomfortable. Now I can see it was all an act, a bluff, she just wanted to get closer to him. Lying bitch. Why did she marry me if she wanted him? Anyway, there's no point picking over the details now. They deserve each other. I'm better off starting again on my own. Clean break...'

Clusters of tiny paper balls lay on the table in front of him. He swiped them away but most of them just stuck to his hand. 'At least we don't have kids to worry about.'

'Assumption,' Charlie said. 'Don't they say it's the mother of something or other?'

It's not the mother who's in question here, Jack thought to himself.

'Fuck-ups,' Tom said under his breath. 'Mother of all fuck-ups.'

Charlie gave Tom a sideways look, 'Have you spoken to your wife since the accident?'

'I suppose I've left her to sweat for long enough,' Tom muttered as he pulled out his cell and saw the number of messages she'd left. 'I guess I ought to let her know I'm alive, at least. Not that she even cares.'

Tom stood up, slid past Jack, and disappeared into the crowd of hotel guests.

'God, I hope he's wrong about his wife, otherwise we're going to have another crisis on our hands,' Jack said. 'We'd better keep a careful eye on him tonight.'

Charlie nodded in agreement.

'What was it you wanted to tell us about?' Charlie asked as he reached over and lifted the magnum of Bollinger out of the extra-large ice bucket. In his huge hands, the bottle seemed almost normal-sized.

'Let's just wait until the others get back. There's something I need to get off my chest and I'd rather say it in front of everyone,' Jack tried to avoid Charlie's eyes.

Charlie poured the champagne into two flutes without spilling a drop. 'It's about the ransom, isn't it?' he said as he handed one of the flutes to Jack. 'The money you miraculously won playing roulette.'

Jack felt Charlie's gaze honing in on him like a laser beam. It was as if Charlie could see right through to his insides. He sipped at the ice-cold champagne but it did little to cool his flushing cheeks.

'I played enough poker with you at university to know when you're bluffing, Jack,' Charlie continued.

'JD. How the devil are you?' exclaimed Piers as he appeared at Jack's shoulder. 'My dear boy, allow me to introduce you to this young lady. Her name's Honey. Isn't she the most beautiful thing you ever saw?'

Honey smiled, flashing her perfectly straight white teeth. She shone out like a showroom car in a scrap yard. Jack stood up and took her outstretched hand. He wasn't sure whether to kiss it or shake it. In the end, he opted for a limp handshake.

'You must be Jack? The treasurer, right? Piers has told me all about you,' she said, smiling broadly. 'It's so nice Piers has such good friends. Charlie said you stayed with Tom in hospital so he didn't have to wake up alone. That's so sweet.'

She glanced across at Charlie and nodded at him with a knowing smile.

Jack was dumbstruck. She was gorgeous. He took in her long black dress. It hugged her perfect curves and showed enough leg to test the most faithful eyes. Her caramel hair was parted in the middle, framing her flawless face. She was holding on to Piers' arm like they were an item. Jack didn't know what to say. He was confused and jealous. How come this girl was talking as if she knew everyone? She looked familiar but he was struggling to place her.

'Jack?' Charlie said, breaking the uncomfortable silence.

'Sorry. How do you do?' Jack said at last. 'I feel like we might have met before. I was just trying to place—'

'Champagne, Honey?' Piers interrupted, reaching over and picking up a champagne flute from the table.

Jack rifled through his hazy memory for clues, trying to remember where he might have seen her before. He drew a blank.

Charlie picked up the bottle of Bollinger and expertly poured another two glasses.

'So tell me, I'm intrigued, how did you two meet?' Jack asked as he handed a glass to Honey, unable to keep his eyes off her angelic face.

Both Piers and Honey seemed to look to Charlie for his approval.

'Why don't we wait for Tom to get back?' Charlie said, 'I think it's time we all laid our cards on the table.'

Card 49

The Nuts: The best possible hand available.

Las Vegas, 14 July 2009
TOM'S HAND

Tom stood in the dazzling hotel lobby to make the call home. His wife answered on the first ring.

Time for the truth.

'Hello, Victoria.'

'Oh dear God, Tom. Are you all right? It's so good to hear your voice, darling. I haven't been able to think straight since I heard you were in hospital. I've been worried sick.'

'I'm OK. The knock on the head did me the world of good, funnily enough. Gave me a new perspective,' Tom said abrasively.

'Thank God ... Jonny told me all about your game and your university friends. He said you'd asked him to cover for you. What were you thinking, darling? Why on earth didn't you just tell me the truth?'

He felt hot and unbuttoned his collar with one hand. 'I bet he told you. I suppose he's been telling you all sorts of things. Goddamn Brutus.'

'Hey, what's wrong, darling? You sound angry.'

'Of course I'm bloody angry. What do you expect? You think I don't know what's going on? Listen, if it's a divorce you want, you can have one.'

'What the hell are you talking about, Tom? You're scaring me. You seriously think I'm having some kind of affair when you've been gone for less than a week!'

'Well, aren't you?'

'Don't be ridiculous. And with Jonny? I find that man barely tolerable at the best of times. You really think I'd cheat on you with your best friend? Christ, that knock on the head really has shaken you up.'

Tom didn't answer. Victoria continued. 'Jonny's a creep – honestly, I only put up with him because you two are such good mates, or at least I thought you were. I've always found him so ... full-on. He gets really familiar when he's had a drink, tells me he wishes he'd made a move when we first met all those years ago. As if he ever had a chance!' Victoria paused for a moment. 'You know, the day you left for your supposed interviews in New York, he came straight over with a bottle of my favorite wine and told me what was really going on.'

'I knew it!' Tom exclaimed. 'The scheming little shit. And you fell for it – he was the rich shoulder to cry on, right? Couldn't help yourself, could you? He told you I was away in Vegas and you wanted to get back at me in some way? It's OK, Victoria, you can admit it.'

'Tom, have you listened to a word I've just said? I find the man unbearable. I didn't touch the wine. Then, when he started saying you were having doubts about our marriage, I got really upset and told him to leave.' Victoria let out a tired sigh before continuing. 'You're my husband, darling. I love you. I can't believe you think I'd jump into bed with your best man. Jesus, Tom, listen to yourself,' she finished with more than a hint of exasperation.

'Jonny's got everything,' Tom answered meekly, 'why

shouldn't he have you as well? I don't blame you; he can look after you better than I ever can and I get it. Your husband is useless, unemployed, has no prospects...'

'Just stop it.' She raised her voice. 'Stop it right now. There's nothing going on between me and Jonny. He's tried but it hasn't worked, Tom. I'm in love with you. God, my heart nearly stopped when your friend called to tell me you were in hospital. I love you more than anything, you idiot. Can't you see that?'

Four seconds of silence passed between them while Tom finally let her words sink in.

'I'm sorry, Victoria,' he started. 'I shouldn't have doubted you. You must think I'm a real shit. Listen, I'll make it up to you, I promise. I guess I've been pretty depressed. It's just, I felt I'd let you down, and somehow I thought hitting the sauce would solve all my problems. Instead, it's just fueled the paranoia and made everything so much worse.'

Victoria took a deep breath. 'I suppose in a way I have been hiding something from you, Tom.'

'What?' Tom responded quickly, his mind going into overdrive again.

'Actually, I've been hiding someone ... I'm thirteen weeks pregnant,' she hesitated and then after a moment's pause quickly clarified, 'We are thirteen weeks pregnant, darling.'

Tom went weak at the knees and almost dropped his cell.

'Tom? Are you still there?'

'Sorry. Yes, yes. I'm just taking a moment... You mean, we're having a baby? Oh my god, I need to sit down.' Tom spotted an empty seat in the busy lobby and took it gratefully.

'So,' Victoria said nervously, 'what are you thinking?'

'Honestly, darling. I couldn't be happier.' Tom smiled.

'Oh, thank God! I wasn't sure how you'd take it. You've

been so distant since the redundancy, and then with the Vegas trip...'

'Listen, Victoria,' Tom cut in, suddenly upbeat, 'things are really going to change from now on ... as soon as I get home I'm going to start looking for a new job, I promise. I'll definitely need to start earning again now we're having a baby.' He beamed as the words left his mouth and for the first time since their honeymoon he really felt he had something to look forward to. The faraway roar of an erupting crowd filtered through from the Palace Casino and swept through the lobby.

'I love you, Tom,' Victoria said, her voice almost drowned out by the noise. 'Enjoy your last night in Vegas, darling.'

Card 50

The Tell: *A change in a player's behavior that can provide clues to their assessment of their hand. A player gains an advantage if they observe and understand the meaning of another player's tell, particularly if the tell is unconscious and reliable.*

Las Vegas, 14 July 2009
JACK'S HAND

Jack sat in the red leather booth, looking down at his glass of champagne and waiting for Tom. In his head, he was going over exactly what he wanted to say. He imagined Charlie's eyes trying to bore into his subconscious and a prickling heat crept over him, putting him even more on edge.

'So what do we all do now? It's our last night in Vegas, right? I know—'

'Before anything else happens, we need to talk.' Charlie cut Honey off mid-sentence. 'Then we'll assess where we all stand and where we want to go from here.'

Honey kissed Piers on the cheek and whispered in his ear. He managed a brief smile, but didn't respond. Jack noticed Piers was sweating.

Tom bounced back to their table with a beaming grin on his face and his arms wide open. 'Guys, you'll never guess what!' His smile was as big and bright as the casino floor but he was quickly forced to change tack. 'Hello. Who do we have here?'

'Hey there. You must be Tom? I'm Honey – I'm with Piers,' Honey said, standing up and offering her hand. 'I heard about the accident. I hope your head is OK? It musta been quite some fall.'

Tom touched his Band-Aid and looked a little embarrassed as he shook her outstretched hand.

'How the hell have you managed to find a girlfriend, Piers?' Tom asked as he placed himself next to Jack in the red booth. 'No offense intended,' he said, pausing and looking towards the intruder. 'Honey, did you say?'

Honey smiled at him warmly and nodded.

'Well quite,' said Piers, 'this is something we probably need to talk about, I think. We were waiting for you before we started.' His eyes fixed on the stem of his champagne flute as he spoke.

Charlie took over. 'OK everyone, I know a lot's happened since university and we've all grown up and gone our separate ways but the friendships we made at Cardiff, well, they're still strong today – if anything, they've grown even stronger over the last few days. It's our last night together and it seems there's still a lot that needs explaining. I think we owe it to ourselves to be honest with each other. No more secrets, no more lies.'

Jack felt the sweat roll down his spine.

If you don't know who the sucker is at the poker table, it's probably you, he thought. He felt sure Charlie's speech was directed at him but then Piers began to speak.

'I think I should start,' Piers' brow furrowed and he spoke in a rush: 'The whole kidnapping was fake. Well, it wasn't fake, exactly. It was real, but I was involved in the planning. It's just I didn't remember anything about it.'

What the hell? thought Jack.

'You are kidding, right?' Tom said.

'It was my idea,' Honey said quickly. 'First, I was going to con Piers and you guys, too.' She looked across at Jack and Tom unapologetically. 'I hustle for a living so when I saw you high rollers come into the club the other night I thought there was easy money to be made.'

'You what?' Tom said, his face pinched, angry and puzzled.

Jack's mind darted back to the Mad House. *Kitty. Sindy. Honey. High Rollers. Dom Pérignon. $100 bills.*

'Relax, Tom,' Charlie cautioned, 'let them finish.'

'Piers and me got to know each other in the Mad House and we really connected. He told me about his life, everything from being sent away from home at such an early age to his troubles with gambling and his debts and I shared my story with him. The thing is, in my line of work, you have many stories, you wear different masks – and I suppose that's what keeps it interesting, you know? Playing a different character for the night, pretending to be something you're not. Sometimes, you need to hide from reality. Sometimes, you need to conceal your motives... But I told Piers my real life story. No bluffing. No mask. I admitted I was a con artist, that I hustled men to make extra money – I told him about my deadbeat brothers who run the scams with me. I never told anyone that kinda stuff before. And Piers listened – didn't you, baby? He understood and he saw me for who I was...'

'A misguided girl from Detroit who'd got herself tangled up in a web of mistakes,' Piers finished, looking her in the eye.

'Is this a bloody joke?' Jack exclaimed, fearing that it wasn't.

'How do we know you're not conning us now?' Tom said with ill-disguised bitterness.

'You don't,' she replied. 'But I'm not. I promise you I'm not. You'll have to trust me. Today marks the beginning of a new chapter, a new book – for Piers and me. Together.'

Tom laughed. 'Seriously, Piers – tell me this isn't for real. This girl is nothing but—'

'So who's got the ransom, then?' said Jack. 'Where's the half a million dollars we gave to Michael Jackson and Elvis – your brothers?'

Jack could see the confusion flooding Tom's face. They hadn't had time to fill him in on the details of the kidnapping.

'Yes, those were my brothers, Danny and Kyle,' Honey replied. 'I put the whole kidnapping idea to them, said I met some punters at the club and they had plenty of cash to burn in Vegas. Piers had told me about your Deadly Famous game, so I knew you were good for it. Obviously, my brothers never knew that Piers and I were double-crossing them. They were skeptical at first – we'd never done anything as big as this before – but I managed to persuade them it would be our last big score...' She paused for a brief moment as she looked at Charlie, 'I guess that much was true. I never meant for it to turn out like this. May God have mercy on my soul.'

'I don't get it, why the hell did you go along with any of this?' Tom asked Piers. 'You of all people. You don't need the money. You're the heir to a bloody mining empire, right? Or is that just a big lie as well? Christ, I don't know what to believe anymore.'

'I'm awfully sorry, chaps, I haven't exactly been honest with you. The thing is, I got myself into a bit of a financial pickle and lost a small fortune. Close to seventy million dollars, to be exact.' Piers hesitated as he took in Jack's and Tom's gaping faces. 'I made some stupid mistakes investing in what turned out to be a Ponzi scheme and then doubled down and lost a bucket-load of money in the US bond markets. Terrible run of luck, really.'

'It's OK, baby, just tell the truth. Tell them what you told me,' Honey said as she gripped his arm and looked into his eyes encouragingly.

Jack couldn't believe what he was hearing – seventy million dollars!

'I've been cut off completely by the family. My only income is the dividends from my shares. I tried to gamble my earnings and got deeper into debt. Then I borrowed money from a man who turned out to be some ringleader of a Triad gang. All rather foolish, really.'

'Holy shit, Piers,' said Tom.

'That's why he needed half a million dollars to pay his debt. His life was in danger if he didn't,' Honey said. 'That's why I came up with the kidnapping idea.'

'What was in it for you?' Tom asked.

'We were going to use some of the money to run away. Leave Vegas and my brothers behind. Get the hell out of here and start a new life together, just the two of us.' Honey squeezed Piers' forearm again.

'So why are you still here? Where are your brothers?' Jack said. His heart was pounding. He felt dizzy with confusion.

'Where's the ransom?' snapped Tom.

Piers and Honey looked across at Charlie as if needing his permission to answer.

'Maybe you should tell us how you got the money first?' Charlie said, honing in on Jack.

Jack's heart thumped. It was his turn to show his hand. He breathed in deeply. 'OK … I guess, like Piers and Honey, it seems, I haven't exactly been honest with you all. There's no easy way of saying any of this, and I want to start by apologizing … I did something I never should have done … I betrayed your trust.'

'Sorry for what, JD? What the hell are you talking about?' Tom turned towards Jack.

'Over the last five years, I've had my hand in the till, so to speak. I've been taking money from the Famously Dead account.'

He looked up to see three faces staring at him with shock and disappointment in their eyes.

'You stole from us, Jack?' Tom said.

After a pause Charlie asked, 'How much did you take?'

'Well, it wasn't exactly stealing. I kind of used the account as collateral. I borrowed money to make investments ... I gambled with it.'

'Sounds like stealing to me,' Tom said.

'Why?' Piers said. 'You're a partner at a global law firm, I thought your life was perfect?'

'Looks can be deceptive. Right, Charlie?' Jack replied.

Everyone seemed to look down in agreement.

'It was greed and envy, I suppose,' Jack continued. 'I saw what my clients had and I wanted the same things. The money in the bank account was too much of a temptation. I knew it didn't belong to me but I was under its spell – I couldn't stop myself. I know that doesn't sound like much of an excuse but let me try and explain.'

Jack took a deep breath and expelled the air slowly.

'You have to understand that in my job I'm constantly surrounded by wealth and excess. Every day, other people's riches land in the palm of my hand, yet they're totally beyond my grasp. There's no escaping it. The absurdly inflated property market; the private cars; penthouses; high-end boutiques selling unaffordable luxuries; designer clothes; handbags; watches; cars. I'm surrounded by the unobtainable wealth of my clients. I know I'm well-paid compared to most people, but my own prosperity and lifestyle pale in comparison to the bankers, the fund managers, the traders who monopolize the world I inhabit. My clients are some of the richest people in the world. I help them buy and sell businesses, strip assets, leverage off inflated balance sheets and pay themselves dividends with cheap debt. I provide legal services to the rich, help them conceal gains and avoid taxes – basically, I make rich people even richer. I guess what I'm trying to say is that I live vicariously through them – the lavish lunches, the sailing vacations, corporate hospitality, private parties, VIP treatment – all expenses paid. But while this lifestyle is a reality for them, it was nothing but a dangerous game of pretense for me.'

'I know exactly what you mean,' Honey said, offering him a warm smile. 'I've often felt I deserved a better hand than the one I was dealt.'

'It doesn't matter how much you have, there's always someone better off than you,' Tom said, with feeling. 'Someone who hasn't worked so hard, doesn't deserve it as much as you do.'

The others seemed understanding; not angry, as Jack had expected. He felt encouraged to continue with a little more confidence.

'After a while, I couldn't help taking advantage of my position. I took £35,000 from the account just to impress a girlfriend – a trainee solicitor, obsessed with cars. She was beside herself the night I picked her up in a brand-new Porsche 911. The sex was amazing for weeks afterwards but it soon fizzled out and so did our relationship. I treated the money as an interest-free loan and I did pay it back over the course of a year. I convinced myself it was just a one-off. But I'd got away with it once and the temptation lingered like a bad smell. In the end, I convinced myself it was OK to dip into the account, as long as I repaid everything I borrowed.'

Jack paused, glanced at the faces in front of him and took a sip of champagne. As he continued, he began to feel a weight lifting from his shoulders. 'My envy grew, and so did the size of the withdrawals. I used the money in the account as collateral for a smaller mortgage on a bigger flat and a year later, when I sold it and made £150,000, I repaid the money and banked a tidy profit. After that, I flipped three properties in three years. I timed the purchases well. Each sale made a bigger profit than the last. I used the money to gamble – on the housing market, the stock market and all kinds of financial instruments. I used my network to glean information and bought and sold equities and securities at the right time for the right prices. I did lose out occasionally, but mostly I made good returns on the trades.'

'So you repaid everything you stole?' Charlie asked.

'How much did you make?' asked Tom.

'I repaid every penny, I promise. The money in the group account remained constant but the side pot grew ... I made nearly £660,000.'

There was a brief, startled silence. It was Charlie who broke it. 'So you lied when you told me the ransom came from the roulette tables?'

'Yes,' Jack looked down at his hands. 'I borrowed the money from the casino and used the side pot to repay them, then I cashed it in for chips. I hoped you'd believe I won it at the tables in the casino – I was too ashamed to admit where it had really come from. I wasn't going to tell any of you what I'd done but then, in the hospital, seeing Tom lifeless in that bed, I had a kind of epiphany. I found myself praying that he'd recover and I realized then that life's too short. All this around us,' Jack gestured to the casino floor. 'All this money and luxury - it doesn't really matter, does it? True friends, like you lot, are far more important.'

Piers and Honey looked across at Charlie. Tom placed his hand on Jack's shoulder. 'If it hadn't been for your gambling, JD, we wouldn't have been able to rescue

Piers. In many ways, we should be grateful.'

Piers nodded at Jack and half-smiled.

'I guess it's my turn,' Charlie said, fixing his gaze on Piers. 'It's possible I've been more deceitful than the lot of you put together, but I never really had a choice. The thing is ... my dad works for Mrs. Clayton-Hill – Piers' mother – and has done for the last thirty years, since he left the army. Actually, he's employed by the family business.'

'Clayton-Hill?' Tom asked, confused. 'I thought his surname was Upwell.'

'Your *dad* works for my *mother*?' Piers was completely taken aback.

'Yes,' Charlie said sheepishly, 'and in a way, so did I.'

Now everyone turned toward Charlie. The evening was growing more bizarre by the moment. 'I was sent to Cardiff to keep an eye on you, Piers. Your mother was worried that if people found out your true identity they might take advantage. She was especially anxious you might be kidnapped,' Charlie flashed a glance at Honey then turned back to Piers and carried on. 'But she wanted your student life to be as normal as possible. I was about your age and the family felt I could be trusted so it was agreed that I would act like a kind of covert bodyguard, on hand to protect you from any danger.' He paused again, his eyes still fixed on Piers. Jack detected a hint of regret in Charlie's voice as he spoke. 'She just wanted you to lead an ordinary life, out of the spotlight, away from the attention of the Australian media. But at the same time, she wanted to be sure you were being looked after – weren't being led astray.'

Piers focused his sight on the table in front of him and didn't respond.

'So for the three years we were at university you were just Piers' bodyguard pretending to be our friend?' Tom said.

'Explains a lot, I suppose,' Piers muttered just loudly enough for everyone to hear.

'Yes, I was at Cardiff, living with you all, because I was protecting Piers. But the reason we became friends, and the reason we still are friends, has nothing to do with any of that. I grew to like you all and I know I don't always show it, but I thought of you all as my closest friends. I still think of you as my closest friends. I hope you feel the same way.'

Jack couldn't believe he hadn't realized sooner. Suddenly, so many things fell into place. It didn't change the way he felt about Charlie. He was still his old friend from university, the friend who'd saved his life all those years ago. But, at last, he felt he could start to understand him.

'You owe me fifty quid,' Tom declared suddenly. All heads swiveled towards him. 'I told you he wasn't gay.'

The laughter that followed relaxed the atmosphere a little and Jack nodded in agreement, though he didn't really see that Charlie's admission had any bearing on his sexuality.

'JD and I had a wager on you,' Tom explained. 'He was convinced you were following Piers everywhere because you fancied him. Now we know the truth,' he smiled cheekily.

'I'm not gay,' Charlie said with a deadpan expression, 'but I feel very protective towards you all.'

Piers still looked confused, trying to take it all in. 'What happened to my protection after university?' he said eventually.

'Your mother thought you were old enough and mature enough to lead your own life by then. My part ended after graduation, that's why I joined the army a year later.'

'So what you did in the basement of the souvenir shop,' Piers said, looking Charlie in the eye. 'Who was that?

Charlie Preston the friend or Charlie Preston on the payroll?'

'It was me – Charlie – your mate – a concerned friend. I was just looking out for you.'

'Well, this has been revealing,' said Tom, sitting forward with an earnest look on his face. 'Let's see now, we've established that Piers has no money and he's fallen out with his family – who it turns out are the Clayton-Hills, not the Upwells. He owes money to the Triads, faked his own kidnapping with the aid of a stripper – no offense, Honey – and helped her double-cross her two brothers. Jack, the supposedly respectable lawyer, has been stealing our money to satisfy his insatiable gambling habit, and Captain Preston here was a bodyguard all through university, employed by a paranoid mother to spy on her son.' He collapsed back in his seat in mock exhaustion.

Jack smiled. The way Tom put things, they did sound ridiculous, and in truth he was relieved not to be the only one round the table who needed to ask for forgiveness. Everyone seemed relaxed about the various breaches of trust and Jack was grateful for that, but the question of the ransom money was still niggling him. Earlier that day, he and Tom had returned to the Presidential Suite to find Charlie and Piers sitting in silence. He hadn't felt suspicious at the time but now he was curious. 'So what exactly happened when Tom and I were at the hospital?' he asked.

Honey took up the explanation. 'I told my brothers I was gonna meet Piers at MLK but the real plan was for him to meet me at the shop. We were gonna run away from there with the ransom.'

'Of course, I had no idea I was being followed by the Triads. I led them straight to us,' said Piers.

'One of them grabbed me and threatened to kill me unless we gave up the money,' Honey continued.

'That was Mr. Yang,' Charlie added.

'Then Honey's brothers came back to the shop and started shooting the place up,' Piers took the reins. 'I can hardly bear to think about it. There was blood everywhere, it was like a Tarantino movie. I thought Honey had been shot dead, I witnessed her brother murder one of the Triads right in front of me. I was convinced I would be next. Thank God Charlie showed up when he did. I thought I'd killed one of Honey's brothers too until Charlie explained the gun I was using contained blanks.'

'Luckily, I got there just in time,' said Charlie. 'It was too late for Honey's brothers. They were already dead but Honey was only unconscious.'

Honey touched the back of her head and grimaced briefly. 'One of the Triads hit me over the head with his gun when I tried to wrestle free from his hold.'

'Holy shit,' said Jack and Tom at the same time. *Jinx,* thought Jack but on this occasion he chose not to say it.

'It sounds like a bloodbath. What happened to your brothers?' Tom asked.

Honey let go of Piers' forearm and made the sign of the cross with her right hand. Now it was Piers' turn to comfort Honey and whisper something in her ear.

'And the Triads?' Jack was hoping they weren't still on the scene.

'What about the ransom?' added Tom.

'One of the Triads, Mr. Yin, survived,' said Charlie. 'We made him clean up the mess and get rid of the evidence. Of course, he knew exactly what to do. I agreed he could take the ransom to give to his boss in final settlement of Piers' debt. Hopefully, that's the last you'll be hearing from any Triads.' He held Piers' gaze.

'I promise I'm done with gambling,' Piers said. 'And when I get back on a more secure financial footing, I'm going to make it up to you all. I'm really sorry, guys. I hope you'll find it in you to forgive me for everything I've put you...'

'I'm sorry, too,' Honey said, looking at Piers. 'In the club, I saw you as just another mark, but I soon realized you were much more than that. Someone, like me, down on your luck, in need of an out.'

A stunned silence filled the air, everyone around the table in a state of shock as they grappled with the evening's revelations and tried to reconcile old secrets with new truths. Apart from Charlie, of course, who, Jack suspected, was the only one of them who knew the full story.

Eventually, Tom broke the silence. 'So what about the gambling winnings? By my calculation, there's still a couple hundred thousand pounds left in Jack's side pot, am I right?'

Jack nodded. There was £274,823.40 left in his Coutts account after paying for the ransom.

'All on black?' Piers suggested with a wry smile.

'Or red,' Tom said.

'Well, we still need to settle the hotel bill and a few extras, but I thought we might split the rest,' said Jack.

'Or maybe we put it in an account and we continue playing the game; you know, let JD pick another celebrity?' Tom suggested.

'What does the contract say?' Charlie asked with a grin.

Jack looked back at his friends and smiled.

Card 51

Double Gut Shot: A reference to a hand in which a player has two inside straight draws at once.

London, 15 July 2009
MR. YIN'S HAND

Mr. Yin was sitting in one of Mr. Lee's bunker-like offices in Chinatown, looking across the black lacquer desk at an empty chair and waiting for the Dragon Master to appear. He had been there for nearly forty minutes.

The office was dark, windowless, and sparsely decorated. Apart from the antique Chinese desk and two matching black chairs, the only other piece of furniture was a metal filing cabinet in the corner of the room. Three pictures hung on the wall above the desk: traditional Chinese characters painted in black ink on ancient-looking scrolls.

At last, Mr. Lee entered the room and took his seat in front of Mr. Yin.

Harald Lee was a curious-looking man. Less than five-foot-tall, he wore platform shoes to make himself seem taller and always arranged for the seat of his chair to be higher than that of his guests. He had a wispy mustache and a huge bouffant of dyed-black hair that looked strangely as if he had an eight-armed mollusk perching on top of his head. Despite being the Dragon Master of the 14K, his incredible hair had earned him another nickname: the Black Octopus.

'That's all of it,' Mr. Yin said as soon as Mr. Lee sat down. '$450,000 – £275,000 at today's rate of exchange. Plus, this watch.'

He placed the GMT Master II wristwatch on the lacquer desk, next to the black canvas bag full of $100 bills.

Mr. Lee pushed one of the jet-black tentacles of hair to the side of his face with his left index finger and observed Mr. Yin silently.

'I've had it valued. It's worth close to £20,000 despite the engraving...'

Silence.

'Like I told you, Dragon Master, Mr. Yang was shot in the chest by one of the kidnappers. I managed to kill two of them but I was ambushed by Captain Preston. He spared my life but insisted I took the money in settlement of the asset's debt.

'It seemed like a fair deal. He was offering to pay you more than was owed. I had no other choice, Dragon Master. He literally had a gun to my head and, like I said, Mr. Yang was dead. They could've easily killed me too and taken the money for themselves.'

Harald Lee picked up the watch, examined it cautiously, and finally broke his silence.

'Happy Birthday Son,' he said, reading out the inscription on the back of the watch before putting it on his pale, bony wrist. Mr. Lee looked and sounded like an oddball. People who didn't know him sometimes sniggered at the sound of his high-pitched voice and didn't take him seriously. It was hard to imagine he held the highest office in one of the most vicious organized gangs in Europe. 'Time is interesting construct, don't you think, Yin?'

No answer was required or expected.

'It means lot to some people and little to others. Some people rush without thinking about consequences. Others bide time, wait patiently. Time goes quick or slow, depending on perspective. When you have fun, like in casino, time fly, but when you in prison, like hostage, time stand still. These both just states of mind, because we all know time is constant.'

He looked down at the Rolex and then up at Mr. Yin, the silhouette of his hair forming a full furry octopus on the wall behind him. 'I lent money to the asset not because I want him to pay back, but because I want him to remain in debt for as long as possible. He was very good debtor because who he was. Who his mother is. The Clayton-Hill family are one of richest family in world and over time debt would build – much more than just for small gambling debt.'

There was a brief pause and Mr. Yin felt a palpable rise in tension in the room.

Mr. Lee slammed his fist on the desk and leaned forward on his fists. 'Now, because stupid Yin and Yang, I lose opportunity.' He scrutinized Mr. Yin with undisguised hostility.

The Black Octopus went on to explain that one of his first assignments as a young Triad had been to extort money without violence. He had spent months planning the perfect kidnapping. They'd taken a hostage for just three days, and returned him for a ransom of fifteen million dollars – 'Three million for every year of hostage's life,' Mr. Lee clarified. There'd been no need to harm the boy, he said, but careful planning had ensured a satisfying reward.

Mr. Lee regarded Mr. Yin in silence. Staring into his eyes, he seemed to be searching for something. An awkward ten seconds passed before he continued, hammering his point home. He explained that he and his cohorts had become famous in the organization because of that result. 'Those three days change life forever,' Mr. Lee asserted. It was the reason he had risen through the ranks so quickly and set up the European branch of the 14K.

'You have three days too, in Vegas,' Mr. Lee said slowly. 'It change your life forever, don't you think?'

Mr. Yin nodded.

Mr. Lee scratched the top of his bouffant and one of his black tentacles seemed to come alive. He pointed with his small hands at the three Chinese symbols that were hanging above his head.

'You know what those characters mean in Hanzi?'

Mr. Yin shuffled in his seat but didn't reply, knowing the question would soon be answered.

'Patience. Luck. Reward,' Mr. Lee said. 'Sometime threat of kidnapping, like threat of pain, enough to get what you want.'

He explained how, in the '70s, his gang had extorted money from wealthy families without needing to kidnap anyone at all. One family, though, had gone to extreme lengths to out-maneuver them. The Clayton-Hills had hired an ex-Special Forces soldier, Peter Preston, for protection. 'He nearly catch us. We forced to disband, go into hiding,' Mr. Lee said. 'But I bide time, gather intelligence.'

Over the years, Mr. Lee had established that Peter Preston's son had studied at Cardiff University, then joined the Royal Military Police. It was only much later, when Piers Upwell had walked into a Paris casino asking to borrow money and offering up the family name, that Mr. Lee finally found the opportunity he'd been waiting for. Mr. Lee now pointed to the Hanzi script behind him. 'Patience. Luck. Reward. Youngest son of family I threatened to kidnap long time ago walked straight into my arms.'

'I'm sorry, Dragon Master,' Mr. Yin said slowly, bowing his head low with shame. 'I had no idea.'

A minute of silence passed until the door to Mr. Lee's office opened and two henchmen carrying broad swords entered. They stood behind Mr. Yin with their heads bowed.

'Tell me, Yin. You remember thirtieth oath?' Mr. Lee asked, using his index fingers to part the two tentacles which had fallen in front of his dark eyes.

Mr. Yin. swallowed hard. 'I must not give support to outsiders if so doing is against the interests of any of my sworn brothers. If I do not keep this oath I will be killed by a myriad of swords.' Mr. Yin had no difficulty recalling the oath; it was one of the thirty-six that all Triads were required to learn by rote. He knew what was coming but his expression betrayed nothing, his voice was flat. He rose from his seat, neatly set it to one side, and bowed his head.

Mr. Lee looked at the oversized Rolex on his bony wrist. 'This is it, Yin. Your time is up.'

The two henchmen raised their swords in unison and in a matter of seconds they had sliced Mr. Yin into bloody pieces.

Card 52

The Final Call: Where a player matches a bet or a raise for the last time. The betting round ends when all active players have bet an equal amount and the player whose bet has been called has to turn over their cards to reveal their hand.

Las Vegas, 14 July 2009
CHARLIE'S HAND

'What happened? Did you track down Piers?' Charlie's dad sounded tired.

'Yes, I got to him in the end. He's safe now and hopefully all the trouble is behind him. He seems to have found a new love interest, too.'

'Good. Good. That all sounds promising. Hopefully, his mother will approve.'

Charlie smiled to himself. 'I think it might be a little early for that,' he said, imagining the meeting in his head. 'How is Mrs. Clayton-Hill coping?'

'She's getting better. The doctor thinks she could be back on her feet in the next few weeks. We'll still need to shield her from much of the truth for some time, though.' Charlie could hear the sound of his dad's rasping chest. 'When do you fly back to the UK?'

'Tomorrow night. I'm not due in Portsmouth until September, though, so I was thinking maybe I'd pay you a visit, if that's OK?'

'Of course, Charles. It would be lovely to see you. I can't remember when we last spent time together.'

'January 2005. For your 70th – I came to visit before my tour of Afghanistan. I bought you those night-vision binoculars, remember?'

'Oh, yes. Well, it's been far too long, anyway. Let me know the dates and I'll make sure everything's squared away at this end.'

Peter Preston coughed. He sounded unwell. Charlie wanted to ask about his health, but his dad was a proud man and not one for sympathy, especially from his son. After a brief pause, Charlie said, 'Dad, I told Piers my ... our secret. I felt he deserved to know the truth.'

'Well?'

'He was shocked at first, then embarrassed, I think, but eventually he seemed to understand.'

There was a moment's silence.

'I'm proud of you, son. You've always been a good friend to him.'

'Dad?' Charlie hesitated. 'I need you to be honest with me now.'

'About what?'

'When I told you Piers had been kidnapped, how did you know where he was?'

There was a brief silence before his dad responded, as if he was unsure whether to reveal his source. 'His wristwatch,' he finally said. 'The Rolex Mrs. Clayton-Hill gave him for his sixteenth birthday. I had a GPS tracker installed for a bit of extra protection. His mother wanted to be able to locate him in case he went AWOL ... or was kidnapped.'

The Rolex with the distinctive red-and-blue face.

'Piers didn't know this, did he?'

'No. We thought about telling him, but decided against it in the end. The same way we didn't tell him about you. Why panic him unnecessarily? Changing his name, sending him to Eton, the Rolex and a bodyguard in his inner circle at university – they were all just precautionary measures. After a while, the threats became less frequent, and eventually they stopped altogether. I think the last letter came on his seventeenth birthday.'

Peter Preston coughed and cleared his throat. 'We barely needed to use the GPS,' he continued. 'I tried it a few times in the beginning to check it worked, but that was all. It wasn't until you called me to say he'd been taken hostage that I remembered its original purpose. Spot of luck the tracker still worked and he still wore the watch. I'm surprised he hadn't sold it. Were the locations accurate? Did they help you to find him?'

'They certainly did.'

'And you say he got himself into trouble with some gangsters? Anything more I need to know about, son, or have you contained the problem?'

'He owed nearly £300,000,' Charlie explained, 'to someone called Mr. Lee – the boss of a Triad gang called the 14K. But everything's fine, we've settled the debt and now—'

Peter Preston started coughing loudly, interrupting Charlie mid-sentence.

'Are you alright, Dad?'

'I'm fine. I'm fine. It's just a cough,' his dad said with obvious irritation. 'We never found out who was behind the threats but I always suspected a Chinese gang. They'd plotted several kidnappings around the time Piers was born. The leader of that gang was a young Triad called Lee. I nearly caught him a few times in

Australia but he always seemed one step ahead of me. In the end, he simply vanished and the trail went cold. He was an evil bastard, by all accounts. I'm just wondering – it might be the same person. What do you think, Charles?'

Charlie paused for a moment. 'I don't know, Dad.' He looked down at his black G-Shock and half-smiled. I'm not sure. But I have a good idea how we can find out.'

Annex 1

The Contract

This Agreement is made on   13th JANUARY 1991

BETWEEN:

(1)   JACK EDWARD DAVIDSON, whose address is Room 2, House M, Flat B, Talybont North, Cardiff, Wales CF14 3UA (**'Jack Davidson'**);

(2)   PIERS LAWRENCE FRASER UPWELL, whose address is Room 1, House M, Flat B, Talybont North, Cardiff, Wales CF14 3UA;

(3)   CHARLES PETER PRESTON, whose address is Room 3, House M, Flat B, Talybont North, Cardiff, Wales CF14 3UA;

(4)   THOMAS ANDREW PATTERSON, whose address is Room 4, House M, Flat B, Talybont North, Cardiff, Wales CF14 3UA; and

(5)   VINCENT DEAN EGFORD, whose address is Room 5, House M, Flat B, Talybont North, Cardiff, Wales CF14 3UA,

(each a **'Player'** and together the **'Players'**).

BACKGROUND:

For the avoidance of doubt, each of the Players intends that this agreement shall create legally binding relations. The Players agree that Jack Davidson shall be the custodian of the monies paid into the Account and shall hold the same on trust for himself and each of the other Players in accordance with the terms of this agreement.

IT IS AGREED:

1. PAYMENT

a. Each Player agrees to pay into the Account (as defined below) the sum set out opposite the relevant dates in Schedule 2 on the 1st day of each calendar month until this agreement comes to an end. If this agreement continues beyond 1 January 2013, the payments shall remain at £1,300 until one of the Celebrities (as defined below) dies.

b. Failure to pay a sum in accordance with clause 1(a) above will result in the relevant Player forfeiting his rights to the monies in the Account and the right to participate in the Vacation (as defined below). Once a Player has forfeited his rights by failure to make a payment or to comply with another term of this agreement, and his chosen Celebrity is the first to die, the game shall continue as if that Celebrity had not in fact died.

2. ACCOUNT

a. Jack Davidson will open a risk-free, interest-bearing savings account at a reputable UK bank (**'Account'**) in his name by no later than seven days after the date of this agreement and notify the Players immediately upon doing so.

b. All monies paid into the Account in accordance with clause 1(a) above shall be held on trust for the Players and shall be kept separately from Jack Davidson's own finances.

c. No individual Player shall have any severable and individual claim to the monies in the Account other than pursuant to the terms set out in this agreement.

d. Save in the case of manifest error, once payments have been made by an individual Player in accordance with clause 1, they shall not be returned to the Player other than in accordance with clause 6.

3.   **TERMINATION**

a. This agreement terminates and shall cease to have any further effect once the following events have occurred:

(i) One of the celebrities listed in Schedule 1 (**'Celebrities'**) dies;

(ii) The Vacation has taken place; or

(iii) All the money in the Account has been spent on and during the Vacation (as defined below) in accordance with clause 6.

4. **NEW PLAYERS**

    a. A new Player may only join the game with the unanimous consent of the existing Players.

    b. Any approved new Player may join the game at any time before this agreement comes to an end if the following conditions are satisfied:

        (i)   The new Player must accede to this agreement; and

        (ii) The new Player must pay the Joining Fee (as defined below) into the Account on the date of the accession.

        (iii) The joining fee is calculated on the proposed accession date by dividing the monies standing to the credit of the Account by the number of existing Players (**'Joining Fee'**).

5. **DEATH OF A PLAYER**

If a Player dies before one of the Celebrities dies, the monies standing to the credit of the Account at the time of the deceased Player's death shall be divided by the number of remaining Players (including the deceased Player) and such sum shall be paid to the deceased Player's surviving wife or parents as the case may be.

6.   WINNING THE GAME

a.   A Player wins the game if their chosen Celebrity dies first. Following the death of their Celebrity, all monies standing to the credit of the Account shall be transferred to a reputable UK bank account of his choice within seven days or as soon as practicably possible (whichever is the latest).

b.   Once the monies have been transferred to the winning Player in accordance with the clause above, the Player shall have no more than seven days to make contact with the remaining Players to inform them of the location and details of the proposed vacation (**'Vacation'**).

c.   The Vacation shall take place no later than one month after the death of the Celebrity. It is the individual Player's responsibility to ensure he can participate in the Vacation. The dates of the Vacation are to be chosen by the winning Player at his absolute discretion and shall be irrevocable.

d.   All the monies in the Account must be used by the winning Player at his discretion but must be spent on or relating to the Vacation and cannot be used to purchase anything of value which cannot be enjoyed by the Players during the Vacation. By way of example, the Players cannot purchase a car on the Vacation and return to the UK with the purchased car.

7. **GOVERNING LAW AND JURISDICTION**

   a. This agreement and any dispute or claim arising out of or in connection with this agreement, its subject matter or formation (including any non-contractual dispute or claim) (**'Dispute'**) are governed by and shall be construed in accordance with English law.

   b. Each party irrevocably agrees that the courts of England and Wales shall have exclusive jurisdiction to settle any Dispute.

SCHEDULE 1
Celebrities

Player	Celebrity
Jack Davidson	Michael Jackson
Piers Upwell	Ozzy Osborne
Charles Preston	Arnold Schwarzenegger
Thomas Patterson	Fidel Castro
Vincent Egford	Corey Feldman

SCHEDULE 2
Payments

Period	Payment per month per player
From 1 February 1991 to 1 July 1991	£25
From 1 August 1991 to 1 January 1992	£50
From 1 February 1992 to 1 July 1992	£100
From 1 August 1992 to 1 January 1993	£200
From 1 February 1993 to 1 July 1993	£300
From 1 August 1993 to 1 July 1995	£400
From 1 August 1995 to 1 July 1997	£500
From 1 August 1997 to 1 July 1999	£600
From 1 August 1999 to 1 July 2001	£700

From 1 August 2001 to 1 July 2003	£800
From 1 August 2003 to 1 July 2005	£900
From 1 August 2005 to 1 July 2007	£1,000
From 1 August 2007 to 1 July 2009	£1,100
From 1 August 2009 to 1 July 2011	£1,200
From 1 February 2011 to 1 January 2013	£1,300

This agreement has been signed and delivered on 13th January 1991 by:

Signed by JACK EDWARD DAVIDSON:

Signed by PIERS LAWRENCE FRASER UPWELL:

Signed by CHARLES PETER PRESTON:

Signed by THOMAS ANDREW PATTERSON:

Signed by VINCENT DEAN EGFORD:

Author's Acknowledgments and Notes

But for the Polish national rugby team this book would not have been written. In 2014, my head found itself unexpectedly on the wrong side of a tackle during a rugby game at an international 7s tournament in Munich, Germany. I fractured my nose, split open my forehead and broke my neck. It was painful, the last time I played rugby, and required me to take time off work. During this time, the idea for *Famously Dead* was born. The journey since then has been long, cathartic and rewarding.

I have many people to thank for getting this book published. I am incredibly grateful to all those friends, family members and colleagues who provided support, feedback and comments on the early iterations of the book; the story is infinitely better as a result of your input. I would particularly like to mention my good friend Robert A. H. Chidley who, in true lawyerly fashion, provided his comments on a very early draft of the manuscript in red pen! Thank you, Robert, for your diligence, patience and support during this early stage. You persuaded me not to turn back and encouraged me to keep going on this journey.

It would be remiss of me not to express my gratitude to my wife, Sophie, who had to endure many a late evening, long weekend and frustrating holiday without my undivided attention. Your love, good humor and support were inspiring and allowed me to persevere. Thank you, darling.

Finally, I would like to express my appreciation to C. Taylor and Helen G for their respective professional insight in helping shape my story at the beginning, and to Katharine Smith at Heddon Publishing who provided me with the final direction and guidance required to finish my journey.

Inspired by movies like *Memento*, *Pulp Fiction* and *Reservoir Dogs*, I have always been a fan of non-linear storytelling. As the reader will be aware, *Famously Dead* is written in such a way. Nevertheless, images of playing cards at the start of each chapter signpost the linear chronology of events, allowing the reader to follow the story in "real time". It is worth noting that the story begins at Card 3 (the ace of clubs) and the sequence of suits for this purpose is clubs, diamonds, hearts followed by spades.

For the record, I am a lawyer at an international law firm. I am not Jack. I have never stolen money from my friends and I no longer play poker.

Not all of the above statements are true and correct.

I hope you enjoyed the book as much as I enjoyed writing it.

24137192R00189

Printed in Great Britain
by Amazon